PAST TENSE

Also by William G. Tapply

THE BRADY COYNE NOVELS

Scar Tissue
Muscle Memory
Cutter's Run
Close to the Bone
The Seventh Enemy
The Snake Eater
Tight Lines
The Spotted Cats
Client Privilege
Dead Winter
A Void in Hearts
The Vulgar Boatman
Dead Meat
The Marine Corpse
Follow the Sharks
The Dutch Blue Error
Death at Charity's Point

NONFICTION

Pocket Water
Upland Days
Bass Bug Fishing
A Fly-Fishing Life
The Elements of Mystery Fiction
Sportsman's Legacy
Home Water
Opening Day and Other Neuroses
Those Hours Spent Outdoors

OTHER FICTION

Thicker Than Water (with Linda Barlow)

Past Tense

A
BRADY COYNE
NOVEL

William G. Tapply

St. Martin's Minotaur
New York

www.minotaurbooks.com

Design by Michael Collica

ISBN 0-312-28442-X

First Edition: October 2001

10 9 8 7 6 5 4 3 2 1

For Vicki,
who keeps me young

ACKNOWLEDGMENTS

If this book works, it's because of the following people:

Ken Quat, my lawyer and legal consultant, without whom I'd have to fake it;

Jed Mattes, my good shepherd;

Keith Kahla, my peerless editor, who really cares about books;

H. G. Tapply, my father and my first editor, who taught me the power of verbs, and whose voice will forever echo in my head;

and Vicki Stiefel, my best (and worst) critic, my friend, my virtual spouse, and my love.

If it doesn't work, don't blame them.

PAST TENSE

ONE

C ool, brine-flavored night air came wafting in through the
sunroof and the open windows. The Sagamore Bridge
hummed under our tires, and in the darkness far below us, the
ebbing tide washed through the Cape Cod Canal.

ZZ Top was singing on the CD player. Beside me, Evie
Banyon was singing with them. " *'She's got legs. She knows
how to use 'em.'* "

Evie had splendid legs, and she certainly knew how to use
'em. She was wearing a short white skirt, and she'd hitched it
up to the tops of her thighs. She'd pushed her seat back as far
as it would go, and those long, smooth, tanned legs were
stretched out in front of her.

Evie was in high spirits. A long August weekend on the
Cape in a cute little rented cottage overlooking the water in
Brewster? Beachcombing and antiquing, napping in a ham-
mock and reading on a screened porch, making love and eating
lobster? What could be more fun?

Me, I was pretty grouchy. A long August weekend on the most crowded peninsula on earth? Fighting smelly traffic and rude sidewalk mobs, sweating under a blistering sun, waiting in line at overpriced restaurants crowded with screaming kids and hostile adults? What could be more aggravating?

Well, the lobster part sounded okay, and the making-love part would be fine.

I'd let Evie talk me into it despite a vow I made years ago after sitting in traffic on Route 3 for an entire Friday afternoon in July. The sun had been blazing, the exhaust fumes nauseating, the wife bitching, the two boys whining. Never again, I promised myself, would I voluntarily drive down to Cape Cod between Memorial Day and Labor Day. For about a dozen years, except for a few unavoidable, involuntary meetings with clients, I'd managed to keep my promise.

And now here I was, driving across the Sagamore Bridge on a Thursday night in August. It wasn't exactly voluntary, of course. Evie had arranged it without asking me how I felt about it.

She put her hand on my leg. "We made it," she said. "We're here. We've crossed the bridge and we're on the Cape. You can stop sulking."

"I wasn't sulking," I grumped. "I was being pensive."

She laughed. "You can pretend to be an old poop if it makes you feel better, but you can't fool me."

"I'm not pretending," I said. "I *am* an old poop."

I turned onto Route 6A, heading east for Brewster. Six-A is a winding, two-lane country road that follows the coastline along Cape Cod Bay. It passes over tidal creeks and skirts salt marshes as it wanders easterly through the self-consciously picturesque little villages of Sandwich, Barnstable, Cummaquid, Yarmouth, and Dennis before it arrives at Brewster, out there toward the inner elbow of Cape Cod.

On a map, the Cape looks like a half-flexed arm, with Provincetown, the hand at its tip, giving the rest of the world the finger.

"You really are quite sweet, you know," murmured Evie.

"I am not."

"I know this isn't your cup of tea."

"Actually," I said, "it's my cup of hemlock."

"That's what I mean," she said. "You're doing it for me. That's sweet."

"Well, don't tell anybody. I've got a reputation to uphold."

She leaned over the console and laid her cheek on my shoulder. Her fingers moved along the inside of my leg. "The flowers were gorgeous."

"Yeah?"

"There's nothing a girl likes better," she murmured, "than having a big bouquet of flowers from her honey delivered to her office. It shows the whole world that she is adored."

Julie, I thought. Julie must've sent them. It would be just like her. My smart secretary knew that Evie's honey was dreading the damn weekend on the Cape. I'd been crabby for a month, thinking about it. Julie knew the power of flowers. A woman who knows she's adored will put up with anything, even an old poop like me.

I probably should've told Evie right then that it wasn't exactly I who had sent them. But I didn't want to spoil her happy illusion. I'd tell her later.

Down on the south side of the Cape, Route 28, the outer coastline road, would be clogged all the way from Falmouth to Chatham at ten-thirty on a Thursday evening in August. There the T-shirt emporiums and nightclubs and souvenir rip-offs and clam shacks and miniature golf courses stayed open at least till midnight. But here on 6A we moved quietly through the darkened villages. Even the gas stations were closed.

"It's not so bad, is it?" said Evie. "Smell the ocean?"

"Low tide," I grumbled. "Rotting seaweed and outboard-motor fumes and dead shellfish."

She jabbed me in the ribs with her elbow. "You really are an old poop."

Just past the traffic light at the little cluster of enterprise at what passed for the center of town in Brewster, Evie said, "Okay. Slow down. I've got the directions here."

We took the second left past the light, another left at the fork, the dirt road on the right, and the third driveway through some scrubby pines, and then we rolled down a long, curving slope to our cottage.

It sat in a moon-bathed opening on a little sandy knoll. An L-shaped screened porch ran around the front and one side. Weathered shingles, fieldstone foundation, brick chimney. Beyond it, the salt marsh merged with the bay.

I parked in front. "Not bad," I said.

"I thought you'd like it," said Evie. "The woman sent me pictures. She said it's totally private. There's a deck out back with a hot tub. We can get naked and drink gin and tonics, and if you want, we can just stay here the whole time." She opened the car door and slid out. "Come on. Let's look."

I followed her onto the porch. She found the key under the doormat where the woman had told her she'd cleverly hidden it, and we went in.

The entire left half of the cottage was a single open room—kitchen, dining room, living room, with floor-to-ceiling bookcases, woodstove, braided rugs, and sliding glass doors along the back that opened onto the deck. A bathroom and two bedrooms occupied the right half of the cottage. The ceiling was open to skylights in the roof. Copperware hung from big rough-hewn beams over the kitchen.

"Isn't it great?" said Evie.

"It is," I said. "It's really nice." I went over to the glass sliders and gazed out on the salt marsh, which reflected a sky full of stars.

Evie came to where I was standing and wrapped her arms around my neck, and the next thing I knew, she was pressing herself against me and kissing my mouth.

"About those flowers," I murmured.

"I was deeply touched," she said, and she grabbed my hand and tugged me toward the bedroom, and I decided that this was a good time to keep my mouth shut and let her think what she wanted if it made her happy.

Evie got up early the next morning to go running. I declined her invitation to join her. I knew she'd leave me in the dust.

When she got back an hour or so later, her slender body was sheened with sweat. She shed her T-shirt and shorts and sneakers on the deck and climbed into the hot tub.

I fetched coffee for both of us and joined her.

We sat naked across from each other in the tub with the hot water swirling around us, drinking coffee and playing footsie.

"I want to explain about those flowers," I said after a few minutes. "I—"

Evie put her finger to her mouth. "Shh," she whispered. "What's that?"

I listened. It sounded like someone standing right around the corner whistling. "It's a bobwhite quail," I said.

"That's so cool," she said. She slid around to my side of the tub. "Let's be quiet. Maybe we can see him."

Pretty soon we forgot about the quail. We ended up back in bed, and the subject of flowers got lost along the way.

Later in the morning, Evie took the car and went shopping for food and booze. I stayed at the cottage and read a Nick Lyons fishing book in the sunshine out on the deck.

We had tuna sandwiches and potato salad and iced tea on the deck, and while we were eating, the wind shifted, the temperature dropped, clouds gathered in the sky, and a fogbank settled over the marsh.

Evie had planned to go to the beach, but now, she said, she wanted to go exploring. Maybe it was guilt about taking credit for my secretary's thoughtfulness, so even though I'd been thinking about hammocks and books and classical music on the radio and maybe firing up the woodstove, I volunteered to go exploring with her.

"You don't have to," she said. But her tone told me that it would make her happy.

"No, really," I lied. "I'd like to."

We ended up driving in slow traffic all the way to Provincetown. We visited several art galleries and antique shops and used-book stores along the way, and in P-town I bought Evie a life-sized quail that had been carved from a single block of pine by a local artisan. Evie had a collection of hand-carved birds. She loved birds.

In my mind, that quail made up for our little misunderstanding about the flowers Julie had sent.

On the way back, we stopped at a rough-shingled seafood restaurant in Eastham. It was perched right on the edge of a tidal creek overlooking a long narrow dock and a small marina, so close to the water that high tide would wash around the pilings that held up the back porch, and even though it was a Friday night in August, we got a table by the window without having to wait.

My kind of restaurant, regardless of how good the food was.

We had gin and tonics, and both of us ordered a two-pound boiled lobster, onion rings, cole slaw, draft beer. We had barely finished our gin and tonics when the lobsters arrived.

Evie was an eat-as-you-go gal. Crack a claw, fish out the

meat, dip it in the butter, and down the hatch. My method was to withhold gratification by picking out the entire lobster, filling a bowl with the meat, and eating only after I'd finished the dirty work. Our approaches to eating lobster pretty much defined the differences between us.

When Evie ate, she mumbled and groaned the way she did in bed. When I pointed that out to her, she laughed. "My grandfather in Maine had a boat," she said. "He had a string of lobster pots, and we always had lobster. When I was a kid, lobsters were a staple in my grandmother's house. I can remember my mother and my grandma and me sitting around the kitchen table all afternoon picking out lobsters. Grandma had a big glass punch bowl, and we'd fill it with tails and claws till it was full and mounded over. When we were done, we rewarded ourselves by picking the bodies and sucking the legs. I ate so much lobster when I was a kid, you'd think I'd be sick of it. But I'm not. I love lobster."

"You can pick my body," I said, "if I can suck your leg."

She smiled, picked up a lobster leg, looked at me cross-eyed, and sucked it suggestively.

"That's the first time you ever mentioned your grandmother," I said. "Or your mother, come to think of it. I didn't know you were from Maine."

"I'm not," she said. "My mother was."

"I don't really know anything about your childhood," I persisted.

"Does it matter?"

I shrugged. "It's part of you. I'm interested in you."

"Nothing interesting in my childhood," she said. She cracked a claw, pulled out the meat, dipped it in butter, and ate it. The drawn butter dribbled down her chin. "I've just had this ordinary life. Anyway, I like being mysterious."

"What about me?" I said. "Am I mysterious?"

"Sure."

"Don't you want to know about me?"

"I know I love you," she said. "What else is there?"

"We never talk about our lives before we met. It doesn't seem natural."

"So what do you want to know?"

"Well," I said, "what about—"

Suddenly Evie's head jutted forward and her eyes narrowed. She was glaring over my shoulder. "Shit," she hissed.

"What?"

"Don't turn around. There's somebody at the bar. He followed me. Bastard."

"Followed you?"

"This is no coincidence." She wiped her mouth and hands on her napkin, pushed back her chair, and stood up. "I'm gonna take care of this."

"Want me to—?"

"You stay right here, Brady. I can handle it."

Evie headed to the bar, which ran the full length of the wall behind me. I turned to watch.

The place had gotten crowded since we'd arrived. People were clustered at the bar, talking and laughing and having a drink while they waited for a table.

Evie marched right up to a man who was neither talking nor laughing. He was a stocky guy with straw-colored hair and a good tan. He had a draft beer in his hand, and he was leaning back with one elbow propped on the bar behind him, smiling at her as she approached him.

He looked to be in his late twenties, which would make him a few years younger than Evie. He had pale eyes and a shy, expectant smile.

I don't think he expected Evie to walk right up to him and slap his face.

It was no love pat. She started it somewhere around her hip

8

and pivoted her body into it, and when her palm cracked against his cheek, it rang out like a gunshot, and the murmur and mumble of voices in the place suddenly subsided so that everyone could hear Evie growl, "You son of a bitch. God-*damn* you. You better leave me alone."

The guy barely reacted to her slap, but he flinched at her words, then shook his head and held up his hand. He tried to smile, and I heard him say, "Come on, honey, just listen . . ." before the other conversations in the room resumed and his voice was drowned out.

Evie stood in front of him, pointing her finger at his face and spitting words at him, and I recognized her anger by the hunch of her shoulders and the angle of her neck. I'd seen it before.

He looked at her with a little bewildered smile, and when she was done, he leaned toward her and said something. Evie lifted her hand as if to hit him again, and he held up his hands, stepped back, nodded quickly, turned, placed his glass of beer on the bar, and walked out of the place.

Two

Evie stood there with her arms folded across her chest and watched him go. Then she turned, came back to the table, sat down, and picked up her fork.

"What was that all about?" I said.

She scowled at me. "I'm so mad I could explode."

"That's pretty obvious. So who was that?"

"I don't want to talk about it." She blew out a quick, exasperated breath, then picked up an onion ring and stuffed it into her mouth. "I just want to enjoy my dinner."

"But you can't—"

"Brady, goddamn it, I do *not* want to discuss it. Okay?"

"Sure," I said. "Okay."

A minute later our waitress came over. "Are you all right, miss?" she said to Evie.

Evie waved her away without looking up. "I'm fine."

"The manager wants to know if—"

"Tell him I'm sorry if I made a scene."

"That's not—"

Evie lifted her head and glared up at the girl. "Look," she said. "It's private and it's over with, all right?"

The waitress, who looked like a high-school kid, hovered there for a minute, then shrugged and wandered away.

I had the good sense not to say anything.

We ate in silence. After several minutes, Evie reached across the table, touched my hand, and said, "Let's leave that girl a nice tip, okay?"

"Sure."

"I'm sorry if I bit your head off."

"Forget it," I said.

"I just don't like being stalked."

"Is that what that was?"

"What else would you call it?"

"If that guy's stalking you, we should tell the police."

"A lot of good that'd do." She shook her head. "He's harmless. Annoying, that's all."

"Stalkers—"

"Forget it, okay?"

"Right," I said. "Sorry."

We finished eating without saying much, and when we were done, we went outside and strolled down to the long T-shaped dock that extended out over the tidal creek. A few sailboats and sportfishing boats were moored there, along with several blocky craft that might've been lobster boats.

We walked out to the end of the dock and stood there watching the water. The afternoon clouds had blown away, and now the tide was coming in and the moon was rising over the marsh. Night birds were swooping around chasing mosquitoes. The air was still and quiet. Somewhere out there a fish sloshed. Some lights glowed from the cockpits on a couple of the sailboats, and from them came the soft murmur of voices, an occasional burst of laughter, the clink of glasses, all muffled by the damp, briny night air.

I lit a cigarette. "You okay?" I said to Evie.

"Yeah, I'm all right." She found my hand and held on to it, and we stood there in silence, watching the boats and the night birds and the rising moon.

After a few minutes Evie said, "Did you ever spend the night on a boat?"

"No," I said. "I don't think I ever did."

"I've always wanted to live on a houseboat," she said. "Get rocked to sleep every night, hear the slosh of waves on the other side of the hull, inches from your head. If you don't like where you are, you just start up the engines and move your house and your whole life somewhere else."

I flipped my cigarette butt into the water. "It's a lovely notion. Impractical, maybe, but lovely."

She chuckled. "Mr. Practicality."

"I fight it constantly."

She squeezed my hand. "I'm sorry, Brady."

"For what?"

"For making a scene."

I shrugged. "It was your scene."

She chuckled. "For being a bitch, then."

"You were angry. You're entitled."

She snuggled against me. I put my arm around her shoulder, and she laid her head against my shoulder.

"I went out with him a few times," she said quietly. "His name is Larry. Larry Scott. It was three or four years ago. He worked where I worked."

"In Cortland?" I said. "The medical center?"

"Yes. He was the janitor. He'd been a Marine. Served in Desert Storm, where he had some hairy experiences, I guess, and after he got out he tried several jobs. He's a good-looking

13

man, terrific body, all that. But it didn't take me long to figure out that he was a little weird, and pretty boring besides. Self-absorbed, narrow-minded, a bit paranoid. So I stopped going out with him."

"And he didn't like it," I said.

"No." She was quiet for a minute. "He started calling me on the phone at odd hours," she said. "Sometimes he'd wake me up late at night. He had this idea that I'd dumped him because he was just a janitor and lived at home with his mother and didn't have much money."

"How did you handle it?"

"At first I tried to reason with him. Told him I thought he was a nice man but that we had no chemistry, and that money had nothing to do with it. He'd argue with me, insist that we did have chemistry. He knew it, he said, because he could feel it, and I was a bad person for rejecting him because he was poor. At the time, I was going out with a doctor who was quite a bit older than me, and Larry figured it was all about money. I told him I didn't give a shit about money, but he never would believe that. After a while, I told him to stop calling me, he was annoying me. He kept calling anyway. I got so I stopped answering my phone. I screened all my calls, and Larry would fill my answering machine with . . . I don't know what to call it. Crazy stuff. He loved me, he'd always love me. I loved him, he kept saying, and I should just admit it. We were destined for each other. He'd rant on about how he was going to have money one day, and then we could be together. And sometimes he'd talk about how he couldn't take it, I was driving him insane, that he was going to kill himself if he couldn't have me."

"Did he ever threaten you?"

"No, not really. I mean, it all felt threatening. But he never actually threatened to hurt me or anything."

Evie put her arm around my waist and burrowed against me. I held her tight against me. She was shivering.

"Finally I got an unlisted phone number," she said. "Within a few days, he somehow got ahold of it. Sometimes when I went out, Larry would follow me. Like tonight. I'd be in a restaurant or a store or something, and I'd look up, and there he'd be, watching me. And I'd find him hanging around my office pretending to change a lightbulb or something when I was working. Sometimes at night I'd look out my window and see him parked outside, sitting there in his car. He'd stay there for hours. Just sitting there, watching my window."

"You should've called the police."

"I did," she said. "They were nice to me, and understanding and all. But the Cortland cops were mostly local guys. They all knew Larry. They grew up together. Old small-town buddies, played football together in high school. So when Larry would be out there in his car, I'd call, and the police would come by in their cruiser, stop, talk with him for a while, and Larry would leave, and a few minutes after the cops left, he'd show up again. One day I went to the police station, told them he was stalking me. They asked me some questions, then told me that what Larry was doing wasn't stalking. He was surely bothering me, they said, but that was no crime, and there was really nothing they could do about it."

"If he didn't actually threaten you with death or bodily injury," I said, "it's not stalking according to Massachusetts law."

"Yes," said Evie. "That's what they said. I even talked to a lawyer about taking out a restraining order. She asked me a lot of questions and was very sympathetic, but she said no judge would go along with it. Larry and I had never been married or lived together, and he'd never hurt me or threatened to hurt me or anything like that. She said the bottom line was, ours wasn't a domestic relationship, and besides that, I wasn't in fear of him. I guess there's no law against driving somebody crazy."

"It sounds like a nightmare," I said.

"It got worse," she said. "He began leaving me gifts."

"Gifts?"

"Jewelry, lingerie, perfume. Stuff like that. Personal, intimate things. I'd come home, and there would be a gift-wrapped box on my kitchen table."

"He got into your house?"

"Yes."

"How? Did he have a key?"

"I don't know how he got in."

"Jesus," I said. "What did you do?"

"I called him. I pleaded with him to leave me alone. I threatened him. Said I'd get a lawyer, take him to court. He just laughed. See, I was playing into his hands. He'd made me call him. It seemed to convince him that I cared about him."

"You should've told your lawyer. I mean, he was trespassing."

"Oh, I did," she said. "Problem was, I couldn't prove it was him leaving those gifts." She blew out a long breath. "It got so I was convinced that I was the crazy person, that it was all my fault. I even started feeling sorry for him, guilty about the way I was treating him. I was going nuts. Fortunately, I knew I was going nuts, and I knew why. So finally I found the job at Emerson, and I left Cortland, and I didn't tell anybody where I was going. That was over three years ago, and until tonight, I thought I'd left Larry Scott behind forever."

"You haven't seen him since you moved?"

She shook her head. "Tonight was the first time. It's way spooky."

"Maybe it was a coincidence," I said. "He just happened to be here and spotted you."

16

"No. He followed us. I'm sure of it."

"Well," I said, "we'll have to put an end to it."

"How?"

"When we get back I'll talk to some people. I know some state troopers who'll put a scare into him."

"Well, I wouldn't mind if you did that." Evie hugged me, then tilted up her head and kissed me. "I'm getting chilly."

"Hot tub, glass of brandy," I said. "I'll fire up the wood-stove."

"Mmm," she said. "Then a warm bed."

"Mmm, indeed," I said.

We held hands and walked back to the car in the moonlight. The restaurant parking lot was still jammed with cars, and Friday-night laughter and loud voices filtered out from the screened windows. We'd parked in the far corner of the lot, and when we came to my car, we both stopped short.

Larry Scott was leaning against the fender.

I squeezed Evie's hand. "Stay right here," I said. I walked up to Scott. "Get away from my car."

He didn't move. "I need to speak to the lady."

"The lady doesn't want to speak to you."

He looked over my shoulder. "Come on, honey," he said. "You gotta listen to me."

"She's not your honey," I said. "Now move."

"This is none of your business, Mr. Lawyer," he said. "This is between Evie and me." He looked at her. "I gotta tell you about your saint. And I got money now. So—"

"I said get away from my car." I grabbed his arm.

He shook it loose. "You don't wanna mess with me, pal." He started toward Evie.

I stepped in front of him and put my hand on his chest. "Stay away from her."

He hesitated for a moment, then gave me a shove with both hands.

17

I staggered backwards, got my balance, and went after him. I was several inches taller than him, but he was stronger and younger and quicker, and I didn't see his fist coming at me. He caught me on the side of the head and followed it with a punch to the middle of my chest, and I went down.

Lights flashed in my head, and Evie was yelling, and my brain was whirling, and then there were people around us, and loud, angry voices.

Evie knelt down beside me. "I'm sorry, baby," she said. "Are you okay?"

I took a couple of deep breaths. My chest and my head both hurt. "Sure," I said. "Aside from my masculine pride, I'm fine." I sat up, rubbed my head, and looked around. "Where is he? Where'd he go?"

"Some people from the restaurant took him away," she said. "He's gone."

A couple of men were hovering near us. "You gonna be all right?" one of them said.

I waved my hand in the air. "I'm okay."

"Want me to call the cops or something?"

I glanced at Evie. She shook her head. "No," I said. "Don't worry about it."

"I'm the manager here," he said. "I apologize for this."

"It's not your fault," said Evie.

"Come back," he said. "Please. Be my guest. Lobster dinner on the house. I'll be sure that fellow leaves you alone."

"Thank you," I said. "Maybe we'll take you up on it." I got my feet under me, and Evie helped me to stand up. I leaned on her until a wave of dizziness passed.

"Sure you're okay?" said the manager. "I can call an ambulance."

I shook my head. "Forget it. Really."

He looked at me for a minute, then nodded. "Come back, okay?"

"Sure," I said. "Thanks."

We got into the car and sat there for a minute. I lit a cig-arette.

"You okay to drive?" said Evie.

"I'm fine," I said. "A little embarrassed, that's all."

"I'm the one who should be embarrassed."

"You nailed him with a good shot," I said. "Me, I got my ass kicked."

"You think you should be able to beat up a man fifteen years younger than you, an ex-Marine?"

"Hey," I said. "I'm a guy. No guy likes to get whipped. Especially in front of his woman."

She reached over and put her hand on the back of my neck. "We girls go all melty when a white knight comes riding up to defend our honor. And when he gets knocked off his steed, our maternal instincts kick in."

"You gonna nurse my wounds?"

"Umm," she said. "Not just your wounds."

"We better get going, then." I started up the car, pulled out of the lot, and aimed for our cottage in Brewster.

We rode in comfortable silence for several minutes. Then Evie said, "I just figured something out."

"What's that?"

"You didn't include a note with those flowers that you had delivered to my office."

I didn't say anything.

"I thought that was a truly romantic notion," she said. "No note, but no note needed, of course. Who else could possibly send them but my very own sweetie? Flowers say everything all by themselves."

"Honey," I said, "actually—"

"You didn't send those flowers, did you?"

"Well, no. Not exactly."

"It was Larry."

"I thought it—"

"You lied to me," she said.

"Well, I never said—"

"All along, I'm thinking . . . I'm so touched that my adorable curmudgeon would do something so out of character. So old-fashioned. So romantic. And it wasn't you at all."

"I thought it was Julie," I said. "Sending them on my behalf."

"You could've told me."

"I was going to," I said. "But I liked how it made you happy."

"If you'd told me it was Julie, I would've laughed," she said. "I know you. You don't think of things like sending flowers."

"You're right. I don't. I wish I did, but I don't."

"So you lied to me."

"Well, technically—"

"Brady, goddamn it, don't you even think about playing lawyer with me."

"Sorry."

Evie sighed. I recognized that particular sigh. Exasperation and disappointment, mingled with anger. She hitched herself as far away from me as she could in the seat beside me and turned her face to the side window.

After a minute, I said, "Larry called me 'Mr. Lawyer.' And he knew which one was my car. How's he know about me?"

"I don't know how Larry knows things. He knows where I work. He knows we're down here on the Cape."

"But—"

"You're not listening to me," she said. "I told you. I do *not* want to talk about it."

When we got back to the cottage, I poured us each a snifter of brandy. I handed one to Evie and said, "How about that hot tub?"

She shook her head. "I'm not in the mood anymore."

"We can't let Larry spoil our time."

"It's not Larry," she said. "It's you."

I took my brandy out onto the deck, and after a few minutes Evie came out. We leaned our elbows on the rail and looked out over the marsh. The fog had evaporated, and the moon reflected off the glassy water.

"Pretty, huh?" I said.

"Yes," said Evie softly. "It's pretty."

"You going to be mad for a while?"

"I think so."

"What do you want me to say?"

"Nothing."

I put my arm around her. She stiffened for a moment, then allowed me to hug her against me.

"I'm sorry for deceiving you," I said. "It'll never happen again."

She hesitated, then chuckled. "It probably will. Don't worry about it. It's no big deal, and it's stupid of me to hold it against you. Compared to every other man I've known, you are positively saintly."

I snapped my fingers. "Saintly. Something Larry said. He said he had something to tell you about your 'saint.' What was that all about?"

"Can we please forget about Larry?"

"None of my business, you mean."

"I mean exactly what I said. I don't want to talk about Larry. I don't want to think about Larry. Okay?"

"Sure," I said. "Okay."

Before we went to bed, I retrieved the key from under the doormat and locked the doors and the glass sliders.

Evie was at the sink putting together the coffee for the morning. "What are you doing?" she said.

"Locking up."

She shook her head. "God*damn* him. I refuse to let him ruin our weekend."

"No harm in locking the doors."

"And what?" she said. "No more wandering around the house naked? No playing footsie in the hot tub? The hell with that. Larry is harmless, and I'm going to pretend he doesn't exist."

"Good," I said. "Me too." But I didn't mean it.

When I woke up the next morning, the light was gray through the windows. Somewhere out there a pair of bobwhites were whistling to each other.

Evie was sitting on the edge of the bed.

"What time is it?" I said.

"Little after five. Go back to sleep."

"What're you doing?"

"I can't sleep. I'm going running." She came around to my side of the bed, bent over, kissed my forehead, then turned for the door. Evie was tall and slim and curvy, and she had long auburn hair. This morning she'd pulled it back into a ponytail, and it hung halfway down her back. She was wearing a white T-shirt and pink running shorts cut high on her hips. She looked trim and athletic and incredibly sexy.

I gave her a bobwhite whistle.

She paused in the doorway, put one hand on her hip and the other behind her head, thrust out her pelvis, licked her lips, and flashed a parody of a half-lidded Marilyn Monroe smile. "I'll be back," she said. "Don't you move, big guy."

"Wait," I said. "What about . . . ?"

She held up her hand. It held a cylinder about the size of a shotgun shell. "Pepper spray," she said. "I carry it for dogs. All species of dogs. Don't you worry about me. Go back to sleep."

"Yes, ma'am." I bunched a pillow under my head, listened to the bobwhites for a few minutes, and eventually I drifted back to sleep.

Sometime later I woke up from a disturbing dream in which people were screaming, and it took me a moment to realize I was awake and I was still hearing the screaming. It came from somewhere outside the cottage, and it was Evie and she was yelling for help.

THREE

I scrambled out of bed, pulled on my pants, and ran barefoot out of the house.

Evie was still screaming. "Help! Brady, help! Oh, please, somebody help me!"

I followed the sound of her voice up the driveway, and around the bend about a hundred yards from the cottage I saw her kneeling at the side of the dirt road.

I ran up to her. A man was lying in the weeds. He was sprawled on his back. It was Larry Scott. He was wearing khaki pants and a blue polo shirt. His pale eyes were staring blankly up at the sky. The front of his shirt was shiny with dark, wet blood.

He looked thoroughly dead.

My first thought was that Evie had killed him.

She was kneeling there, pounding her thighs with her fists. Her face was wet with tears and her eyes were wild and her chest was heaving. Her breaths came in shuddering gasps. I knelt beside her and put my arm around her. She turned to me and burrowed her face into my chest.

I held her tight in my arms. "It's okay," I murmured. "It's okay, baby."

"He's dead," she whispered. "Isn't he?"

I reached over and pressed two fingers up under Larry's jawbone. I found no pulse. "Yes," I said. "He's dead."

Evie looked up at me. "I didn't . . ."

"I know, honey. Tell me what happened."

She pressed her palms over her eyes. I took out my handkerchief and handed it to her. She wiped her face and blew her nose, then balled the handkerchief up in her hand. "I ran out to the end of the dirt road," she said. "I saw rabbits and quail along the way. I turned right on 6A, ran into town, hooked around a back road down to the ocean, and the sun came up and burned off the fog, and when I figured I'd gone about two miles, I turned around and started back. And I was just coming along here and . . . and I saw him. He was just . . . lying there. Like that. Like he is." She looked up at me with wide, pleading eyes. "After what happened last night," she said softly, "I was thinking, I was wishing he was dead. I thought about killing him, I really did."

"But you didn't," I said, although the thought still lingered that she might have. "Somebody else did. It's not your fault. You didn't see him on your way out?"

She shrugged. "The sun wasn't up then. It was shadowy and foggy, and I was running pretty fast, looking ahead for rabbits on the road. No, I didn't see him. Maybe he was there then. His body. I don't know."

"We've got to call the police. Can you do that?"

She frowned at me. "Me?"

"One of us should stay here with him."

"Not me," she said. "I'm not doing that."

"Then you've got to make the call."

"What do I say?"

"Dial 911. Just tell them that we have a dead person here. They'll ask where you arc and tell you to stay there. After that, come back here. Bring my cigarettes with you."

She nodded. "Want coffee?"

"Absolutely."

I got to my feet, reached down, and helped Evie up. She held on to me.

"You going to be all right?" I said.

She shrugged.

I kissed her forehead. "Go call the cops."

She gave me a quick hug, then started jogging to the cottage. She ran a few steps, then stopped and turned back to me. "I didn't do it, you know," she said.

"I know."

She frowned, nodded, and headed to the cottage.

After Evie disappeared around the bend, I squatted down beside Larry Scott's body. The entire front of his shirt was soaked with blood. I touched it with my finger. It had just begun to coagulate. He hadn't been dead for long.

It looked like too much blood for a gunshot, unless he'd been shot in the back and the bullet had exited his stomach. If he'd been shot in the back, I figured he'd've fallen on his face. But he was lying on his back.

A knife wound, I guessed. I bent and looked closer, and under the thick shiny blood I saw two rips in his shirt, one just to the left of his navel and another a bit higher, right under his rib cage.

Whoever killed him had been standing directly in front of him, close enough to ram a knife into him. Twice.

Who?

Evie? I couldn't believe it. Not Evie. Maybe she'd have

squirted her pepper spray in his face if he'd approached her. The lawyer in me tried to be objective, but the Evie I knew was incapable of murder.

Then I thought: How well do I really know her? Before yesterday, I didn't even know her mother was from Maine, or that her grandfather was a lobsterman. Before yesterday I'd never heard of Larry Scott. She'd never told me about any of her old relationships or why she'd left her job in Cortland and gone to work at Emerson Hospital in Concord.

I really didn't know much about Evie Banyon's life.

But I knew *her*.

Evie couldn't stick a knife into anybody—even a man who had stalked her and haunted her until she thought she was crazy; who had finally driven her away from her home and her job; who had somehow managed to track her down here to Brewster on Cape Cod after being out of her life and her thoughts for more than three years.

Evie?

Evie wore her maple syrup–colored hair in a ponytail and got butter all over her face when she ate lobster and mocked herself with a funny, seductive, half-lidded Marilyn Monroe smile. Evie loved Monet's paintings and Debussy's music and Jane Austen's novels and Jim Carrey's dumb movies. She loved ducks and birch trees and daisies and cows. She loved jogging before sunrise and throwing a frisbee on the beach. She loved making love.

She loved me.

I squatted there, looking at Larry Scott's body.

Not Evie.

If not Evie, who?

She might have an idea, but I didn't.

I knew better than to move Larry's body or tromp around the area. But I stood up and looked around. If there was a murder weapon nearby, I didn't see it.

After a few minutes, Evie came back. She'd pulled on a pair of blue jeans and one of my flannel shirts over her T-shirt, and she was carrying two mugs of coffee.

She'd washed her face and brushed her hair. It looked like she was done crying.

I stood up and took a mug from her. "You made the call?"

She nodded. "They're on their way." She reached into her shirt pocket, took out a pack of cigarettes, and handed it to me. "Light one for me, will you?"

I lit two cigarettes and gave her one. Evie was one of those lucky people who could smoke half a pack of cigarettes in an evening and then go for two months without wanting one. She liked to share a cigarette with me after we made love. We'd pass it back and forth as we lay on our backs looking up at the ceiling, blowing plumes of smoke into the darkness. Sometimes, when she was upset about something, or upset with me, she'd ask for a cigarette. She'd puff at it furiously until it was half gone, then stab it out as if she were angry at the ashtray.

"So what's going to happen?" she said.

"The local cops will come, verify that there's been a homicide. Then the state cops will come. They're the ones who handle homicide investigations. They'll separate us and ask us questions. This whole area"—I swept my hand around—"will be a crime scene."

"What kind of questions?" she said.

"Everything," I said. "You'll have to tell them all about Larry."

"It's a long story."

"They'll want to hear it all, and you'll probably have to tell it several times." I hesitated. "Don't volunteer anything. Just answer their questions. You might want to have a lawyer with you."

She cocked her head and frowned at me. "Why would I want a lawyer?"

I shrugged. "Their questioning might get pretty intense and confusing. A lawyer can help you through it."

"No offense," she said, "but I don't need a damn lawyer."

"Well, you know you can change your mind at any time. All you have to do is ask for one, and they'll have to stop questioning you."

"Are you reading me my rights?"

I shook my head. "No, honey. Just trying to tell you what'll probably happen."

Evie took a quick drag on her cigarette, threw it down onto the dirt road, and ground it out under her foot as if she were squashing a poisonous bug. Then she folded her arms across her chest, turned away, and gazed off into the woods.

I touched her shoulder, and she flinched away from me.

So we stood there beside Larry's body, and after a minute, sirens howled in the distance, and then two police cruisers came barreling over the hilltop. Their sirens squawked as they skidded to a stop, and they left a billow of dust in their wake.

Each cruiser held two police officers. Three of them got out, leaving the driver of the second cruiser behind the wheel to tend the radio.

One cop went over and looked down at Larry Scott's body. The other two approached Evie and me. One was a middle-aged guy with gray showing under his cap. The other was an olive-skinned young female officer who looked like she'd been cultivating the hard scowl on her face.

The female spoke to Evie, then led her over to one of the cruisers. The gray-haired guy stood in front of me. "Sergeant Costello," he said. "Brewster PD."

"Brady Coyne," I said. "I'm a lawyer in Boston. We're renting this cottage for the weekend." I held out my hand.

He didn't seem to notice it. "I want you to come over and sit in the cruiser, sir. We've got to wait for the state police to get here."

"I know how it works," I said.

He nodded. "I'm sure you do, sir."

He led me to the second cruiser. Evie was sitting in the back seat of the first one. The doors were closed and the female officer was sitting in front. Evie was staring out the side window, and when I tried to catch her eye, she shifted her gaze to somewhere behind me.

I climbed in the back. Costello put his hand on top of my head to steer me in, closed the door behind me, then got in front. He left his door open. A wire mesh separated us. He mumbled something that was not intended for my ears to the cop behind the wheel, who turned and grinned at him.

After about five minutes I said, "Do you mind if I smoke?"

"Yes," Costello said without turning around.

A few minutes later two more cars rolled up behind us. They were both unmarked sedans, and they had not heralded their arrival with sirens. State cops in plain clothes.

Costello got out and went over to talk to them.

"Now what happens?" I said to the officer behind the wheel.

He did not answer me.

After a while Costello came back, slid into the front seat, slammed the door, and said, "Let's go."

The driver managed to turn around on the narrow dirt road, and we headed into town. Costello spoke into the car radio. I couldn't make out what he said.

At the station Costello led me into a small room in the back. It had one square window high on the wall. It was covered with thick wire mesh. In the middle of the room stood a single rectangular steel table with six straight-backed wooden chairs around it. A big metal ashtray brimming with old cigarette butts sat on the table.

"Have a seat, sir," said Costello. "You can smoke in here if you want. Can I get you some coffee?"

"Sure," I said, "thanks. Black."

He shut the door behind him, and I didn't need to check to know it was locked from the outside.

A few minutes later he was back. He put a heavy ceramic mug in front of me and left without saying anything.

It wasn't bad for police-station coffee. I sipped it and smoked and sat there in the uncomfortable wooden chair. I assumed Evie was getting the same treatment in an adjacent room.

I didn't need my lawyer training to realize that we were both prime suspects. Dozens of people had witnessed Evie's confrontation with Larry Scott at the restaurant. Several others had seen him beat me up in the parking lot. The police wouldn't have much trouble learning that Larry had harassed Evie back when she was living in Cortland and that he'd tracked us down here to the Cape.

Means, motive, and opportunity. Either or both of us had plenty of all three. I didn't know anybody else who'd want Larry dead, but I didn't know anything about him. I hoped Evie could come up with somebody.

I waited nearly an hour before the door opened and two men came in. The bulky, bald-headed one introduced himself as state police homicide detective Neil Vanderweigh. He wore a gray summer-weight suit with a solid-blue necktie that he'd pulled loose. His collar button was undone. The younger blond guy was Sergeant Lipton. He wore a green sports jacket, gray slacks, pale blue shirt, no necktie.

They both shook hands with me. Then Vanderweigh took off his suit jacket, draped it over a chair, and sat across from me. Lipton put a portable tape recorder on the table between us, then went over, leaned against the wall, and crossed his arms.

"Any objection if we record this?" said Vanderweigh.

I shook my head.

He clicked the machine on, recited the date, time, place, and our names into it, then looked up at me. "Why don't you just tell us what happened this morning, Mr. Coyne."

I told him about hearing Evie scream, running out of the cottage, and seeing her there with Larry's body.

He asked if either of us had touched the body. I told him I'd touched his bloody shirt with my fingertip, that was all.

He asked what we'd done at the crime scene. I told him we'd each smoked a cigarette and ground out the butts on the dirt road.

He asked several clarifying questions. They mostly had to do with time—what time Evie had left to go jogging, how long she'd been gone before I heard her scream, how long we'd waited before calling the police. I answered the questions as best as I could.

He led me through the events at the restaurant the previous night, and it was clear he already knew all about it.

"Did you threaten him?" said Vanderweigh.

"I don't recall threatening him," I said.

"You didn't tell him to leave the woman alone—or else?"

I shook my head. "I don't think I said 'or else,' no."

"You don't *know* what you said?"

I shrugged. "I was angry. He was upsetting Evie. He shoved me and I went after him, and he punched me."

"You know that Ms. Banyon had a relationship with Mr. Scott in Cortland a few years ago."

"I only learned that last night."

"That he harassed her for almost a year?"

"That's what she told me."

"Did you kill Larry Scott, Mr. Coyne?"

"No."

"Did Evelyn Banyon kill Larry Scott?"

"No."

"You're a lawyer," said Vanderweigh. "Be precise, please."

I nodded. "To the best of my knowledge, Evelyn Banyon did not kill Larry Scott."

He smiled at my lawyerly precision. "When Ms. Banyon left to go jogging, did she bring a knife with her?"

"No. She had some pepper spray."

"Why did she bring pepper spray?"

"We were both concerned that she might encounter him."

"Scott?"

"Yes."

"And you feared he might try to harm her?"

I shrugged. "It occurred to me."

"Do you know for a fact that she didn't bring a knife with her?"

"No," I said. "I guess I don't. I stayed in bed."

"And you went back to sleep."

"Yes."

"So you have no idea what she did between the time she left the bedroom and when you heard her screaming."

"I have a very good idea," I said. "She told me."

"But she could be lying."

I sighed. "She's not lying."

"In fact," he said, "if you're telling the truth, you really cannot tell us anything about Ms. Banyon's actions this morning between the time she walked out of your bedroom and when you heard her screaming and came upon her with Scott's body in the driveway, is that right?"

"I am telling the truth," I said.

I wondered what they were asking Evie. Probably establishing the fact that *she* couldn't account for *my* actions while she had been jogging in Brewster.

They had themselves two excellent suspects.

Vanderweigh led me through his questions again, and then Lipton came over and sat with us and asked me the same damn questions. I asked for more coffee, and Vanderweigh went and

34

got it. I'd had no breakfast, and I was feeling woozy and light-headed. The coffee helped a little.

It seemed like I'd been in there for several hours when there came a soft knock on the door. Lipton got up and went out of the room.

He was back a minute later. He was holding a plastic zip-pered bag. He put it on the table between us. It held a knife. The blade was five or six inches long with a serrated edge. It looked like a steak knife.

"Recognize this, Mr. Coyne?" said Lipton.

"No. Is it the murder weapon?"

"Maybe." He glanced at Vanderweigh, then turned back to me. "It appears to match a set of knives from the kitchen in the cottage you were renting."

I said nothing.

"It was found in the bushes about twenty feet from Larry Scott's body."

"So it's probably the murder weapon," I said.

"That remains to be seen," said Vanderweigh. "Take another look at it."

I looked at it and shrugged. "We've only been in the cottage since night before last. We haven't cooked or eaten there, except for cereal yesterday morning and sandwiches for lunch. We didn't use any sharp knives. The woman who owns the place kept the key under the doormat. Anybody could've gotten in there."

They asked me a few more questions—the same ones they'd been asking me before—and then the two of them looked at each other, and Vanderweigh said, "Terminating interrogation at—" He glanced at the clock on the wall. "—at eleven forty-seven A.M." He snapped off the tape recorder. "You're free to go, Mr. Coyne, but I've got to ask you not to return to that cottage."

"Crime scene and all."

35

"Yes."

"For how long?"

"A couple days, anyway."

"So what're we supposed to do?"

"That's up to you. Go home, if you want."

"All our stuff is in that cottage. My car's there."

Vanderweigh nodded. "I'll have one of the Brewster officers take you back to get your things. I'm afraid you can't have your car for a while, though."

"You think we killed him somewhere else and transported his body to our driveway?" I said. "So we could find it and report it and make ourselves logical suspects?"

He shrugged. "Why don't you go clean out the cottage? When you get back, I'm sure someone'll be happy to help you find a rental."

"What about Evie?"

"You can wait here for her."

They'd had me for more than three hours. And they still weren't done with Evie.

I hoped she was doing all right.

I hoped they hadn't caught her in a lie.

A young Brewster patrolman drove me back to the cottage. A pair of sawhorses sat in the driveway at the turnoff. A cruiser was parked there, and an officer sat behind the wheel with the door open. When we pulled up, the officer got out and moved one of the sawhorses. We drove down the drive-way. Two unmarked sedans were stopped near the place where Larry's body had lain. There was a long string of yellow crime-scene tape around the area. A man with two cameras hanging from his neck and another in his hand waved us around it.

My chaperon followed me through the cottage while I packed up Evie's and my stuff. He watched me closely and didn't offer to help me lug it to his cruiser. I told him I had some things that I needed in my car. He said I'd have to leave them.

Then he drove me back to the station.

They were still questioning Evie.

The receptionist at the front desk scribbled down the number for a local Ford dealer, told me they rented cars, and pointed to a pay phone on the wall. My friendly Ford salesman told me he could hold a Taurus sedan for me. Sixty-eight bucks a day, which was robbery, but I agreed to it and recited my credit-card number to him.

I got two bags of peanuts and a Coke from a vending machine, sat in the waiting room, and waited. Police officers came and went. None of them looked at me.

Poor Evie. I figured they were grilling her. Maybe she'd asked for a lawyer, and they were holding off their interrogation until he arrived.

I couldn't serve as her attorney. I was a witness in their investigation.

Maybe they'd arrested her.

That niggle of doubt came back. Actually, it had never quite left me. Maybe Evie *had* done it. The more Vanderweigh had questioned me, the more I'd realized that I had no idea whether she had done it or not.

Means? A knife from the kitchen of our cottage.

Motive? Larry Scott had made her life miserable.

Opportunity? No witness could say where she'd been or what she'd done for the hour or so after she'd left the cottage in the morning.

I didn't want to think about it. I didn't want to invent scenarios in which Evie came jogging back to the cottage and found Larry Scott standing in the driveway blocking her way, begging to talk with her. I tried not to visualize Evie going up to him and stabbing him twice in the stomach.

But it was hard not to.

It was almost two o'clock in the afternoon when Evie came into the waiting room. She glanced around, saw me, and shook her head. She looked dazed and pale and frightened.

I stood up, went to her, and put my arms around her. She laid her forehead on my chest but did not return my hug.

I kissed her forehead. "You all right?" I whispered into her hair.

"No," she said.

"I'm sorry, babe."

"Not your fault. Can we get out of here?"

"You're free to go?"

"For now. They think I did it."

"They think I did it too," I said. "But we didn't. They'll figure it out."

She looked up at me. "Will they?"

"Of course they will."

The same officer who'd driven me to the cottage took us to the Ford place, and pretty soon we were in a new-smelling Taurus driving west on Route 6A, heading back to Boston.

I started to say something about my old vow never to visit the Cape in the summer. But when I glanced at Evie beside me, I recognized that jut of her chin and hunch of her shoulders, and I decided she was in no mood for stupid jokes.

FOUR

It was early afternoon on that sunny Saturday in August, and westbound Cape Cod traffic on 6A was stop-and-go. More stop than go. There were frequent turnoffs and stoplights all along 6A, not to mention antique shops and used-book stores and nurseries and coffee shops and views of the marsh and the bay—all of which any dyed-in-the-wool Summer Person was obliged at least to slow down for.

Evie rode silently beside me. She'd found some classical music on the radio of our rented Taurus, and she slouched back in her seat with her eyes closed and her hands folded in her lap. I didn't think she was sleeping. I figured she just didn't feel like talking.

We put Brewster behind us, and as we passed through Dennis I said, "How about something to eat?"

"I'm not hungry," she said without opening her eyes. "I just want to go home. Get something for yourself if you want."

I decided the couple of mugs of cop coffee, two bags of peanuts, and the Coke would last me. I wasn't very hungry either.

When we got to the Sagamore Bridge, which spans the canal that separates Cape Cod from the mainland, I pointed to the big sign. *Desperate? Call the Samaritans,* it read. Probably intended for folks who were tempted to leap off the bridge, although I've always suspected that the Samaritans got a lot of business from desperate weekend drivers stuck in the traffic.

"Shall we give 'em a call?" I said to Evie.

She opened her eyes and glanced at the sign. "I'm not desperate," she said. "I'm not in a very good mood, either. Don't make jokes, please."

I shrugged. Under the circumstances, I figured she was entitled to any mood she wanted.

Once we got over the bridge and were heading back home on Route 3, the traffic thinned out and we zipped along. I made a few conversational forays, all of which Evie either tartly rebuffed or ignored entirely, and we pulled up in front of her townhouse in Concord at a little after four-thirty without having talked about our experiences at the Brewster police station.

I wanted to know what they'd asked her, what she'd said, how they'd treated her, and I was disappointed and a little hurt that she didn't want to tell me or to hear about what I'd been through.

But I knew Evie better than to push it. That's how she was. I'd experienced her dark withdrawals before. Evie liked to think things through on her own before she talked about them. Eventually she'd get a handle on it. Then we'd talk.

I got out of the car, opened the trunk, took out her duffel bag and her backpack, and started to lug them to her door.

"I've got them," she said.

"I'll carry them for you," I said. "They're heavy."

She touched my arm. "I said, I'll take them."

I shrugged and handed the bags to her. "I assume that means I'm dismissed?"

She nodded. "I need to be alone."

"It's Saturday," I said. "Maybe our weekend on the Cape got ruined, but we always—"

"I've spent enough time today with people who think I murdered somebody," she said. Then she turned and trudged up to her door.

"I don't think you murdered anybody," I called to her.

"Yes you do," she said without turning around.

I stood there and watched Evie unlock her door and drag her bags inside. Then I turned, got into my car, and headed home to my solitary apartment on the waterfront in Boston.

I've been renting the same condominium unit on Lewis Wharf on the Boston Inner Harbor ever since I split from Gloria eleven years ago. My landlord keeps threatening to put the place on the market, and if he ever does, I suppose I'll have to decide either to buy it or to move to something permanent.

My place has one big bedroom, where I sleep, and a smaller one, where I store things. There are cardboard boxes in there that I haven't opened in eleven years.

The living room, dining room, and kitchen are one big room. It has floor-to-ceiling sliding glass doors that open onto a narrow iron balcony overlooking the harbor. Across the water lie East Boston and Logan Airport. Way off to the left sits the old Charlestown Navy Yard, and beyond it looms the Mystic River Bridge. The nighttime view from my balcony features traffic lights and city lights and airplane lights and the lights of the ferries and barges and tankers and fishing boats and pleasure craft that chug around the harbor at all hours. I can spit over the railing and hit the ocean six stories down.

On a damp night, I can hear a friendly bell buoy clanging in slow, comforting rhythm. The harbor smells are strongest on a foggy night—salt air and seaweed, dead fish and diesel fumes.

I know my neighbors in the building only well enough to nod to in the elevator that runs up from the parking garage in the basement.

I furnished my place with discarded stuff from the house Gloria and I used to share in Wellesley, and in eleven years I haven't replaced any of it.

I can walk to my office in Copley Square, and I usually do. Even in the winter, coming home is a pleasant stroll up Newbury Street, across the Public Garden and the Boston Common, and through the financial district and Quincy Market. I can walk to Chinatown and the North End and the Fleet Center and Fenway Park and the New England Aquarium from my place. Skeeter's Infield, which serves a hundred varieties of beer and the best burgers in the city, lies halfway between my office and Lewis Wharf.

I moved there in a hurry when Gloria and I agreed we couldn't live together for another day, and at the time I figured it was a stopgap until I found something that suited me, or until Gloria and I decided we needed to be together after all.

After eleven years, it still felt temporary. Eleven years, and I was still waiting to see where my life was headed.

"Simplify, simplify," Thoreau said. He moved to a one-room cabin in the woods on Walden Pond to get away from people and figure things out, and I guess I was doing the same thing.

It had taken Thoreau only a couple of years. For me, it had been over a decade and I hadn't made much progress.

I got home around five-thirty. I dropped my duffel bag on the bed, got a Coke from the refrigerator, and went out onto the balcony. I lit a cigarette, leaned my forearms on the railing, and gazed at the water.

I wondered what Evie was doing.

She believed that I thought she had killed Larry Scott. I had to fight the urge to call her and try to convince her that I knew her better than that.

Actually, she was half-right. I wasn't sure what I thought.

Evie had powerful intuition. She always seemed to know what I was thinking—sometimes even better than I did.

When she was ready to talk, she'd call me.

I finished my cigarette, flipped it over the railing, and went back inside. I turned on my old black-and-white television for company, found a ball game, then went into the bedroom. I unzipped my duffel bag, turned it upside down on the bed, and started putting my weekend stuff away.

On the bottom of the pile I found the little carved quail I'd bought in Provincetown for Evie. When I'd collected our things from the cottage under the watchful eye of the Brewster police officer, in my haste I must have stuck the little bird into my bag instead of hers.

I held it in my hand and looked at it. The artist had not painted it. Instead, he'd used the grain of the wood to suggest the texture of the feathers. It looked so real that I wanted to stroke those feathers with my fingertip.

I suspected that I'd slipped the little wooden bird into my bag with some subconscious intent. A hostage, maybe, against the easily imagined possibility that Evie would go into one of her withdrawals—as, in fact, she had done. An excuse to call her. *I've got your quail, honey. Why don't I just bring it over, and while I'm there, we can have a drink.*

Nope. She'd call me when she was ready, and she'd be ready quicker if I respected her distance.

* * *

43

She didn't call that night, or all day Sunday or Monday, either, and finally, when I was ready for bed on Monday night, I took a deep breath and dialed her number.

Her machine answered. "It's Evie. I can't come to the phone right now, but your call is important to me, so please leave a message and I'll get back to you, I promise."

I did not leave a message. I had a feeling that if I did, she'd break her promise.

On Tuesday I called my old friend Roger Horowitz, who was a state police homicide detective. When he picked up the phone, the first thing he said to me was, "I can't talk to you."

"There was a homicide in Brewster," I said.

"Why do you think I can't talk to you?"

"Am I a suspect?"

"Read my lips, Coyne."

"Roger," I said, "you know me. I didn't kill anybody. You know Evie, too. Are your colleagues making any progress on this thing?"

"If you don't want to chat about the Red Sox or something," he said, "then I'm hanging up."

"Okay," I said. " 'Bye."

State police detective Neil Vanderweigh called me at the office on Wednesday afternoon. "We're done with your car," he said. "You can come get it whenever you want."

"That was quick," I said. "I expected to be driving this clunky Taurus for a month."

"We aim to please," he said.

Another midsummer trek to the Cape, I was thinking. But I wanted my BMW back. And I definitely wanted to talk with Vanderweigh. I checked my calendar, saw nothing that couldn't be moved around, and said, "How's tomorrow?"

"Good. The sooner the better. Tell me what time you'll be here, and I'll bring your car, meet you at that Ford place where you got your rental."

"That's awfully nice of you," I said.

"Not really. We've got to talk."

"Yes, we do," I said. "You're required to tell me if I'm an official suspect, you know."

"I'm aware of my obligations," he said. He cleared his throat. "You have killed two men. Shot 'em both at point-blank range with that thirty-eight you keep in your office safe. That's a lot of dead guys for a mild-mannered lawyer who devotes his life to helping rich people guard their money."

"That's my job, not my life," I said. "Anyway, both of those guys were—"

"I know," he said quickly. "They were bad guys." He hesitated. "You were protecting a woman in jeopardy both times."

He let that thought linger there. I didn't know if Larry Scott was really a bad guy, but Evie certainly had seemed to be a woman in jeopardy.

I said nothing.

After a minute, Vanderweigh chuckled. "Look, Mr. Coyne. I'm just trying to solve a murder here, and I could use some help, okay?"

"Okay," I said. "Good. I'd like to get this murder solved too. I'll be there around noontime."

My rented Taurus had no sunroof, no CD player, no leather seats, no clutch, no stick shift. It was no fun, and I couldn't wait to get rid of it.

And so a week to the day after Evie and I had driven to the Cape for our fateful encounter with Larry Scott—*fatal*, for him—I found myself driving down there again. This time

I was alone on Route 3 with only my thoughts for company, and instead of dwelling on how much I hated Cape Cod in the summer, I thought about Evie.

We had not spoken since I'd dropped her off at her door on Saturday afternoon, and I missed her. This was a long silence, even for her, and it caused me again to wonder what had really happened that morning when she was out jogging.

I tried to think: If Evie really had knifed Larry Scott that morning, would she have told me? We'd been friends for almost a year and lovers for several months. One of the things I'd learned about her was that she was absolutely direct. If she didn't want to talk about something, she said so. If she did talk about it, she said exactly what she felt. There had been many times in the year I'd known her when the easiest, kindest thing for her to do would have been to lie, and she never did.

On the other hand there were many things she refused to talk about, including virtually her entire life up to the time we'd met. If I asked her casual questions about her childhood or her family or her old lovers or previous jobs, she'd accuse me of idle curiosity, as if that was unworthy of me. She always said her past life was irrelevant, that now was what counted, and up until a week ago, I'd pretty much agreed with her. I didn't talk about my past much, either, and Evie had expressed no idle curiosity about it whatsoever.

I loved the Evie I knew, not the Evie who'd existed before that. Whatever had happened before I met her was relevant only insofar as it had made her the person she had become.

Now it seemed Larry Scott had contributed mightily to the person she'd become, and it made me understand that we are all a sum of our experiences, for better or worse, whether we like it or not.

Maybe she had lied to me. Maybe she had expected to encounter Scott there in our driveway that morning. Maybe she

46

had taken a knife from the kitchen. If she had, and if she'd killed him with it, it would give state police detective Neil Vanderweigh a good argument for malice aforethought. Intent and premeditation. Not just murder, but murder in the first degree.

How well did I really know Evie?

That was the question.

I figured Vanderweigh planned to try some misdirection on me. A pleasant lunch, some casual conversation. He'd already shown me his inquisitor side. Now he'd probably try to show me what a nice guy he was.

I assumed he still suspected both of us, either as alternate suspects or as a team.

Objectively, we were both damn good suspects.

Well, it didn't matter. Vanderweigh could think whatever he wanted, and he could pick my brain to his heart's content. I wasn't hiding anything, so telling the truth would be easy.

I arrived at the Ford place in Brewster a few minutes before noon, and just about the time they finished checking the Taurus for dents and scratches and verified that I'd topped off the gas tank, my green BMW pulled into the lot and Detective Neil Vanderweigh got out. He was wearing a Red Sox cap, and without his bald head showing, I didn't recognize him at first. He came inside, saw me signing papers with the salesman, lifted his hand and nodded, and went back outside.

I joined him a minute later. We shook hands and got into my car. I waved my hand around the inside. "So what'd you find?"

He smiled. "If we found anything incriminating, I wouldn't tell you. On the other hand, if we found anything incriminating, I probably wouldn't be returning it to you. Feel like some lunch?"

"Sure. Where to?"

He directed me back to Dennis, then down a side street to a low-slung shingled place on the water. It was called the Lighthouse Tavern. Poetic license. I knew of no lighthouse on the bay side of the Cape.

I found a slot at the far end of the jammed parking lot, and we went inside. The place featured dim, indirect lighting and soft music and dark woodwork, fishing nets with cork floats draped on the walls, fake portholes, and a solid glass back wall overlooking still another Cape Cod tidal creek. The lobby was crammed with middle-aged men in baggy shorts and tanned women in capri pants and whiny children in foul tempers, but when Vanderweigh took off his cap to reveal his bald head, the hostess looked up, smiled at him, and waved us over.

We shouldered our way through the crowd, and when we got to the hostess, she put her hand on Vanderweigh's arm, kissed his cheek, and led us to a table by the window. "The usual?" she said to him.

He nodded.

"Sir?" she said to me.

"Coffee, please. Black."

She put menus in front of us. "Want to know the specials?"

Vanderweigh shook his head, and so did I.

When she left, I said, "Friend of yours, huh?"

"That's my daughter-in-law. My son owns this place. This is my table. They hold it for me unless I tell them not to. I eat here just about every day."

I picked up a menu. "Any recommendations?"

"The fish is always fresh."

A middle-aged waitress brought iced tea for Vanderweigh and coffee for me, and the two of them talked about her son, who was working on a fishing boat out of New Bedford for the summer and planned to take business courses at UMass Dartmouth in the fall. I ended up ordering a lobster roll. Vanderweigh asked for the turkey club, no mayonnaise.

After the waitress left, he mentioned fishing, and I told him I loved fly-fishing, so we talked about that for a while, and the more we didn't talk about Larry Scott's murder, the more I began to suspect that Vanderweigh knew something, or had what he thought was strong evidence of something, and that he was trying to lull me into dropping my defenses.

Well, that was okay. Since I had no secrets, I needed no defenses.

When our sandwiches arrived, Vanderweigh asked about my family and my job, and I answered all his questions. I had the feeling I wasn't telling him anything he didn't already know.

We finished eating, the waitress cleared our table and brought more iced tea and hot coffee, and still the subject of Larry Scott's murder had not come up.

Then he said, "How well do you know Evelyn Banyon?"

I smiled. "Aha."

"You were wondering when I'd get around to that subject."

"I figured you'd wait till you'd softened me up."

"So?"

I shrugged. "I met her nearly a year ago. We've been—I never know what to call it—in a relationship, I guess you'd say, for five or six months. I know her intimately. But you're not asking about our intimate life . . . are you?"

"No." He smiled. "But if you want to talk about it—"

"I don't."

"Of course you don't." He cleared his throat. "I talked with my colleague and your friend Roger Horowitz the other day. He urged me to consider you an ally. I told him it was impossible to eliminate you as a suspect in this case, and he told me that was a waste of time. I have a lot of respect for Horowitz, but I do have some doubts about you."

"I don't blame you," I said. "I'm a good suspect. I didn't do it. But I guess I'd suspect me, too."

49

"Horowitz rarely places much stock in somebody's character," he said. "We've both seen too many fine, upstanding people with no history of anything criminal committing horrific crimes." He waved his hand in the air. "Anyway, for the record, and in the interest of candor, you should know that I have been unable to find any evidence that you did *not* commit this crime, so you have got to be a suspect. The same goes for Ms. Banyon."

"Any evidence that either of us did it?"

"Compelling circumstances," he said. "As you know."

I nodded. "Means, motive, and opportunity."

"Right. Both of you are obvious suspects, and nine times out of ten it's just that simple. The obvious suspect is the one who did it."

"Occam's razor," I said.

"Sure," he said. "Whatever." He took a sip of iced tea, gazed out the window for a minute, then turned back to me. "We learn in cop school to pay a lot of attention to the obvious. When we don't, we generally end up looking stupid. Remember the Stuart case?"

"Sure," I said. "Chuck Stuart. They found him in his car outside a hospital in Dorchester with a gunshot wound in his gut and his wife shot dead beside him. He told the police some black guy robbed them. Very plausible in that part of the city. So the cops went looking for a young black guy who fit Stuart's description. Found him, too, and dragged him away in a flurry of flashbulbs. Turned out Stuart had set the whole thing up, killed his wife, shot himself, had his brother drive by to collect the weapon and dispose of it, invented the black suspect. Chuck Stuart ended up writing a confession and jumping off the Mystic River Bridge. Got a lot of ink, that story."

"That," said Vanderweigh, "was one of those cases where there were two obvious suspects, and the Boston cops picked the wrong one. There are plenty of robberies and murders in that part of the city, and they're almost always committed by young black men. On the other hand, whenever somebody is murdered, your first suspect has got to be the spouse."

"As I remember it," I said, "when it all shook out, the Boston cops caught hell from the black community for having the temerity to actually suspect a black man from the worst neighborhood in New England of breaking the law."

"How it goes. Everybody fucks up sometimes." Vanderweigh shook his head. "The worst thing is to ignore the obvious, and as it turns out, that's what the Boston cops did. They were too willing to believe the story of a white guy, even if it did make a lot of sense. Hell, the man had a bullet hole in his stomach. Still, they forgot that he was the spouse." He sighed. "Point is, we also learn that sometimes things aren't that obvious. I've spent the last several days trying to find holes in what you and Ms. Banyon told us."

"And?" I said.

"And I see three possibilities." He held up three fingers, then bent one of them down. "One, you're both lying." He bent down the second finger. "Two, you're both telling the truth. And, three"—he bent down the third finger—"one of you is lying and one of you is telling the truth." He shook his head. "I'm bothered by the fact that if you're both lying, and the two of you invented this story, it's seriously flawed."

"Because neither of us can give the other one an alibi," I said. "It's not a very good story, is it?"

He nodded. "I'd expect an experienced attorney to do better. This leads me to believe that one of you, at least, is telling the truth."

"The one who didn't kill Larry Scott, you're thinking."

"Right. Ms. Banyon could've gone running, just the way she said, and on her way back found his body. In which case, you could've killed him."

I started to speak, but he held up his hand. "Or," he said,

"she could've encountered him there on the driveway and knifed him while you were sleeping. Either way, one of you's telling the truth and one's lying."

"Or," I said, "neither of us killed him and we're both telling the truth."

"Of course," said Vanderweigh. "For the sake of argument, let's say you're both telling the truth."

"You might find that line of thought productive," I said, "given the fact that it happens to be true."

"In that case," he said, "somebody else did it."

"I am witnessing a brilliant deductive mind at work."

"Yeah, Horowitz said you had a smart mouth." He smiled. "So the question is, if not one of you two, then who?"

"You asking me?"

He arched his eyebrows.

I shook my head. "I don't have a clue. Do you?"

Vanderweigh stared out the window, and without turning to face me, he said quietly, "When you've got not one but two excellent suspects, what a good detective does is, he starts building the case. He questions the suspects. He takes testimony from witnesses. He checks backgrounds. He gathers forensic evidence. He looks for the anomaly, the fact that doesn't fit, the thing that makes him doubt his case, and he tries to maintain his objectivity. A good detective *does* want to get it right, Mr. Coyne, because he does not want some competent defense lawyer making him look stupid. But when he can't find any anomaly, he doesn't see much purpose in looking around for other, less obvious suspects."

"You're telling me that Evie and I are your only suspects."

He turned his head, looked at me for a minute, then shrugged.

I planted my forearms on the table and leaned toward him. "So why are you telling me these things, Detective? What's this"—I waved my hand around the restaurant—"this friendly lunch all about?"

"Was it that friendly?"

I smiled. "It was friendly enough."

"I didn't give anything away, did I?"

"Nothing I haven't already thought of. I was hoping you'd tell me what your forensics experts turned up."

"Is that a question?"

"Sure."

He shrugged. "They concluded that Lawrence Scott died of two knife wounds to the abdomen sometime between five and seven A.M. on Saturday morning. They found no defense wounds on his hands or arms."

"Meaning?"

"Meaning," he said, "that he was standing very close to his assailant and didn't expect to be attacked, that he didn't see it coming."

"You think he knew his killer?" I said.

"Very likely," said Vanderweigh.

Larry Scott knew Evie well. He had also made my acquaintance. "What else did forensics find?" I said.

"Scott died where he fell," he said. "The sand under his body was saturated with blood. According to the medical examiner, his body had not been moved."

"That's why I got my car back so soon," I said. "You knew we hadn't transported a dead body in it."

"It's more complicated than that," he said.

"But my car was clean."

"Clean?" He laughed. "They found a fully packed overnight bag, not to mention pieces of monofilament, old fishhooks, dirty socks, rubber boots, a couple of hats, dried mud, pine needles, an old Army blanket—"

"That's what a trunk is for," I said.

53

Vanderweigh nodded. "That steak knife was the murder weapon, Mr. Coyne, and it was, in fact, a match for seven other six-inch steak knives that were in the kitchen drawer of that cottage you were renting." He arched his eyebrows at me.

"The key was under the doormat," I said. "Anybody could've gotten in there. Evie and I were gone all afternoon and well into the evening on Friday."

He shrugged. "A serrated knife is a nasty weapon. The ME figured the victim was standing up when the first thrust was made. It went up under the rib cage and ripped into his heart. Right-handed blow, delivered with enough force to make a bruise where it entered. A mortal wound. He fell on his back and died within a couple of minutes. The killer stabbed him again in the belly for good measure, also up to the hilt, then threw the weapon into the bushes."

"You're reading a lot of anger in those blows."

"They weren't halfhearted, that's for sure."

"What about footprints or tire tracks? Find anything in Scott's pockets? Where was his car? Where was he staying? What about witnesses?"

Vanderweigh laughed. "Don't push it, Mr. Coyne. You don't expect me to tell you everything."

"Obviously you didn't find any fingerprints on that knife," I said, "or you'd know for sure that it wasn't Evie or me."

"Or that it was. You're right. It's too bad."

"So none of your evidence exonerates either of us, then."

"No," he said. "It doesn't. Thing is, I'm pretty convinced it wasn't the both of you, working together, who killed Mr. Scott. If it was, one of you would've confessed it, or at least slipped up, when we questioned you, and surely you would've come up with better alibis for each other."

"But you *do* think it was one of us."

He started to say something, then shook his head. "I didn't say that. I guess all I'm saying is, I'm still in the market for suspects. As it is, Horowitz says it couldn't possibly be you, and that leaves me with your friend."

"Evie didn't kill anybody."

"You don't know that."

"Yes, I do."

He arched his eyebrows at me.

"You're the one who's got to make the case," I said.

"We've got a damn good circumstantial case, Mr. Coyne. Means, opportunity, and more motive than you can imagine."

"What do you mean by that?"

"How well do you really know Ms. Banyon?"

I looked at him and said nothing. That was the question he'd started our conversation with.

Vanderweigh picked up his iced-tea glass, tilted it up until the half melted ice cubes clicked against his teeth, drained it, and put it down on the table. "Well," he said, "I gotta get back to work." He started to stand up.

"Wait a minute," I said.

He shook his head. "Go home, Mr. Coyne."

"What about Evie? What did you mean, 'more motive than I could imagine'?"

"You talked to her lately?"

"No," I said.

"Me neither."

I stared at him. "If you needed to have this conversation with me, you certainly wanted to talk with Evie, too."

"When you see her," he said, "tell her it makes a bad impression, not responding to a polite request after a police officer specifically tells you it's important to be cooperative."

"You've tried to reach her?"

He shrugged.

"She's avoiding you?"

"We'd very much like to talk with her," he said. "The fact that we've tried without success . . ."

I knew what he was thinking. He was thinking that Evie was acting guilty.

FIVE

I called Evie after supper that night. When her machine answered, I hung up, hesitated, then dialed her again and left a message. "It's me, honey," I said. "I retrieved my car today down in Brewster and had lunch with Detective Vanderweigh. You and I have got to talk. Please call me."

I kept my portable phone by my feet on the coffee table while I read the newspaper with one eye and watched the Red Sox beat the Tigers with the other. Evie didn't call. I tried her again after the game, got her machine, and didn't bother leaving another message. I called a third time after I crawled into bed around midnight. This time after her message, I said, "It's me again. I know you're listening. Come on, honey. Please pick up the phone. I guess you're still mad at me. Well, I'm sorry about that, but we've got to talk about what happened last weekend. Detective Vanderweigh wants to talk to you, too, and you can't just ignore him. It makes it look bad for you."

I waited. But she did not pick up the phone.

When I got to work on Friday morning, the second thing I did after pouring myself a mug of coffee was call Evie's office at Emerson Hospital in Concord. When she didn't answer, I left a message on her voice mail. "We've really got to talk," I said. "It's important. Call me when you get in."

I had nonstop meetings with clients scheduled for the morning, so I went out to the reception area and told Julie that if Evie called, she should interrupt me, that I absolutely needed to talk with her.

Julie frowned at me. "What's going on, Brady?"

I had told Julie all about the events of the previous weekend. I always told Julie everything. "I can't get ahold of her," I said. "It's starting to look like the police think she killed that man, and she's avoiding them, too. It makes her look guilty. Actually, I'm a little worried."

"You think something's happened to her?"

I shrugged.

"You don't think she actually could have—"

"No," I said quickly. "Not Evie. Evie couldn't kill anybody." I shook my head. "I guess I just don't know. Truthfully, I don't know what to think."

"She's mad at you," said Julie. "I don't blame her. You're easy to get mad at."

"Yeah, well, in this case—"

"Brady, for heaven's sake, think about it. She found the body of that man who'd been stalking her. If that's not bad enough, then she gets interrogated by the police for hours. What should she expect from her best friend, her lover, her— her rock?"

"I thought I was quite supportive."

"Supportive?" Julie rolled her pretty blue eyes. "You've got to do better than *supportive*, Brady Coyne." She pronounced the word "supportive" as if it meant a disgusting animal waste product. "I bet you were all lawyerly and rational, eager to discuss the facts of the case, ponder evidence, devise strategies. Am I right?"

"I had it in the back of my mind that she might've done it," I said. "But I didn't say that to her."

"God!" She shook her head. "If you think she didn't pick up on that, you understand women even less than I thought."

"Well, whatever," I said. "At this point, I need to advise her."

"You," said Julie, "are the last person she wants advice from. Any half-assed lawyer can give advice. From her lover, all a woman wants is unconditional love and understanding and sympathy."

"Are you calling me a half-assed lawyer?"

She rolled her eyes.

I sighed. "You're a woman," I said. "You should know. I guess you're right. So what'm I supposed to do?"

"Keep trying," she said. "Women appreciate persistence. Shower her with messages. Tell her you love her, you miss her, you're miserable, you can't stand it, not talking with her is driving you crazy."

"That's all true," I said.

"Is it so hard to say, then?"

I smiled. "No. I can say it." I leaned across Julie's desk and kissed her forehead. "Thank you."

She pointed to my office. "Do it."

So I went back into my office and left messages of love and misery on both Evie's home answering machine and her office voice mail.

After I ushered my last client of the morning out of my office around one o'clock that afternoon, I arched my eyebrows at Julie.

She shook her head.

"Evie didn't call, huh?"

"No," she said.

So I went back into my office and called Marcus Bluestein. Bluestein was the administrator at Emerson Hospital, Evie's boss, the man who'd hired her. He was a big, shambling man with jug ears and a hook nose and unruly gray hair and gentle brown eyes. He was Evie's confidant, just as Julie was mine. I figured I could convince Bluestein to intercede for me.

When he picked up the phone, I said, "Marcus, it's Brady. I've been trying to reach Evie."

"I was thinking of calling you," he said.

"Me? Why?"

"I've been trying to reach her, too."

"What do you mean?"

"I expected her back in the office from your long weekend on Tuesday or Wednesday. She left it a little vague, and Lord knows she's accrued plenty of vacation time, but—"

"You haven't seen her all week?"

"Well, no," he said.

"And she didn't call you?"

"No." I heard him clear his throat. "You're worrying me, Brady."

"I'm worrying myself. So she didn't tell you about our weekend?"

"Why, no. Did something happen between you?"

"I guess you could say that." I told him as succinctly as I could about our encounter with Larry Scott at the restaurant, and how we found him murdered in our driveway the next morning, and how the state police had questioned us extensively, and how Evie and I had parted uncomfortably when we got home on Saturday.

"That's an awful story," Bluestein said softly.

"Yes. I know Evie's terribly upset, but still . . ."

"You got home Saturday?" he said.

"Yes."

"And you haven't seen her or talked to her since then?"

"No. I've left her messages, but she hasn't responded."

"This isn't at all like her," he said.

"Maybe she just feels she needs some space," I said.

"From you, maybe." Bluestein chuckled softly. "I'm sorry. You know what I mean."

"I know," I said. "She would've talked to you. You said you tried calling her?"

"I left her a couple messages. Just said I hope everything's okay, check in with me and let me know what your plans are. Like that. I depend on her, of course, but she knows we can manage for a while when she's gone." He paused for a moment. "With all those horrible events, she probably just felt she needed to avoid all of us for a while. Evie can be quite headstrong, you know."

"Believe me, I know," I said.

"Independent. Willful. Stubborn. She insists on thinking things all the way through before she acts. I value that in her. It prevents her from making mistakes."

"You're not really comforting me, Marcus," I said.

He sighed. "I'm not comforting me, either. So what shall we do, Brady?"

"I guess I better try to find her."

It was a lazy midsummer Friday afternoon, so we closed down the office early, around four-thirty. Julie packed my briefcase with weekend paperwork, as she always did, and I dutifully lugged it home. Both of us knew that I'd probably drop it in the hallway of my apartment and leave it right there until Monday morning, when I'd lug it back to the office. Julie believed that a lawyer's work was never done, that it was a seven-day-a-week job. I believed that philosophy worked well for young, ambitious lawyers. I was neither young nor ambitious.

But I liked to humor Julie, and confessing on Monday morning that I'd been too busy, or too scatterbrained, or too lazy to do my weekend homework gave her something to tease me about, and that made her happy. I believed in keeping my employees happy.

So when I got home, I dropped the briefcase in its appointed spot beside the door and went directly to my bedroom to check my answering machine.

No messages, from Evie or anybody else.

Marcus Bluestein had disturbed me. I could understand Evie refusing to talk to me. But she hadn't contacted him all week, either. That meant something was wrong.

So I changed out of my office pinstripe, took the elevator down to the parking garage, climbed into my car, and headed for Concord.

Evie's townhouse sits in a development near the Assabet River on the south side of Route 2 just a couple of miles from Emerson Hospital where she worked. The buildings were designed and arranged for maximum privacy, and they'd left plenty of big oak and pine trees standing to enhance the illusion. A tributary to the Assabet meandered through the property. They'd dammed it here and there to form little ponds, which attracted mallards and Canada geese. The management company fed them. I once explained to Evie that the cost of duck and goose food unquestionably came out of her monthly condo fee. She insisted it was money well spent. Both of us liked birds. I liked the wild kind. She said her tame ducks and geese were more fun than the seagulls that liked to perch on the railing of my balcony.

The birds, recognizing a good thing when they saw it, hung

around all year. They didn't migrate, and they didn't burst into wild flight at the sight of a human. Duck and goose turds littered the grass and the flower gardens and the parking areas, and the management company spent still more of the tenants' money cleaning up after the birds. They'd become tame and stupid, and big bunches of them followed people around, quacking and honking for handouts.

So when I parked in the visitors' lot and walked to Evie's townhouse, I quickly attracted a gabbling crowd. I turned around and stomped my foot at the birds. They stopped and cocked their heads at me, and when I continued along my way, they continued to follow me.

Goofy birds.

I rang Evie's doorbell, waited, rang it again.

After a minute, I banged on the door with my fist and called, "Evie. It's me. Come on, honey. Open up."

There came no response from inside.

The blinds were drawn across all of her downstairs windows, so I couldn't peek inside.

Evie and I had exchanged house keys back in the winter when our relationship had evolved to that logical point. I hesitated to use the key. I doubted that she was inside, but if she was, the last thing she'd appreciate would be me barging in on her.

Terrible scenarios had begun to ricochet through my brain. Evie could be stubbornly and unpredictably uncommunicative for a day or two. I'd learned to understand and respect those silences. But now it had been nearly a week.

I took a deep breath, unlocked her door, and poked my head inside.

With the blinds shut and the drapes pulled, the place was dim and shadowy. The motor of her refrigerator hummed softly from the kitchen. Somewhere a clock ticked.

"Evie?" I said quietly. "It's me. Are you here?"

No answer.

I stepped inside and closed the door behind me. I blinked and waited for my eyes to adjust to the gray half-light. For some reason, I was reluctant to turn on the lights.

It smelled musty and unlived-in, but I figured that was my imagination.

I stepped into her living room . . . then stopped. In the middle of the floor sat her blue duffel bag, the same one she'd taken on our trip to the Cape. The last time I'd seen her, she'd been carrying it inside.

It was as if this was as far as she'd gotten back on Saturday afternoon, as if something had happened to cause her to drop her bag, as if she'd been frightened or startled, as if she'd panicked.

I didn't like it.

I went directly upstairs to her two bedrooms.

Now I was hoping I *wouldn't* find her.

The big king-sized bed in her master bedroom, the bed Evie had shared with me on many Saturday nights, was neatly made. The other bedroom, her guest room, looked the way it always did—spartan and comfortable. Clean, neatly folded towels hung on the racks in her bathroom. Nothing out of place there, either.

I peeked into the closets. By now I'd admitted to myself that I might be looking for a dead body. But all I saw in the closets were Evie's clothes, carefully arranged on their hangers.

Back downstairs, I turned on some lights, then opened the door to her little office off the living room. The answering machine on her desk was blinking rapidly. Between me and Marcus Bluestein, I knew, she had several messages waiting for her that she'd apparently not listened to.

Aside from her duffel bag sitting in the middle of the floor, everything was as I remembered it in the living room. I went over and looked at Evie's collection of hand-carved birds in the glass-fronted cabinet in the corner. I had given her the little ruby-throated hummingbird for Christmas and the wood thrush for Valentine's Day. I was lucky, always knowing what I could give Evie for gifts, knowing that they would delight her, knowing I'd never run out of good ideas. I was eager to return her bobwhite quail to her so she could add it to her collection.

I moved into the kitchen. Everything was neat and orderly there, too. I opened the refrigerator and checked the dates on the milk and orange-juice cartons. They had both expired earlier in the week. Both cartons were about half full. I figured she'd bought them sometime before we went to the Cape.

I judged orange juice by its taste, but Evie, I knew, threw away everything the moment it became outdated, whether it tasted all right or not.

It was obvious that she hadn't been here for a while. In fact, it seemed as if she'd turned around and left as soon as I'd dropped her off back on Saturday.

That duffel bag sitting there in the middle of her living room was ominous. It suggested she'd left in a hurry.

Or that she'd left against her will.

I looked out the living-room window to the slot under the trees in front where she parked her black Volkswagen Jetta. It wasn't there.

I went back into the living room, sat on the sofa, and lit a cigarette. I tried to think. Larry Scott was following Evie. Then someone murdered Larry Scott—someone, apparently, that he'd known. Evie had been questioned hard by the state police. Scott knew Evie. She was a good suspect.

Then she'd disappeared.

I was just stubbing out my cigarette when the phone rang.

I jumped up and went into her office. I debated answering it versus letting her machine take it and listening to the message, then grabbed it while it was still ringing.

"Yes?" I said. "Hello?"

There was no response. I sensed rather than heard a person breathing on the other end of the line.

"This is Brady Coyne," I said quickly. "Who is this? Evie? Is that you?"

There was a perceptible hesitation, then whoever it was hung up.

I sat at Evie's desk. The answering machine kept winking at me.

I felt like a snooper. But I pressed the PLAY button.

The machine whirred for a minute, clicked, beeped, and then a woman's voice said, "Evie? This is Charlotte Matley, returning your call. It's, um, Sunday evening. I'm sorry I couldn't get back to you sooner, but I've been away from the office for the weekend. You sounded like you had something urgent. I hope everything's okay. You can call me here at home tonight, or catch me in the office in the morning." She left two phone numbers, then hung up.

The machine beeped again, and then came a message from Sergeant Lipton, Vanderweigh's partner, politely asking her to call him. Then there was another message from Lipton. This time he was less polite. "Ms. Banyon," he said, "you must call us immediately."

Then I heard my voice asking Evie to call me. Then me again, sounding both annoyed and concerned. Then came Marcus Bluestein, then me again, telling her I loved her and missed her.

After the last message, I pressed the SAVE button and the machine rewound itself.

Who was Charlotte Matley? I didn't remember ever hearing Evie mention anybody named Charlotte. On the other hand,

I was realizing that there were a lot of things about Evie I didn't know.

I replayed the messages and jotted down the two numbers Charlotte Matley had left. Then I picked up Evie's phone and pressed the redial button.

It rang five times. Then a recorded message said, "You have reached the offices of Hagan and Matley, attorneys-at-law. Our regular hours are eight-thirty to five, Monday through Friday. To speak to Attorney Michael Hagan, please press one. To speak to Attorney Charlotte Matley, press two."

I pressed two. "This is Charlotte Matley," said the same, rather throaty voice that had left Evie a message. "Please leave your name and number along with a brief message and I'll be sure to return your call."

I hit the OFF button on Evie's phone without leaving a message.

Hmm. Evie had mentioned consulting a lawyer back when she lived in Cortland and Larry Scott was driving her crazy. I thought I remembered that Evie had referred to the lawyer as "she." An inspired leap of deductive analysis suggested to me that Charlotte Matley might be that same lawyer.

I dialed the home number that Attorney Matley had left on Evie's machine, and after a couple of rings, a woman's voice said, "Yes?" It was the same voice I'd been listening to on Evie's answering machine.

"Hi," I said. "I'm sorry to bother you at home. My name is Brady Coyne. I'm an attorney and a friend of Evie Banyon, and—"

"How did you get this number, Mr. Coyne?"

"Well, to tell you the truth, I'm at Evie's house and I got it off her answering machine."

"Really." Her voice dripped with disapproval.

"Well, yes," I said. "You see, she and I are, um, good friends, and we've been out of touch, and I've been worried about her. I haven't spoken to her for a week, and she hasn't been returning my calls, and so finally—"

"You broke into her house?"

"No," I said. "I have a key."

"May I make a suggestion, Mr. Coyne?"

"Sure, but—"

"Evie doesn't appreciate being hounded."

"Hounded? I'm worried about her, Ms. Matley. She's been through a very traumatic experience."

She didn't say anything.

"Ms. Matley?" I said. "Are you there?"

"Yes." She cleared her throat. "You might as well call me Charlotte. So you haven't heard from her in what, a week?"

"Right. I dropped her off here last Saturday. Her duffel bag is still sitting on the living-room floor. She has a week's worth of messages on her answering machine. The state police are trying to reach her. I know she tried to call you. Did you speak with her?"

"Mr. Coyne," she said, "you know better."

"I'm not asking what you talked about, Charlotte. I'm just asking if you spoke with her. I just want to know that she's all right. And you should call me Brady."

"Right," she said. "Brady it shall be, then." She hesitated. "Well, no, I didn't actually speak with her. She left me a message, and I returned her call. But she didn't answer, and she didn't get back to me, and I haven't seen her. I wish I could assure you that she's all right."

"What was her message?"

"I don't think—"

"Look," I said. "Client privilege and all that. But I heard your return message to her. You said her call sounded urgent. Well, I'm sure it was. Last Saturday Evie found the dead body of a man who'd been following her and harassing her. Did you know that? His name was Larry Scott. He'd been knifed twice in the stomach, and the state police think she killed him. So she called you, her lawyer, and when she couldn't reach you, it looks to me like she left here in a hurry." I paused. "Or else something happened to her."

Charlotte Matley said nothing. In the background, I heard what sounded like television laughter.

"Charlotte?" I said.

"Yes," she said. "I haven't gone anywhere. To tell you the truth, I've got my two children here with me, and we were just putting supper together when you called. They're hungry. This is not a good time."

"What is a good time?"

She laughed quickly. "It's my weekend with the kids. It's precious to me. There is no good time. Why don't we talk on Monday?"

"Doesn't it concern you that Evie called you, and it sounded urgent, and you haven't heard back from her in a week?"

"I don't know," she said. "I just figured whatever it was, it wasn't that urgent after all, or it got resolved."

"How well do you know Evie?" I said.

"Quite well, actually."

"Would you say Evie panics easily?"

"No. Evie Banyon does not overreact. She's a calm, confident, very self-contained person."

"Well," I said, "she's gone. She called you, and she didn't get you, and now she's gone."

"Are you trying to make me feel responsible?"

"No. I'm just telling you what happened."

"Just because she's not there, it doesn't mean—"

"She hasn't showed up for work all week. She didn't even call her boss. He's concerned, too."

"I see," she said softly.

"The state police can't find her," I said.

"Yes, you said that."

"Would you say that's typical of Evie, not showing up for work, and not calling in, and avoiding the police like that?"

"Certainly not."

"In her message to you, she didn't say what she wanted?"

"I told you—"

"Sure," I said. "Privileged. Fine. But she's a suspect in a murder case, and she seems to have disappeared, and I, for one, intend to do something about it."

"Of course," she said. "Okay. Why don't you meet me in my office tomorrow. Say around ten?"

"Why wait?" I said. "Talk to me now."

"No. My kids are hungry, and right now they're my priority. I'm sorry, but it'll just have to wait. I don't usually go to the office on Saturday mornings, Brady. I'll have to arrange a baby-sitter. So do you want to do this?"

"Okay. Yes. How do I get there?"

She gave me directions. Her office was in Cortland, the town where Evie had worked, where she'd been followed and harassed by Larry Scott.

Evie had told me that Scott had lived his entire life in Cortland. The town was full of people he had known—people who could walk up to him and stab him in the belly before it would occur to him to raise his arms to defend himself.

It was a good place to start.

SIX

I spent Friday night second-guessing myself. I never should have left Evie alone on Saturday without clearing the air. Finding Larry Scott's body and then being interrogated by the state police had spooked her, and she'd reacted in a perfectly normal way—by taking her frustrations and fears out on me. I should've understood that. I shouldn't have taken it personally. I should have insisted that she let me carry her luggage inside. Then I should have hugged her and held her and told her I loved her. I should have let her be angry with me if she wanted, and I should have waited while she cried or beat on my chest with her fists, or yelled and cursed, if that's how she felt.

I should have been there for her, even if she didn't want me to be.

Instead I'd shrugged and left her there, alone with her anger, or her fear, or whatever it was she was feeling. So she had gone inside, dumped her duffel bag on the floor, and called her lawyer, and when she didn't reach her, she . . . what? What had she done?

Disturbing scenarios bounced around my brain all night, and I slept poorly.

Finally, around five o'clock, I gave up trying to sleep. I made coffee, and when it had brewed I took a mug and my road atlas out onto the balcony to watch the sun come up.

I found Cortland a little southwest of Foxboro about halfway between Boston and Providence, on the old Route 1 where it paralleled Interstate 95. Charlotte Matley had told me her office was on Main Street—which is what they called Route 1 in town—directly across from the village green. I guessed it would take me less than an hour to drive there from my apartment in the light traffic of a summer Saturday morning.

I forced myself to wait until quarter of nine before I left. I was eager to get there, eager to talk with Charlotte, eager to begin looking for Evie. But there was no reason to get there early. I'd just have to wait.

I hated waiting.

It was a straight shot down Interstate 95 to the Cortland exit, and then I found myself heading south on Route 1. I crossed the town line into Cortland a little after nine-thirty A.M. I passed cornfields, now shoulder-high, and motels that looked as if they'd been built in the 1950s, and an old drive-in movie theater with weeds growing out of cracks in the paved parking area. The marquee read, COMMERCIAL PROPERTY FOR SALE.

Once upon a time, Route 1 was the most-traveled highway in America. It started at the very northern tip of Maine on the New Brunswick border and traced the zigzags of the Atlantic coastline all the way to Key West, Florida. Commerce flourished all along Route 1. Gas stations, souvenir stores, motels,

72

antique shops, ice-cream parlors, taverns, restaurants—all were excellent investments. Any small town lucky enough to be located on Route 1 was guaranteed at least modest prosperity in the early postwar years when all of America owned automobiles, and gas was cheap, and motoring was the national pastime.

Then the Eisenhower administration launched its interstate highway program, and the old meandering prewar two-lane roadways like Route 1 became byways, and their villages became commercial ghost towns. Now you could hop onto Route 95 in Houlton, Maine, set your cruise control for 70, and in two days of steady driving you'd be in Miami.

I'd always dreamed of driving the length of Route 1. I'd start in early September in Madawaska, Maine, where the leaves would already be turning, and I'd follow autumn southward, and by the time I arrived in southern Florida, it would be snowing at my starting point. I'd stop at ten thousand stoplights and school crossings. I'd stay in rental cabins and eight-unit motels, and I'd eat in coffee shops and diners with the locals, and I'd visit every World War One and Civil War memorial along the way.

Well, I'd probably never do it. It was a romantic notion, but the older I got, the less inclined I seemed to be to pursue romantic notions.

I pulled into the tree-shaded parking area in front of the neat white colonial where Charlotte Matley's office was located around nine forty-five. Several other cars were already parked there.

A flea market had been set up on the village green across the street, and families were prowling the tables and booths, sipping from paper cups, eating cotton candy, carrying balloons. I crossed the street and bought a cup of coffee and a donut from a pair of elderly women at the Friends of the Library booth, then went back and sat on the front steps of Charlotte's office building.

At five minutes of ten, a red Subaru wagon pulled in beside my BMW, and a stocky, thirtyish woman with short blonde hair slid out. She waved at me. "Brady?"

"Yes, hi," I said.

She opened the back door of her Subaru, and two girls came bursting out. They both wore red sneakers and striped overalls and crisp white T-shirts, and they looked four or five years old. Twins.

Charlotte ushered them to the front of the building where I was sitting on the steps. "Couldn't get a sitter," she said. She jerked her head back over her shoulder. "Everyone's at the fair. Most excitement we've had in Cortland since the senior prom." She held out her hand. "I'm Charlotte Matley."

I took her hand. "Brady Coyne."

She knelt beside the two girls. "I'm going to be talking with Mr. Coyne," she said to them, "and I want you to behave yourselves. If you're good, we'll go to the fair after I'm done, okay?"

"Can't we go now?" said one of the girls.

"No. You can watch TV in the back room, and you can use the coloring books, and I don't want to hear a peep out of you."

"Can we have cotton candy?"

"If you behave. End of discussion." She stood up. "Come on in," she said to me.

She unlocked the front door, and I followed her inside. She opened one of the inner doors and said, "Have a seat. Let me get these two settled." Then she led the girls toward the rear of the building.

Charlotte Matley's office appeared to have originally been the library in the old colonial house. It was large and square,

74

with high ceilings and tall windows and floor-to-ceiling bookcases built into three walls, with a bricked-over fireplace in the corner. There was a leather sofa and two matching easy chairs on one side, and a big oak desk against the opposite wall.

I sat on the sofa, and a minute later Charlotte came in. She was wearing a short-sleeved blouse, a knee-length skirt, and sandals. She sat in one of the easy chairs. "Being a single parent is a full-time job," she said. "So is being a lawyer." She blew out a long breath, then smiled at me. "Well, enough about me. You want to talk about Evie Banyon."

"Yes," I said. "I'm concerned."

"Since I talked to you yesterday, I guess I am, too. I'm not sure I'll be able to shed much light on it. As I told you, I just got that one message from her a week ago. I called back and left her a message, but I haven't heard from her."

"You said her message sounded urgent," I said. "What did she say?"

"Unfortunately, I erased it. There was an urgency in her tone, I remember. She said something like, 'I need to talk to you.'"

"She used the word 'need'?" I said.

Charlotte nodded. "Yes. That was the word that got my attention."

"Do you know what time she called?"

"I can tell you exactly." She got up, went to her desk, opened a drawer, and came back with a leather-bound notebook. "My machine records the time of my calls, and I log them all in." She opened the notebook, flipped a couple of pages, then looked up at me. "Evie called at four fifty-two P.M. last Saturday."

"That was no more than ten or fifteen minutes after I dropped her off," I said.

"Is that significant?"

I shrugged. "I don't know. She'd just been through a long interrogation with the state police. Maybe she decided she needed to consult a lawyer. I'd mentioned that to her." I shook my head.

"You don't seem convinced," said Charlotte.

"Well," I said, "it's unlike Evie to leave her duffel bag in the middle of the living room. It's as if she panicked when she walked into her place."

"Why would she panic?"

"Maybe she had a message on her answering machine, though if she did, she deleted it. I guess I was hoping you might have an idea."

She shook her head.

"Evie told me she'd consulted a lawyer about Scott back when she lived in Cortland," I said. "That was you, huh?"

"Yes. She wanted to take out a 209A."

"The way she explained her situation to me," I said, "she didn't have grounds for a restraining order."

Charlotte looked at me and smiled quickly. "Right. But now I'm feeling maybe I should've tried harder to do something for her."

"She did talk with the local police, though?"

She nodded. "That was before she came to me. Our police are mostly local boys. Cortland is a small town. For better or worse, if you know what I mean. Everybody in town knows—knew—Larry Scott. He was sort of a war hero after Desert Storm. Evie lived here for three or four years, but Scott was born here. Compared to him, she was an outsider."

"So she didn't get any satisfaction."

"Scott was following her and watching her and harassing her on the phone and parking outside her house at night. Evie felt the police weren't taking her seriously. I told her they couldn't do much without a restraining order, and she didn't have legal grounds to get one, and I explained that what Scott

76

was doing wasn't technically stalking. I think the police did everything they could, but Evie was very angry and frustrated by the whole thing. Finally she got a new job and moved away."

"So advising her about the restraining order was the only business you had with Evie?" I said.

Charlotte looked out the window. "Now you're asking me questions I can't answer."

"There was something else, then?"

She shook her head. "She's my client."

"Look, Charlotte," I said. "I'm here as Evie's friend, not as a lawyer. If there's something—"

"The way I look at it," she said, "whatever she wanted you to know, she would've told you. It's not up to me."

"Except she's missing."

She shrugged. "We don't really know that. Just because you can't find her . . ."

"Sure," I said. "You're right." I smiled. "Evie didn't tell me much."

"I guess everybody has their secrets." Charlotte stood up and smoothed her skirt against her legs. "I'm afraid I haven't been much help, but I think I've told you everything I can. You should probably just let Evie work out whatever it is she's doing in her own way."

I stood up, too. "If you knew where she was, would you tell me?"

"Not if she asked me not to."

"But you didn't talk to her."

"No," she said. "I might refuse to tell you something, but I wouldn't lie to you. Hey, I'm a lawyer."

I arched my eyebrows, and she laughed.

"Who were her friends here in Cortland?" I said.

"Friends?" She frowned. "I don't know. We never talked about her friends. She worked at the new medical center and she rented an apartment in a big old Victorian down near the lake. That's about all I know. I was her lawyer, not her confidante."

"Can you tell me how to find the medical center and that apartment building?"

Charlotte smiled. "You are persistent, aren't you?"

"I'm worried about Evie."

She nodded. "Of course you are." She gave me directions. The medical center was on Main Street—Route 1—outside of town a few miles south of the village green. Evie's old apartment building was down toward the end of a side street I'd passed on my way. They both sounded easy to find.

We walked out of her office. She locked the door, then turned and held out her hand. "I've got to round up the kids," she said. "You can find your way out."

I took her hand. "Thanks for seeing me on a Saturday morning. I know it was an inconvenience."

"I'm afraid I haven't been much help."

"It's a start," I said.

She headed for the back of the building, and I went out the front door. I paused on the porch to light a cigarette. It was one of those still, hazy summer mornings that felt like it would evolve into thunderstorms in the afternoon. The crowds on the village green across the street appeared to have grown larger, and now the parking area in front of the lawyer's building was packed with vehicles.

I headed for my car, where I'd left it under the sweeping branches of a big old oak tree. Charlotte Matley hadn't been much help, and this quest was starting to feel quixotic and futile. Evie could be anywhere, and I didn't know where to look, or even whether I should be looking. Maybe Charlotte was right. Maybe I should trust Evie to work out her own problems by herself. She certainly hadn't asked for my help.

But since I was already here in Cortland, I figured I should try to talk to some people. Maybe somebody where Evie used to live or at the medical center where she'd worked had been her friend. An old friend might have an idea where she'd go if she wanted to get away from things.

It also occurred to me that Cortland was populated with people who'd known Larry Scott. The police figured he and his killer had known each other. If Scott had lived his entire life in this town, then about the only people he did know were here.

It was a good place to start snooping.

When I got to my car, I stopped, let out a long breath, and mumbled, "Shit." The left front tire had gone flat.

I squatted down beside it. I figured God, or the Fates—not that I believed in any of them—were trying to tell me something. Mind your own business, Coyne. Go home, or go fishing, or catch up on your paperwork, and forget about Evie.

Except I couldn't forget about Evie after what had happened, and I couldn't go anywhere on a flat tire.

"I hate it when that happens," said a voice behind me.

I turned around. Charlotte was standing there with her two girls. She was shaking her head sympathetically.

"Oh, well," I said. "I've changed plenty of flats in my day."

She fished in her purse and came out with a cell phone. "Let me make a call for you. You don't want to get all sweaty and greasy."

I stood up. "You're right. I really don't."

She pecked out a number on her cell phone, looked up at the sky, then shifted her eyes and said, "Raymond, it's Charlotte Matley. I've got a flat tire here in my parking lot . . . Yes, at my office. Will you send one of your boys down to rescue me?" She paused, smiled, and nodded. "Thank you. You're a dear man." Then she snapped her phone shut and smiled at me. "Someone'll be here in fifteen minutes."

"Thank you," I said.

"If you'd called, it would probably take them two hours to get here. If they didn't forget it completely."

"Me being a stranger here in town."

"Exactly."

She said she should stay with my car because the tire-fixer would be looking for her, so I went across the street, wandered through the crowd until I found the cotton-candy booth, and bought two for Charlotte's girls.

I returned to the parking lot just as a tow truck pulled in. I gave the cotton candies to the twins. They curtsied and thanked me, and Charlotte went over to talk with the young guy who was climbing out of the truck. Then they both came over.

He looked to be in his early twenties. He had brown hair cut in an old-fashioned crew cut, with splotches of grease on his face and arms. He was wearing workboots and overalls with no shirt underneath.

"Mr. Coyne," said Charlotte, "this is Carl. He's one of Raymond's sons."

I held out my hand to Carl. He looked at it, then looked at his own hand, which was black with grease, and smiled at me. "You don't wanna shake this hand, sir." He pointed his chin at my tire. "Looks like you picked up a nail."

I shrugged. "I guess so."

He waved at my car. "Beemer, huh? You like it?"

I nodded.

"Nice car." He glanced down at my flat tire. "Well, we'll throw on your spare, and if you want, we can go back to the garage and I'll patch this one up for you. Shouldn't drive around without a good spare. Where you headed?"

"I'm from Boston."

"Come down for the fair?"

"No," I said. "I had an appointment with Ms. Matley."

80

He looked at me and grinned. "I was joking," he said. "Nobody comes to Cortland for anything, never mind our dumb fair. Pop that trunk for me, willya?"

I opened the trunk, and in a couple of minutes Carl had the spare tire mounted on the front and the flat loaded in the back of his truck.

He climbed in. "You want to follow me?"

"Sure." I turned to Charlotte. "Thanks for everything."

She shrugged. "I wish I could've been more helpful. If you learn anything, please let me know. I'll be thinking about Evie. Thanks for the cotton candy."

"I'll keep you posted."

I got into my car, backed out, waved to Charlotte and her daughters, and followed Carl's tow truck north on Main Street, retracing the route I'd taken to get there. About a mile out of town, we pulled into a two-bay garage with four gas pumps out front. It was a low-slung weathered brick building, vintage 1955, I guessed. A large wooden sign over the door read RAYMOND'S TEXACO.

I bought a Coke from the machine out front while Carl lugged my flat tire inside. I'd just lit a cigarette when he came out. "Uh, sir," he said, "you wanna come here for a minute?"

I followed him into one of the bays. My flat tire was lying on the cement floor.

Carl squatted down beside my tire. "Here, take a look at this."

I squatted beside him. He pointed at the valve. "See this?"

"I'm not sure what I'm supposed to see," I said.

"The valve stem, sir. It's missing."

I shrugged.

"See," he said, "inside the valve there's this thing you press down, right? Well, you can unscrew it, which is what we do to let the air out of a tire. Yours is missing."

"Meaning what?"

Carl looked up at me. "Meaning, somebody unscrewed it for you."

"You saying somebody vandalized my car?"

"That's the only way it could happen. Those things don't just fall out all by themselves." He stood up. "I can fix it. That's no problem. But I ought to report it."

"Hell," I said, "it's just a flat tire."

He shrugged. "Up to you, I guess. Some asshole kid, got nothing better to do, probably thinks it's pretty funny, disabling some out-of-towner's nice BMW. But I don't."

"I don't want to make a fuss," I said.

"Cortland cops don't get much in the way of excitement," said Carl. "Why don't I give 'em a call?"

I nodded. "Sure. Okay."

He went into the office, and a minute later he was back. "Someone'll be along."

I watched Carl fix my tire. It took him about ten minutes to replace the missing valve stem, pump up the tire, and mount it back on my car. When he was finished, he wiped his hands on a rag. "So you got business with Ms. Matley, huh?"

I nodded. "Lawyer business."

"You a lawyer, too?"

I nodded.

He smiled. "So you can't talk about it."

"Right."

I offered him a cigarette. He waved it away. I lit one for myself. "Did you know Larry Scott?"

He turned to me and frowned. "What about him?"

I waved my hand. "He was murdered. He was from Cortland, wasn't he?"

Carl nodded. "Everybody knew Larry. Hear it was a woman killed him. That why you're down here? Something to do with Larry?"

I shook my head. "I can't talk about it. What kind of guy was he?"

Carl shrugged. "Sad."

"How so?"

"Well, he was this big jock in high school. Everybody said he was good enough to play in college. Baseball and football both. He was a halfback. Led the league in rushing two years. Pitcher on the team. Made the *Globe* 'Honorable Mention.' After graduation, he joined the Marines. Said he was gonna get his education that way. He went off to Desert Storm, and when he came back, he was . . . I don't know. Different. Had a mean temper. Used to spend a lot of time by himself. Liked hunting and fishing. Owned a lot of guns. Got a job as a janitor. Didn't seem to have any ambition anymore. Drank a lot. Liked to tell war stories. Guess he had some hairy experiences over there." Carl shrugged. "He was six years older'n me. I used to idolize Larry Scott when I was a kid."

"But not anymore, huh?"

"I felt sorry for him," he said. "It was like the best thing that was ever going to happen to him in his whole life had already happened. He was the town's football hero, and then he went off to war, and when he came home he wasn't a hero anymore. He liked to talk like he was, but nobody gave a shit."

"So what are people saying, now that he got murdered?"

"Not much," he said. "I mean, it's a tragedy, and some people are taking it hard. Folks're remembering what a golden boy he used to be and forgetting what he turned out to be, the way they do after somebody dies. But it's like it's no surprise something like that happened."

"He had enemies, you mean?"

"No, I didn't mean that. All I mean is, ever since he came home, it seems like he was doomed. Like things had gone bad

83

for him. He couldn't play sports anymore, and he couldn't get a good job, and he couldn't even keep a girlfriend."

"He had a girlfriend?" I asked.

"He liked to say he did, but that was all in his imagination."

"What do you mean?"

"Oh, there was this woman, worked where he did. Older than him, real pretty and smart. He liked to brag about how she was his girl. But she wasn't. She finally moved out of town to get away from him. What I hear, he followed her, so finally she killed him."

"Where did you hear that?"

He shrugged. "I don't know. Around. People talk, you know?"

"Did you know this woman?"

"Sure. Miss Banyon. Evie. She got her oil changed here. Everybody knows everybody in Cortland."

"You haven't seen her around lately, have you?"

He cocked his head and frowned at me. "Why are you asking me all these questions?"

"No reason," I said. "Just making conversation until the police arrive."

"Well," he said, "I gotta get back to work. They should be here any minute. Thirty bucks should take care of it."

I gave Carl two twenty-dollar bills and waved him away when he dug in his overalls for change. "Thanks for helping me out."

He shrugged. "It's my job."

I backed my car out of the garage, pulled it off to the side of the paved area, got out, and leaned against the fender. About ten minutes later a black-and-white police cruiser pulled in.

SEVEN

The cruiser parked in front of the entrance to the garage's office. A uniformed officer slid out from behind the wheel, glanced in my direction, then went inside, leaving his engine running and his door hanging open. He stood in the doorway with his hands on his hips, rocking back and forth on his heels, talking with Carl.

He was in there for about five minutes. Then he came out, hitched up his belt, adjusted his sunglasses, and sauntered over to me. "You're Mr. Coyne?" he said.

I nodded.

He was a burly guy, thirtyish, with a round face and pale eyes and curly red hair showing under his cap. He had shaved so close that his pink cheeks shone. "Mind if I look at your license?" he said. The nameplate on his shirt said SGT. J. DWYER.

"Why?"

"May I see your license, please, sir?" he repeated.

I shrugged, took out my wallet, and handed him my driver's license.

He glanced at it, looked at me as if he were comparing the photo on the license with my actual face, and wrote something into his notebook. Then he nodded and gave the license back to me. "So what brings you to Cortland, Mr. Coyne?"

"I thought it would be a likely place to get a flat tire," I said.

He frowned. "What did you say?"

I blew out a breath. "What makes the difference why I'm here? Why are you checking my driver's license? Somebody vandalized my car, and Carl in there, being a responsible citizen, called it in, though I told him I didn't think it was necessary, but when he did I, also being a responsible citizen, waited here for you. Where I come from, having the valve stem removed from your tire doesn't make you a suspicious character."

"You're a lawyer, is that right, sir?"

"Yes."

"From Boston."

"Right."

"Long way from home to be telling a police officer how to do his job," he said mildly.

"It took less than an hour to get here."

He squinted at me. "You want to be respectful, sir."

I nodded. "So do you, Sergeant."

He shrugged, then glanced at my car. "Nice wheels."

"Thank you."

"I don't know anybody in Cortland owns a BMW. Kind of an attention-getter, wouldn't you say?"

"I guess so," I said.

"You have any enemies in Cortland, Mr. Coyne?"

"Until I got here this morning," I said, "I didn't know a single citizen of Cortland."

"Understand you had a meeting with Mrs. Matley."

I nodded. I figured Carl had filled him in.

"Lawyer business?" he said.

"Yes. Lawyer business."

"So I guess she's one citizen you know, then."

"I do now."

"What about Larry Scott?" he said.

"What about him?"

"You know him?"

"I met him once."

"Thought you said you didn't know any citizens of Cortland. Did I hear you wrong?"

"Larry Scott is dead," I said, "so technically he's no longer a citizen of Cortland. Anyway, it's unlikely he's the one who unscrewed my valve stem."

"What about Evelyn Banyon?"

"I don't think she did it, either."

"You know her, though?"

"She's no longer a citizen of Cortland," I said.

"Pretty close to her, are you?"

"That's none of your business." I opened my car door. "If you're not interested in the vandalism to my car, I've got some things to do, so—"

He put his hand on the door. "Hang on a minute, Mr. Coyne. I got a couple more questions for you."

"Well," I said, "I'm really not in the mood to be interrogated because you suspect me of being the victim of vandalism. So unless you'd care to tell me what your agenda here is, I'm on my way."

"Agenda?" Dwyer peered up at the sky for a minute. "Good friend of mine, guy I grew up with, used to open holes in the line for, went fishing with, got drunk with, he goes down the Cape and gets knifed in the belly." He nodded. "Everybody in town knows all about it. People in Cortland have heard your name, sir. We know about you and Ms. Banyon and what happened down the Cape. State cops've been here, asking questions. Us local cops're cooperating with them."

"Good," I said.

He shook his head and laughed quickly. "Look," he said, "this isn't coming out right. I'm just jumpy. Everyone around here is. Not often one of your friends gets murdered. If I came on a little strong, I apologize. It's because Larry and I were buddies since we were in kindergarten." He held out his hand to me. "Okay?"

We shook hands. "No problem," I said. "I guess I'm a little jumpy, too."

"No hard feelings?"

"Forget about it."

"So tell me," he said, "I guess it's no coincidence, you showing up in Cortland, huh?"

"Like I said, lawyer business."

"Sure," he said. "You can't talk about it."

"No, I can't."

He nodded. "Heading back to Boston?"

"Eventually," I said. "I'm in no hurry."

Dwyer smiled and slapped his hand on the roof of my car. "Well, sir, it's a nice little town," he said. "Enjoy your visit." Then he hitched up his belt and went back to his cruiser.

As I started up my car, I noticed that Dwyer was sitting in his vehicle with the door still open, talking on his radio.

I pulled out onto Main Street and headed back to the center of town. I figured that between Sergeant Dwyer and Carl the tire-fixer—and maybe Charlotte Matley—within an hour everybody in Cortland would know about me and the car I drove and my connection with Larry Scott and Evie Banyon. If Cortland was like most small towns, everybody knew everybody else, and knew everything that happened behind closed doors, and had strongly-held theories and beliefs on all issues, and didn't mind circulating and embellishing rumors. Larry Scott's murder was big news in Cortland, of course, and no matter what kind of man he'd become, in the small town's collective memory, he'd forever be a high-school football star, a fallen hero. A "golden boy," Carl had called him.

I passed the village green, where the fair was still swarming with citizens, and headed for the medical center where Evie had worked. I didn't know who'd be there at noontime on an August Saturday, and I wasn't sure what I was looking for. But I thought it might be interesting to shake some trees in this little town and see what might fall out.

A mile or so south of the village green I passed a small strip mall with a supermarket, a hardware store, and a bowling alley along with the usual dry cleaner, Laundromat, take-out pizza, and video rental. That's probably where the cruiser was waiting, although I'd gone another half-mile or so before I noticed it in my rearview mirror.

The cruiser kept its distance behind me. I spotted a speed-limit sign—45—glanced at my speedometer, and eased down to 40.

It stayed behind me all the way out of town to the medical center, and when I turned into the almost-empty parking area, it kept going.

So that's how it was going to be.

The Southeastern Massachusetts Medical Center was perched on a knoll in the countryside with a four-way view of rolling meadows and wooded hills. It was an impressive rectangular brick-and-glass structure. It was four stories tall, and its foundation was about the size of a football field. Bright annual flowers bloomed in neatly kept gardens, and brick walkways curved among Japanese maples and clumps of white birch.

It was modern and classy—an anomaly in Cortland.

I left my car on the bottom level of the open, two-tier concrete parking garage, locked up, and walked to the front of the building. Inside, through the glass doors, I could see a large open room. A long chest-high counter ran along the far wall. It reminded me of the lobby of a fancy hotel. It appeared to be deserted.

I pushed on the door, half expecting it to be locked. But it opened, so I went in.

The lobby featured strategically placed miniature palm trees in big pots, a tasteful scattering of low-slung sofas and chairs, glass-topped coffee tables covered with magazines, plush beige carpeting, and the soft tinkle of piped-in orchestral music.

On the left wall beside the bank of elevators I found the glass-fronted roster that listed all the people who had offices in the building. It was an impressively long list, and it seemed to include a group of medical specialists dedicated to the well-being of every conceivable organ and system in the human body. The list was alphabetical by last name, so it took me a few minutes to find what I was looking for.

The lobby area was empty except for one woman sitting behind the long counter. I went up to her and leaned my elbows on the countertop. She had a paperback book open on her lap.

I cleared my throat and said, "Excuse me?"

She looked up at me. She was, I guessed, around sixty. She had straight dark hair cut chin-length and peppered with gray, with half-glasses perched down toward the tip of her nose. She turned the book upside down on its open pages, took off her glasses, and gave me a quick, practiced smile. "Can I help you?" she said pleasantly.

"I'm here to see Mr. Soderstrom." Thomas L. Soderstrom, I'd learned from the roster, was the medical center's chief administrator.

She frowned. "Do you have an appointment?"

"I'm a lawyer."

Her eyebrows twitched. "I see." She blinked a couple of times. "Is Mr. Soderstrom expecting you?"

"He may not be expecting me today," I said. "I took a chance I could catch him."

"What's your name, sir?"

"Brady Coyne. He might not recognize my name. Then again, he might."

She shrugged. "Just a minute, please."

She picked up a phone, swiveled around so that her back was to me, and spoke into it. After a brief moment, she put her hand over the receiver and turned to me. "Mr. Soderstrom wants to know what your business is with him."

"Tell him it regards Evelyn Banyon."

She nodded as if she expected me to say that, showed me her back, and spoke into the phone. Then she turned and said, "Down there past the elevators." She pointed. "Go through the doors, then turn left. Mr. Soderstrom is in suite 110 at the end of the hall."

I thanked her and followed her directions.

The little waiting room in suite 110 had one sofa and two matching upholstered chairs. It was empty. There was a receptionist's desk, but no receptionist. A narrow corridor led to some inner offices.

I stood in the middle of the waiting room for a minute, then said, "Hello?"

A moment later a small man with pale skin and thinning straw-colored hair and large round glasses appeared. I guessed he was in his early forties. He was wearing khaki pants and a short-sleeved white shirt. He reminded me of Wally Cox, back when he played Mr. Peepers on *Our Miss Brooks*.

"Mr. Coyne, is it?" he said.

"Brady Coyne." I held out my hand.

He shook it quickly. "You're a lawyer."

"Yes."

"What can I do for you?"

"If you're busy . . ."

He nodded. "I'm always busy."

"I thought the easiest thing would be to talk informally," I said. "But if you'd rather, we could meet at my office in Boston."

He smiled. "I do believe you're trying to threaten me, Mr. Coyne. But since I have no idea what you're threatening me about, I'm afraid I don't feel threatened. Helen said you mentioned Evelyn Banyon. Evie doesn't threaten me, but she interests me. Why don't we go into my office."

"You don't feel threatened?"

"Sorry, no."

"Intimidated a little, at least?"

He shook his head.

"Damn," I said. "Well, we better go into your office, then."

Soderstrom's office was cluttered with file cabinets and cardboard boxes and papers stacked in bookcases and piled on his desk. It looked like he was just moving in—or moving out. Julie never would have allowed my office to look like that.

He picked up a handful of manila folders from the chair across from his desk. "Have a seat," he said.

I sat.

"Sorry about the mess." He took the chair behind the desk and folded his hands on the glass top. "I'm between assistants these days. That's why I'm here in the office on a pretty Saturday in August instead of at the lake with my wife and kids." He smiled quickly. "Have I got your sympathy yet?"

"Sure."

"So you wanted to talk to me about Evie Banyon?"

"No," I said. "I wanted you to talk to me about her."

He took off his glasses, wiped the lenses with his handkerchief, and fitted them back onto his face. Then he leaned forward on his elbows. "There's been a good deal of interest in Evie recently. They seem to think she murdered somebody."

"Who's 'they'?"

"Oh, I guess just about everyone who lives in this benighted little town."

"What about you?"

"Me?"

"Do you think she killed anybody?" I said.

He leaned back in his chair and looked up at the ceiling. "It hardly matters what I think," he said.

"You knew Evie, though, right?"

He tilted forward and looked at me. "I hired her, Mr. Coyne. She was my assistant for more than three years. I haven't found anybody like her since. They keep coming and going. Either they can't do the work, or they're too lazy to try. Evie was good. I hated to see her go."

"You must've known her pretty well, then."

He lifted a hand and let it fall. "As well as Evie allows anyone to know her, I guess."

"So do you think she—"

"Mr. Coyne," said Soderstrom quickly, "I think you should tell me exactly what you want and why you're here. I cannot imagine that my opinion of Evie's capacity for murder is of the slightest interest to you. I'm sure you know her better than I ever did."

"Of course your opinion is important to me," I said.

He shrugged. "This murder is a very big story in Cortland," he said. "Everybody knows how Larry Scott stalked Evie, followed her down to the Cape, had a confrontation with you and her at some seafood restaurant, and ended up getting killed. She's a prime suspect, I understand, and since the police are looking for her and questioning everybody who knew her—including me—one can easily deduce that she cannot be found. So is that what it is? Are you looking for Evie?"

I nodded. "Yes."

"Well," he said, "I don't know where she is."

"Could she be here in Cortland?"

"I guess she could be. But if she is, she hasn't told me about it. I haven't seen her, if that's what you're asking."

I smiled. "That would've been too easy." I touched my shirt pocket. "Mind if I smoke?"

"Me? No, personally I don't mind. But there's a policy in this building, and as its chief administrator, I'm obliged to uphold it. It is a medical center, after all." He smiled. "The doctors all sneak out back for their cigarettes."

"As they should, of course," I said. "Look. The truth is, Evie seems to have, um, disappeared, and I'm worried about her. That's why I'm here. I don't know where else to go. I figure she must have friends in Cortland, people she might get in touch with if she felt she was in trouble." I arched my eyebrows at Soderstrom.

"She hasn't contacted me," he said. "But I wouldn't expect her to."

"Why not?"

He shrugged. "I was her boss, not her friend."

"Who, then?"

"In Cortland?" He frowned up at the ceiling. "You might try Win St. Croix. Or maybe Mary Scott." He shrugged. "I can't think of anybody else."

"Did you say Mary Scott?" I said.

He nodded. "She's Larry Scott's mother. As I told you, I didn't know a lot about Evie's private life. We didn't share that. She was single and I was married and we traveled in different circles. But I do know that she and Mary Scott were friends. Mary works here in our cafeteria."

"Do you suppose they're still friends?"

"What? Oh, you mean after . . ."

94

"Yes. After Larry got murdered."

Soderstrom shrugged. "I haven't the faintest idea. A lot of folks in town seem willing to believe that Evie killed him. I don't know how Mary feels about it."

"Who's that other name you mentioned?"

"St. Croix. Winston St. Croix. He's a doctor here in town. A pediatrician. He and Evie saw each other, um, socially, for a while."

"Does he have an office in this building?"

"Actually, no. He's been in Cortland since before they built this place. He's an old-timer, still has his office in his house. They invited him to join the pediatrics group here, but he declined. I hear he's planning to retire."

"Evie dated him?"

"For a while she did, if that's what you'd call it. I don't think anything much came of it. Far as I know, they remained friends."

I thought for a minute. "Mary Scott and this Dr. St. Croix, they're both quite a bit older than Evie, then, right?"

Soderstrom shrugged. "So?"

"I don't know," I said. "I'm a little older than her, too."

He smiled. "What, ten years, maybe?"

"About that."

"I'm not sure there's a useful generalization in that," he said.

I asked Soderstrom how to find Dr. St. Croix and Mary Scott, and he gave me directions. Then I took out one of my business cards and put it on his desk. "If you hear anything about Evie or have any thoughts about where she might be, I'd appreciate a call. Anything. No rumor is too insignificant."

He took the card, glanced at it, then dropped it onto his desktop. "Sure. No reason not to, I guess."

I thanked him and stood up. "I've taken enough of your

time." I waved my hand at the clutter in his office. "I'm sure you want to get back to work. It can't be easy without an assistant."

He stood up and came around from behind his desk. "It's impossible without an assistant."

"You must have been pretty upset when Evie told you she was taking another job."

Soderstrom took off his glasses and rubbed his eyes. "It didn't exactly happen that way, Mr. Coyne."

"Huh? What do you mean?"

"You don't know?"

"What are you talking about?"

"I figured you knew." He blew out a quick breath. "I had to ask Evie for her resignation."

"You fired her?"

He nodded.

"I don't get it," I said. "I thought . . ."

"Right. She was great. The best assistant I ever had. I helped her find that job at Emerson Hospital. Marcus Bluestein is a friend of mine. I recommended her highly. He's been delighted with her. It worked out well for everybody."

"For you, too?"

"I had no choice, Mr. Coyne."

"I don't get it."

He nodded. "So Evie never told you. Not surprising, I guess." He peered at me through his big glasses. "I don't see any harm in telling you about it. It's common knowledge around here." He looked up at the ceiling for a moment. "You know that Larry Scott was, um, harassing her. He was a custodian here. He came on at four in the afternoon. Emptied the trash, replaced the lightbulbs, washed the floors after the building was empty. He always started here on the first floor, worked his way up through the building. I guess that's how he and Evie met. Here, in this suite of offices, when he'd come

96

in to empty the trash, before Evie left for the day. So anyway, one afternoon I'm in my office and I hear these angry voices out in the reception area, and then suddenly there's this terrible loud scream. I go running out, and there's Larry Scott holding his arm"—Soderstrom showed me, gripping his left biceps with his right hand—"and blood is pouring out between his fingers and dripping onto the floor, and Evie's standing there holding a pair of scissors, and . . . and she's screaming at him, Mr. Coyne, out of control like I'd never seen her, telling him if he comes near her again, she swears she'll kill him."

I stared at Soderstrom. "Evie stabbed him?"

"Yes."

"Said she'd kill him?"

He nodded.

"She stabbed him with a pair of scissors?"

"Yes."

I blew out a breath. "Jesus."

"So you see," he said, "I really had no choice."

"What about Scott? Did you fire him?"

"He stayed. He was the victim."

"Even though he'd been harassing her?"

Soderstrom shrugged.

"So was Evie arrested?"

He nodded. "Somebody called the police, and they came and handcuffed her and took her away. It never went to trial, though."

"Why not?"

"I guess they decided they couldn't make a case. Scott was the only witness, and he refused to cooperate with the prosecutor."

"Why?"

He shrugged. "According to the Cortland rumor mill, he said he loved her."

"So you fired her."

"I asked for her resignation, Mr. Coyne," he said. "The board of directors insisted. If I'd refused, they just would've fired me and hired somebody else, and Evie still would've been fired. I called Marcus Bluestein, and I helped her get a better job, far enough away from Cortland to make everybody happy."

"Was Evie happy?"

He shrugged. "I think she was relieved. Evie wasn't a quitter, but Scott was driving her to the edge. It was probably a good thing that, um, incident occurred. If it hadn't, and if she hadn't left Cortland, I don't know what might've happened."

"Except Scott kept following her," I said.

"Apparently," he said. "And now . . ."

He didn't finish his thought, and I didn't finish it for him.

Now Larry Scott was dead. He'd been knifed in the stomach.

Everybody in Cortland knew that Evie had stabbed him with a pair of scissors and threatened to kill him a few years ago.

I wondered if anybody doubted she'd stabbed him with a kitchen knife on Cape Cod a week ago.

EIGHT

It was nearly one in the afternoon. I asked Soderstrom where I might get a sandwich, and he suggested a diner a mile or so down Route 1. I thanked him and we shook hands. As I left his office, he was standing there with his hands on his hips, staring at the stacks of paper on his desk.

I paused outside the entrance to the medical center to light a cigarette. The air was thick and hot and still, a sharp contrast to the chilly air-conditioning I'd just left. If I wasn't mistaken, those were thunderheads building up along the western horizon.

I forced myself to consider the reality: If Evie could stab Larry Scott in the arm with a pair of scissors, she was a logical candidate for stabbing him in the belly with a kitchen knife. The incident with the scissors was what Charlotte Matley had refused to tell me. It's what Homicide Detective Neil Vanderweigh had been thinking about.

It's what everyone in Cortland was thinking, too.

As I was learning, I didn't know much about Evie's personal history.

But, I kept thinking, I knew Evie. She purred when I lifted up her hair and kissed the back of the neck. Cradling her bare feet in my lap and painting her toenails made her want to make love. Evie liked Ella Fitzgerald and Lord Byron and the Muppets. She hated snakes and spiders and professional wrestling.

She loved me. I knew that.

I refused to believe that anyone who loved me was capable of murder.

I followed the curving brick walkway back to the parking garage, climbed into my car, and headed for the diner.

I've always loved diners, and whenever I'm hungry in an unfamiliar place, I seek one out. Traditionally, diners cater to truckers, and truckers always know where to get the best food for the best prices. Diners serve bacon and eggs and hash browns and unlimited coffee refills all day and night, seven days a week, every day of the year including Christmas and Thanksgiving. Diners have their own special meatloaf recipes, and they serve it with lumpy mashed potatoes made from actual potatoes, and thick brown mushroom gravy, and peas and carrots, with warm homemade apple pie and a slab of cheddar cheese for dessert.

This diner looked promising. Three ten-wheelers were parked in the spacious side lot, and half a dozen other vehicles were pulled up in front. The neon sign on the roof read DINER, as it should, and the structure appeared to be a genuine old railroad dining car.

I parked in front, and when I pushed open the door and went in, it seemed to me that the ten or a dozen patrons on the stools and in the booths all paused momentarily in their conversation to size me up.

If they did, they recovered quickly.

Probably my overheated imagination.

I took a booth by the front window, and a glass of water instantly appeared at my elbow. I looked up. The waitress wore a tight-fitting green uniform. Her reddish blonde hair was pulled back in a tight bun. She was fortyish and thin and unsmiling. Her nameplate said RUTH. She plucked a pencil from her bun and held it poised over a pad. "Interested in the specials?" she said.

I looked up at the menu, which was written on a blackboard on the wall behind the counter. "Just a sandwich," I said. "Tuna, wheat toast, and iced coffee."

"Milk in the coffee?"

"Black. Please."

She was back with the iced coffee in about a minute. While I sipped it, I kept glancing outside at my car.

The sandwich arrived about five minutes later. It was at least an inch thick, and it came with a handful of ruffled potato chips and a big dill pickle.

The diner hummed with the drone of conversation mingled with the music from a radio on a shelf behind the counter. The songs were oldies from the seventies. I couldn't make out what the patrons were talking about.

As I ate, a pair of men in workclothes left. They paused outside to look at my car. One of them said something and the other one nodded and laughed. Then they wandered away.

I finished my sandwich and pickle, then ate the potato chips and sipped my iced coffee.

A pickup truck pulled in out front. A pair of teenaged boys got out. They, too, gave my BMW the once-over before they came in.

Ruth appeared. She took away my plate. "Dessert?"

"Tempt me."

"Blueberry, strawberry-rhubarb, lemon meringue. Fresh this morning."

"Did you make them?" I said.

She rolled her eyes. "You kidding?"

"I'll pass on dessert," I said. I cleared my throat. "I've got a question."

She shrugged. "What?"

"Do you know who I am?"

She gave me a quick, cynical smile. "You famous or something?"

"No."

She glanced outside. "You belong to that green BMW?"

"I do."

She nodded. "I know who you are, then."

"Do you mind me asking how you know?"

"I don't mind you asking," she said, "but I do mind telling you."

"Somebody vandalized my car this morning."

"Yes," she said. "I heard that. It wasn't me."

"Did you know Larry Scott?"

She frowned. "Mary's a friend of mine. She's his mother."

"What about Evie Banyon?"

She reached into the pocket of her uniform, took out a slip of paper, and put it on my table. "You can pay at the register on your way out," she said. "More coffee?"

"No, I'm all set, thank you."

When she turned and walked away, I noticed that the radio was playing "Rag Doll" by the Four Seasons, and all the voices in the diner had stopped.

I left three dollar bills on the table, got up and paid Ruth at the register, and it wasn't until I opened the door to leave that conversation inside the diner resumed.

Outside, the clouds in the west had grown darker. Overhead, the sun still shone bright and hot through the sticky haze.

None of my tires was flat. This was progress.

I followed the directions Thomas Soderstrom had given me to Dr. St. Croix's place. Both the doctor's home and his office were in an old shingled Cape with new-looking ells jutting off both ends. It was located on a winding country road off Main Street just north of Raymond's Texaco about a mile out of town. There was a circular driveway with a peastone parking area in front. A little sign hanging from a post read, DR. WINSTON ST. CROIX, PEDIATRIC MEDICINE.

Three cars were parked in the lot—a new-looking silver Oldsmobile sedan with New Jersey plates, a blue Toyota Camry, and a somewhat-battered Jeep Cherokee. A golden retriever snoozed on the steps by a side door on the right-hand ell. His tail flapped halfheartedly when I bent and scratched his forehead.

A sign on the door invited me to *Ring the bell and come on in*, so I did, and I found myself in what appeared to be a children's playroom. There were low tables with crayons and coloring books on them, shelves crammed with books, and colorful kid-sized furniture. Scattered on the floor were dolls and stuffed animals, board games and puppets, toy trucks and puzzles.

For an instant I thought I'd entered the wrong part of the house. Then a voice said, "Looking for the doctor?"

I turned and saw a young man in a summer-weight glen plaid suit sitting on a sofa in the corner. He was reading a magazine. A briefcase sat at his feet.

I nodded to him. "Yes. Is he in?"

"He's with a patient," he said. "I'm next."

"Are you a patient?"

"Me?" He smiled. He was about thirty, a big, tanned guy with curly black hair and dark eyes. "No, I'm a doctor. I'm here on business."

"Me too," I said. "I'm a lawyer."

His eyebrows arched, but I didn't answer his questioning look. If he didn't know all about me, he was apparently the only person in the entire town of Cortland, and I saw no harm in leaving it that way.

I took a chair next to the sofa where he was sitting.

"You from Cortland?" he said.

"Boston."

"Interested in buying the doctor's practice?"

I shrugged. Soderstrom had mentioned that Dr. St. Croix was retiring. This guy could think whatever he wanted about me.

"I haven't gotten far enough to bring a lawyer into it yet," said the dark-haired guy. "But I'm very interested." He reached over to me. "I'm Paul Romano. Up from New Jersey to check it out."

I shook his hand. "Brady Coyne."

He nodded and smiled. Apparently he hadn't been in town long enough to recognize my name, which was refreshing. "This is exactly what I'm looking for," he said. "Nice small town, established practice, modern medical center right down the road, the best hospitals in the world an hour away. I can't think of a better—"

He stopped and looked up when an inside door opened and a visibly pregnant woman in her thirties stepped into the room. She was holding the hand of a boy who looked about ten. His eyes were red, as if he'd been crying. Behind her was a tall fortyish woman wearing a white jacket over a pale blue skirt and flowered blouse. A pair of glasses was perched on top of her head, and a stethoscope dangled from her jacket pocket.

The woman led her boy to the outside door, then turned and smiled at the nurse. "Thank you," she said.

The nurse smiled. She wore her blond hair in a ponytail, and she had clear, pale skin and sharp blue eyes. "Give him an ice cream," she said. "He deserves it for being so brave."

The boy smiled and waved at her. " 'Bye, Claudia."

The nurse lifted her hand. " 'Bye, Bobby. No more rusty nails, okay?"

The woman and the boy left, and the nurse turned to Paul Romano. "He can see you now, Doctor." Then her eyes fell on me. She smiled. "I know you're not a patient."

"No," I said. "I'm a lawyer."

Sometimes telling strangers that I'm a lawyer makes them nervous. I've often found that to be useful. But this nurse didn't even blink. She knew how to handle children needing booster shots. For her, lawyers were no challenge.

"You're here to see the doctor?" she said.

"I'd like to talk to him, yes," I said.

"You don't have an appointment."

"No. I was hoping . . ."

"I'll see what he says," she said. "What did you want to talk to him about?"

"A mutual friend. Evelyn Banyon."

If Evie's name meant anything to her, she didn't give it away. "I'll tell him you're here, Mr. . . . ?"

"Coyne. Brady Coyne." I found a business card and handed it to her. "Please tell him I just want five minutes of his time."

She nodded and went back into the office.

She was out a minute later. "You can go in now, Doctor," she said to Romano. To me she said, "He'll be happy to talk with you if you don't mind waiting."

"I'll wait," I said.

The nurse held the door for Paul Romano. He took his briefcase into the office, and before she shut the door behind them, I heard a deep voice from inside rumble, "I'm Dr. St. Croix. Call me Win."

I read two books about a monkey named Curious George, a Winnie-the-Pooh picture book in which Eeyore, the cynical old donkey, celebrated his birthday, and I'd just picked up

Wind in the Willows, which my father used to read to me, when Claudia, the nurse, came back into the room with Paul Romano.

They shook hands by the outside door, then Romano lifted his hand to me. "Good to meet you," he said.

"You too," I said. "Good luck."

He smiled. "Thanks." To the nurse he said, "I'll be back tomorrow, then."

After he left, the nurse turned to me. "Please try to keep it brief," she said. "The doctor is tired."

"I will," I said. I stood up. "Claudia, is it? You're the doctor's nurse?"

"Claudia Wells," she said. She held out her hand, and I took it. She had a firm, manly grip. "I've been with him ever since he came to Cortland. Twenty-one years, it's been."

"You started when you were in grammar school, huh?"

Her eyes crinkled when she smiled. "Lawyers," she said. "Silver-tongued rogues, every one of you." She touched my arm. "Well, come on in, meet the doctor."

She opened the door and held it for me. The man sitting behind the desk was probably in his early sixties, although at first glance, he looked twenty years older than that. He had thinning white hair and a little white brush of a mustache and pale, papery skin. He was wearing a tan-colored suit, a white shirt, and a jaunty blue bowtie with white polka dots. He was slouched down in his chair, and his eyes were closed.

It took me a moment to realize that he was sitting in a wheelchair.

"Doctor?" said Claudia gently.

He blinked his eyes open. "Oh," he said. He smiled quickly. "Mr. Coyne, is it?" His strong bass voice seemed incongruous, rumbling from such a frail-looking chest. "I'm Winston St. Croix. Call me Win."

He reached a hand across his desk. I leaned forward to shake it. It felt bony and fragile.

He looked up at Claudia. "Thank you, my dear."

She touched my arm. "Five minutes," she said, then turned and left, shutting the door behind her.

"Have a seat, Mr. Coyne," said the doctor.

I sat across from him.

"You wanted to talk about Evie Banyon?"

"I understand you dated her," I said.

He glanced out the window, then turned to me with a smile. "Alas, that would be an imprecise word for it. She did honor me by allowing me to treat her to dinner a few times. A beautiful woman, Mr. Coyne, and most charming. Very intelligent. Excellent company."

"You weren't, um, romantically involved with her, then?"

He closed his eyes for so long I thought he'd gone to sleep. Then without opening them, he said, "I had my silly, old man's notions, but I'm afraid she didn't share them." He blinked and looked at me. He had watery blue eyes. They were almost colorless. "The Cortland rumor mill is churning, Mr. Coyne. This is about the unfortunate death of Larry Scott, am I right?"

"It's about the fact that Evie seems to have disappeared," I said. "I'm trying to find her. I was hoping you might—"

At that moment, Dr. St. Croix's eyes widened and he began to breathe rapidly. "Get Claudia," he gasped. Beads of sweat popped out on his forehead, and his gnarled hands clawed at his shirt collar.

"Claudia!" I yelled. I got up, opened the door to the waiting room, and called again.

She came bursting through a door into the waiting room and brushed past me. "Wait out there," she said to me.

I sat on the sofa, and about five minutes later Claudia wheeled St. Croix out of his office. He seemed to be breathing normally now.

"We can talk tomorrow," he said to me.

"I don't want to—"

"Please," he said. "Can you come by around eleven?"

"Sure."

Claudia patted his shoulder. "Come on, you old goat," she said. "Let's get you tucked in." She looked at me. "I'll be back in a few minutes. Please wait."

I nodded. "I'll be outside."

I went out into the front yard and lit a cigarette. A breeze had begun to ruffle the leaves high in the oak trees, and black clouds had hidden the sun. I listened, but no thunder grumbled in the distance yet. Soon, though. It felt like the temperature had dropped about ten degrees since I'd entered the doctor's office.

I was sitting on the steps smoking my second cigarette when Claudia came out. She sat beside me.

"Is he all right?" I said.

"He overdid it today," she said. "I try to tell him he doesn't need to see patients on Saturdays, but he says he always has, and they depend on him. Some people, it's the only time they can bring their children, be with them in the doctor's office. He's retiring, you know. I just hope it gets settled before he kills himself."

"I thought maybe I upset him."

"No. He's sick."

"It was scary in there," I said.

She nodded. "Multiple sclerosis. He's had it for a couple years, but recently it kicked into a new stage. He tires easily. When he's tired, he loses his balance, gets double vision, shortness of breath, nausea. All the usual symptoms. I try to arrange his schedule so he won't have one of his spells, but today, with Dr. Romano showing up, and then him insisting he see you . . ."

"I'm sorry," I said. "I didn't know."

"He's delivered just about every young person in Cortland for the past twenty-one years," she said. "And he's taken care of them all, too. He's an institution here, Mr. Coyne. You don't find doctors like him anymore. The town won't be the same after he's gone."

"Dr. Romano seems eager to take over," I said.

She nodded. "I hope it works out. There aren't a lot of young doctors who want to buy into an old-fashioned small-town pediatric practice."

"And what about you?" I said. "Will you stay and work for Dr. Romano?"

"It's a possibility, if he wants me," she said. "Though, truthfully, I can't imagine working for anybody but Dr. St. Croix. This has been the only job I've ever had."

I glanced at her left hand and saw no wedding ring. "Do you have children?" I asked.

"Me?" She smiled. "Every kid in Cortland is my child, Mr. Coyne."

I stood up. "You sure it'll be okay if I come back tomorrow morning?"

"He's expecting you. He seems to be looking forward to it, in fact. Told me to tell you that. He'll be fine. He does all right in the mornings. Tomorrow's Sunday. He has no patients—unless some kind of emergency comes up."

"I want to ask him about Evie Banyon. Did you know Evie?"

She nodded. "Win took her out a few times. That was before he got sick." She smiled. "I think he was a bit infatuated with her."

"You've heard about—"

"Larry Scott?" She waved her hand. "Of course. There are no secrets in Cortland. People want to believe that Evie Banyon killed him. It's a neat, simple answer. People in this town like simple answers to complicated questions."

"Do you have an opinion?"

"Me?" She laughed. "What do I know? Evie's a nice person. That's all I know."

"Did you know Scott?"

"Certainly. He was our patient for several years. Which," she said quickly, "means I can't talk about him."

"I understand." I stood up. "Well, my plans seem to keep shifting on me. I've got more places to go, people to see, and now an appointment with the doctor tomorrow morning. Guess I'll try to find a place and spend the night around here. Any suggestions?"

"There's a decent motel a couple miles south of the medical center," she said. "That's the closest place without a leaky roof."

"I'll check it out." I held out my hand to her, and she took it. "I'll be back tomorrow at eleven, then."

"Come to the front door," she said, tilting her head in that direction. "He'll want to meet with you in his living room, not his office."

I waved at Claudia Wells, then went over to my car. Just as I opened the door, I heard the first, distant rumble of thunder.

NINE

I wanted to be sure I could get a room, so I turned back onto Route 1 and headed south to the motel. Just about the time I drove past the medical center, the first fat raindrop splatted against my windshield, and within minutes it was raining so hard that even on high speed, my wipers couldn't keep up. I switched on my headlights, slowed to a crawl, and followed the white line on the side of the road. The wind blew leaves and small branches off the trees, and periodically lightning flashes lit up the world.

When I saw the red neon sign for the Cortland Motor Inn blinking through the rain, I pulled in and parked under the overhang in front of the office where a VACANCY sign was lit in the window.

It was a one-story rectangular brick building with rooms front and back. Twenty units in all. They gave me number 10, a single down at the end on the front.

A pair of plastic chairs sat on the walkway under the

overhang in front of each unit, so after I checked out my room—it was your basic motel room, with a double bed, a bedside table with one of those digital alarm clocks I can never figure out how to operate, a couple of chairs, a bureau, a bathroom, and a color TV—I sat outside in a plastic chair under the overhang and smoked and watched the storm. Now and then a gust of wind blew a mist of rainwater on my face. It was refreshing, and I liked the smell of the air and the grumble of the thunder and the way the sky lighted up in the distance as the storm rolled away.

In about an hour the sun came back out, so I got into my car and followed Charlotte Matley's directions to the Victorian apartment house north of town where Evie had lived.

I found it halfway down a long slope toward the end of a meandering country road. In the distance, the afternoon sun glittered off the surface of a fair-sized lake that nestled in a bowl among the low round hills.

Of the four apartments in the house, only one tenant was home on this summer weekend. He was a garrulous old guy who'd lived there forever with his wife until she "passed on," as he put it, two years ago. The other tenants came and went, he said, and all the others had moved in within the past year or so, long after Evie had moved out. He remembered Evie— "that pretty redhead," he called her—but he said he didn't really know her, and he hadn't seen her since she moved.

He invited me in for a beer, but I declined. I felt petty and selfish, but I wasn't in the mood for a rambling conversation with a lonely old man.

When I got back into my car, I glanced at my watch and was surprised to see that it was after six o'clock. That got me thinking about food. So I drove back to the motel, snagged the overnight bag I always keep in the trunk of my car, and went into my room to clean up.

After my shower, I called my home phone and accessed my

answering machine. No calls all day from anybody, never mind from Evie. It occurred to me that I could spend a week in this nowhere motel on Route 1 in Cortland, Massachusetts, and if I didn't have a law practice and a slave-driving secretary, nobody would notice or care.

Without Evie, I felt aimless and useless.

Where the hell was she?

I walked into the diner around seven. Families with small children and groups of teenagers occupied most of the booths. A few truckers straddled stools at the counter. I spotted an empty booth down at the end and grabbed it.

Someone had left a copy of the *Boston Globe* on the seat. Thank you. I opened it to the sports page.

Ruth, who'd waited on me at lunch, was still there, and she was still wearing the same green uniform and the same sarcastic half-smile. She slid a mug of coffee beside my elbow. "Glutton for punishment, eh?" she said.

"Best food in town is what I hear," I said.

"Only food in town is more like it." She got out her pad and pulled a pencil from her hair. "Know what you want?"

"What's good?" I said.

"You're asking the wrong person, mister," she said. "I work here. I don't eat here." She pointed to the blackboard behind the counter. "Think it over. The dinners come with soup and salad and coffee and dessert. All out of the meatloaf and the fish-'n'-chips. I'll be back."

The blackboard listed fried chicken, turkey dinner, chicken-fried steak, pork chops, shepherd's pie, hot roast-beef sandwich, sirloin tips, spaghetti and meatballs. The meatloaf and the fish-'n'-chips had lines drawn through them. The sirloin tips, at $9.95, was the most expensive.

When Ruth came back, I ordered the shepherd's pie, and I was sipping my coffee and studying the box scores when a voice beside me said, "Mind if I join you?"

I looked up. Paul Romano, the young curly-headed doctor I'd met at Dr. St. Croix's office, was standing there grinning at me.

I waved my hand and said, "Sure."

He was wearing the same glen plaid suit he'd had on at Dr. St. Croix's office. His only concession to informal dining was his necktie, which he'd pulled loose from his throat.

He slid in across from me. "Some storm, huh?"

"I like thunderstorms," I said.

"Me too. They remind you of who's the boss." He took off his suit jacket, folded it, and laid it on the seat beside him. "So you making a weekend of it?"

I nodded. "Got some business here tomorrow."

"Me too," he said. "Great place to spend a Saturday night, huh? Watch the fireflies, listen to the frogs. It's a real happening place."

Ruth came over and gave Romano a mug of coffee. He pushed it away. "No coffee."

"Sorry," she said. She didn't sound sorry. "Something else to drink?"

"I wouldn't mind a cup of tea."

"Tea?"

"You can figure it out," he said. "You boil some water, find a teabag, put the bag in a cup, pour some of the water on it, let it sit there for a minute . . ."

"Sounds complicated," she said. "I'll have to ask the chef. I'm just a lowly waitress."

"Lowly, maybe," he said. "But sexy."

She rolled her eyes, then walked away.

"So what do you think?" he said to me as he watched her go.

"About what?"

"Her. Ruth."

"Overworked, underpaid, bitter, lonely. Sore feet. Probably

got a couple kids at home, an ex-husband behind on his child-support payments, truckers hitting on her all day."

"Not a bad ass."

"I didn't notice."

"You didn't?"

"Getting old, I guess," I said.

"Bet old Ruth there wouldn't mind a little stimulating company on a Saturday night after she gets off work. What do you think?"

"I think she's probably looking forward to a hot bath and a good night's sleep."

"Give her a shot, why don't you?"

"Not me," I said. "Why don't you?"

"Oh, I already got something lined up. But Ruth there, she likes you."

"I don't think so."

"You don't know much about women, do you?"

"No," I said. "I really don't."

"Well, I do," he said. "And I can tell you, that Ruth, she's got her eye on you. Handsome out-of-town lawyer, lots of money, nice car? She'd be easy. You ought to—" He glanced up.

Ruth was standing there holding a cup of tea. She placed it beside Romano. If she'd heard what he was saying, her face didn't reveal it.

He touched her hand. "Thanks, honey."

She slid her hand away from him. "You ready to order?"

"I'll start with the escargots," he said, "then the Bibb lettuce with the vinaigrette dressing. Rack of lamb, mint sauce, roasted new potatoes, fresh green beans al dente."

"Very funny," she said.

"Would you believe the hot roast-beef sandwich?"

"Mashed or fries?"

"Surprise me."

Ruth rolled her eyes. "I got a lot of customers, mister. Why don't you just tell me what you want?"

He grinned. "Really?"

She shrugged. "You get mashed, then." She looked at me. "Want me to hold yours till his is ready?"

"No," I said. "I'm in a hurry."

When she left, Romano said, "You *do* have something lined up, huh?"

I nodded. My motel room had cable, and I figured the Saturday-night movies would start at eight.

"So," he said, "you interested in St. Croix's medical practice?"

"I'm a lawyer," I said. "I can't talk about it."

"Oh, right," he said. "Sorry." He poked my arm. "Guy comes into a bar, grabs a stool, okay? He's muttering and sputtering and swearing, and everyone stops and looks at him. Someone says, 'What's the matter, pal?' 'Fuckin' lawyers,' the guys says. 'Assholes, every damn one of 'em. I hate lawyers.' And the guy goes on this long rant about lawyers, how they're out to screw you, how they've got no morals, how all they want is money. 'Assholes,' the guy says. 'Lawyers are god-damn assholes.' Everyone is nodding and murmuring sympathetically. Then the guy notices this older man down at the end of the bar who's frowning and shaking his head. 'Hey,' says the guy to this older man, 'what's the matter? Did I insult you? You a lawyer?' And the older man looks up and says, 'Yes, you insulted me, and no, I'm not a lawyer. I'm an asshole.' " Romano laughed. "Lawyer joke, huh?"

I tapped the newspaper that lay on the table beside me. "Want a section?"

"What's the matter?" said Romano. "I didn't hurt your feelings, did I? You offended?"

I shook my head.

"I thought it was a pretty funny story."

116

"Sure," I said. "A good one."

"Ah," he said. "I guess I did offend you."

"I'm trying to read my newspaper."

"You mean, shut up and leave you alone, huh?"

"I've got the sports," I said. "You can have the rest of it."

"I like to be sociable when I eat."

"I like to read the paper when I eat," I said. I propped it up in front of me and took a sip of my coffee.

He slapped his hand on the table. "Well, fuck me, then." He slid out of the booth, put his suit jacket back on, and picked up his tea. "Sorry to bother you."

"Enjoy your sandwich," I said, without looking up from my newspaper.

Romano went over to the counter and sat on a stool. I resumed my study of the box scores.

A few minutes later Ruth delivered my shepherd's pie. "Thought he was a friend of yours," she said, jerking her chin in Romano's direction.

"He thought so, too," I said.

"I figured, two strangers . . ."

"He's a doctor, I'm a lawyer. Natural enemies."

"I don't trust lawyers *or* doctors," she said. "Lawyers want to screw you out of your money. Doctors just want to screw you."

"You're a wise person."

She shrugged. "You keep your mouth shut, you can learn a lot in a place like this." She touched my shoulder. "Enjoy your dinner."

I did enjoy it, and I enjoyed the hot apple pie afterwards. When I paid Ruth at the cash register, Dr. Paul Romano, who was still sitting at the counter, glanced up at me, narrowed his eyes, then leaned his head to the guy sitting beside him and said something out of the corner of his mouth. The other guy, who had long stringy hair and a thick neck and wore a baseball cap and overalls, slowly lifted his head and looked at me. Then he turned to Romano and nodded.

If it hadn't been for the nasty undercurrent, the two of them sitting at the counter in this small-town diner—Romano in his spiffy New Jersey suit and the other guy in his small-town workclothes—would've made a classic Norman Rockwell *Saturday Evening Post* cover.

As I opened the door to leave, Ruth called, "Have a good evening, Mr. Lawyer."

When I turned to wave to her, I saw that everybody in the diner was looking at me.

I lay on my bed with my shoulders propped up against the headboard and the color television playing between my feet. It was not a big night for cable movies, and I'd finally settled on an old Dirty Harry adventure featuring Clint Eastwood. It wasn't a very demanding story, but still I kept losing track of who was who. I was thinking about Evie, and the fact that for the past several months I'd been spending all my Saturday nights with her, and that without her, a Saturday night in a cheerless motel room in Cortland, Massachusetts, felt about as lonely as it could get.

It might not have felt so bleak if I'd managed to latch on to a trace of her, or if I'd learned something about the murder of Larry Scott. I was beginning to understand that Evie wouldn't come back until Scott's murder was solved.

All I'd learned was that Evie had stabbed him with a pair of scissors a few years ago, which made her an even better suspect than I'd thought.

All in all, this had not been the best day of my life.

In spite of Clint's best efforts to hold my attention, I guess I dozed off, because when a noise from outside the motel snapped my head up, some stand-up comic was telling dirty jokes on the television.

I lay there for a moment before I realized that the noise was somebody tapping sharply at my door.

My first thought was Dr. Paul Romano, looking for company, and I was tempted to ignore it.

But the tapping became more persistent, so I muted the television, slid off the bed, went to the door, and cracked it open.

Somebody pushed past me and hissed, "Shut the damn door. Quick."

I shut it and turned around.

Evie was standing in the middle of the room. Her hair was piled under a man's felt hat that she had pulled low over her forehead. She wore sunglasses and a man's blue shirt and loose-fitting khaki pants.

"What are you doing here?" I said.

"No," she said. "What are *you* doing here?" She took off her sunglasses and put them on the bedside table, then pulled off the hat and shook her hair loose.

"I came looking for you," I said. "You're . . . missing."

"I don't suppose it occurred to you that if I wanted to be found, I would've told you."

"I was worried." I went over to where she was standing and put my arms around her. "I'm glad you're okay."

She stood stiffly in my embrace, neither returning it nor pulling away. "Who said I was okay?"

"You're alive," I said. "And that's a relief."

She laughed softly against my chest, and then I felt her relax. She put her arms around my waist and laid her cheek on my shoulder. "How's about a kiss?" She tilted up her face.

I gave her a kiss, and she gave one back to me.

"Now," she said, "please go home."

"I will if you'll come with me."

She shook her head.

"Honey—"

"I've got to do this," she said. "It's my thing, and I've got to do it by myself."

"What?" I said. "What exactly are you doing?"

Evie sat on the bed. She clasped her hands between her knees and looked down into her lap. "They think I murdered Larry. I didn't, but everybody thinks I did." She glanced up at me. "Even you."

I started to speak, but she glanced sharply at me and held up her hand. "You do," she said. "Or at least, you've got some doubts. You don't have to deny it. It's understandable. The point is, I've got a problem, and I've got to deal with it."

"You're innocent," I said. "You don't have a problem."

She shook her head. "You know better than that."

"We should go to Detective Vanderweigh. He's a reasonable man. He thinks you're avoiding him. Hiding out—it makes you look guilty, you know. Charlotte Matley can come with us. She can—"

"How do you know Charlotte?"

I sat beside Evie on the bed. "I, um, I heard her message on your answering machine. So I called her. I saw her this morning in her office. That's when my valve stem—"

"You *what*?"

"My valve stem. It—"

"You listened to my messages?"

I nodded. "I talked with Marcus, and he said he hadn't heard from you, and you were supposed to be at work, and I had terrible thoughts, so I went to your condo and used my key."

Evie shook her head. "I know I'm supposed to be flattered," she said softly, "you caring so much . . ."

"Loving you so much," I said.

"Sure," she said. "Whatever. But I don't feel flattered. Or loved. Mainly, I feel crowded. Jesus. Going into my home

120

when I'm not there, listening to my messages? I suppose you pawed through my underwear, too."

"I didn't know you weren't there. I actually thought you might be there. I thought something might have happened to you."

"Yeah, you said that. Well, now you know I'm okay, so you can go back to Boston and let me finish what I started, okay?"

"Let me help you, at least."

"No, damn it. You can't help. You can only get in the way. Please."

I let out a long breath. "Whenever I have a problem," I said, "I want to solve it right away. I am not patient. I don't do well, waiting for things to work themselves out. I'm never comfortable leaving them in the hands of somebody else."

"So you understand how I feel," said Evie. "I'm the same way. Maybe it's selfish of me, not caring if you're uncomfortable. But I've got to figure this out for myself. I know you love me. I know you're worried, and I understand it makes you feel better, ramming around Cortland, feeling like you're doing something. But you're not helping, Brady. You're only making it more complicated than it already is."

I sighed. "I understand how you feel."

"Do you?"

"Sure. If I were in your place, I guess I'd feel the same way."

"So will you go home?"

I shrugged. "I don't see how I can just turn around and forget this, forget you. You're a murder suspect. The cops are looking for you. Actually, we're both suspects. But we didn't do it. I'm willing to bet that somebody from Cortland did. That's what you think, too, right?"

She shrugged.

121

"Two brains are better than one," I said.

"But," she said, "this is *my* problem."

"No," I said. "It's *our* problem. Your problems are my problems. We share good times, we share problems. That's what it's all about."

Evie was quiet for a long moment. Then she hitched herself close to me and took my hand in both of hers. "That's very sweet," she said.

"Have you forgiven me about those flowers?"

She chuckled. "Never."

"I'm glad I found you."

"You didn't find me," she said. "I found you."

We stood there in the middle of the little motel room and undressed each other in the flickering light of the muted television. We went slowly, taking turns, a button here, a zipper there, a tug on a sleeve, with many pauses for touching and kissing.

When we were both naked, Evie took my hand and led me to the bathroom. She turned on the shower and let it run until the room filled with steam. Then we stepped under the water. We took turns soaping each other, running our slippery hands over each other's slick skin, and pretty soon we couldn't wait any longer, so she wrapped her arms around my neck and I held her butt and she clamped her thighs around my hips, and I braced her back against the glass shower door, and she bit my shoulder and held on tight. We moved together, finding our rhythm, feeling it build, and I don't remember ever sensing such desperate hunger from her. And then her fingernails dug into my back, and she said, "Oh!" and we shuddered and spasmed together under the water, and for the first time in more than a week there was no empty place in me.

* * *

I lay on my back staring up into the darkness. Evie had one leg hooked over mine. Her arm lay across my chest, and her cheek rested on my shoulder, and her breathing was slow and soft.

After a minute, she whispered, "You awake?"

"Yes."

"You know I love you," she said.

"Yes, I do."

"If you love me, you'll do what I want."

"What do you want?"

She kissed my throat. "I want you to go home."

"No," I said. "I can't do that."

"It's not safe in this town."

"That's why I'm staying," I said.

"You're a stubborn man," she said. It almost sounded complimentary, the way she said it.

A few minutes later, I said, "So are you making any progress?"

"Maybe."

"Do you know who killed Larry Scott?"

"I haven't gotten that far."

"Want to share?"

"No," she said. "Not yet."

"But if—"

She put her fingers on my lips. "Shh," she said. "Go to sleep."

After a while, I did.

I was awakened by a disturbing dream that slipped away instantly, leaving only a sense of dread that lingered like a cold stone in my chest. Gray light was seeping in around the edges of the curtain across the front window, and it took me a moment to realize that someone was banging on my door and calling my name.

"Mr. Coyne." It was a man's voice. "Open up." He banged on the door again. "It's the police."

I slipped away from Evie, sat on the edge of the bed, and pulled on my pants.

"What is it?" mumbled Evie.

"There's a cop at the door."

"Shit." She scrambled out of the bed, grabbed her clothes off the floor, slipped into the bathroom, and shut the door behind her.

I went to the outside door and pulled it open. The same cop who I'd met at the garage in the morning when my tire was being fixed—Sergeant J. Dwyer, of the Cortland PD—stood there.

"Sir," he said, "I want you to please come with me."

TEN

"What's going on?" I said to Dwyer. I yawned. "What time is it, anyway?"

"It's ten after five," he said, "and what's going on is, I need you to come with me."

"I've got to get dressed." When I turned back into the room, he followed me in and turned on the light.

I noticed that Evie's sunglasses were on the bedside table and her felt hat was sitting on the bureau. As I bent over to pick up my shirt, I saw her panties crumpled on the floor next to my socks. I quickly shoved them under the bed with the side of my foot.

When I glanced up at Dwyer, he was looking around the room. To me, it was obvious that two people had been sleeping in the bed, and I was aware of Evie's scent lingering there.

If Dwyer noticed anything, he didn't mention it.

After I'd buttoned my shirt and slipped on my shoes, I said, "Okay. Where to?"

He led me out of the room. I checked my pocket to make sure my key was there, pulled the door shut, then followed him around the corner to the back side of the motel.

Down at the far end were two or three Cortland PD cruisers and several other vehicles parked at random angles in the middle of the lot. A couple of uniformed cops were keeping a small gathering of people away from a vehicle parked in front of one of the units. That car seemed to be the center of attention.

As we got closer, I saw that the vehicle in question was a new-looking silver Oldsmobile. I'd seen that car—or its twin—parked in Dr. Winston St. Croix's driveway the previous afternoon.

Dwyer put his hand on my elbow. "Wait here, sir."

"I'm not going anywhere," I said.

He shouldered his way through the crowd, and a minute later state police detective Neil Vanderweigh appeared.

He smiled and held out his hand. "Mr. Coyne," he said. "We meet again."

"Yes." I shook his hand. "What a swell surprise."

"Come on. I want to show you something."

I followed him over to the silver Oldsmobile. The driver's door was hanging open, and somebody was slumped behind the wheel.

"Recognize him?" said Vanderweigh.

He had curly black hair, and his chin rested on his chest. His formerly white shirt and light-green glen plaid jacket were now dark with dry blood. He was surely dead.

"They cut his throat, huh?" I said.

"Ear to ear."

"His name is Paul Romano," I said. "He's a doctor from New Jersey. He was looking into buying a pediatric practice here in Cortland."

126

Vanderweigh nodded. He already knew that. "Let's talk," he said.

He led me away from the crowd to an unmarked sedan, and we leaned against the side. "You want some coffee?" he said.

"Desperately."

Vanderweigh got the attention of one of the uniformed Cortland cops, lifted his cupped hand to his mouth in a drinking gesture, and held up two fingers. The cop nodded.

Vanderweigh turned to me. "So tell me about Dr. Paul Romano."

I told him what little Romano had told me.

"You had supper with him last night, I understand."

"Not really. He sat with me for a few minutes. But I ate in a booth and he moved to the counter."

"You had an argument." It was a statement, not a question.

"I just let him know that I preferred to eat alone. I didn't like him."

"Why not?"

I shrugged. "Not my kind of guy, that's all. He was making suggestive comments about the waitress. He hinted that he had a woman 'lined up'—I believe that's the term he used—for the evening."

"And you found this offensive?"

I smiled. "I found it boring."

"Did he mention who this woman he had lined up was?"

"No. At the time, I didn't necessarily believe him. He struck me as one of those guys who like to brag about their conquests."

"And that kind of guy bores you."

"Yes. Even when I was a teenager I thought they were boring. I figured they were all lying. I'd rather read the sports page than listen to that crap, and that's more or less what I told Romano. He got the hint and moved to the counter."

"The way I hear it," said Vanderweigh, "it was more than a hint."

"I don't know how you heard it," I said, "but we did not exactly exchange blows. I was sitting peacefully in a booth, and he came along and sat across from me, and I made it as clear as I could in the most civil manner I was capable of that I'd prefer not sharing my booth, and he moved to the counter. If you've got yourself some witness who wants to make a motive for murder out of that . . ."

Vanderweigh patted my arm. "Relax, Mr. Coyne. I've questioned plenty of eyewitnesses in my day."

The uniformed officer came over with two Styrofoam cups of coffee. "Hope black is all right," he said to Vanderweigh.

Vanderweigh shrugged and gave me one of the cups.

I took off the lid, sipped it, and felt a tiny spark of life tingle in my veins.

Vanderweigh blew on his coffee. "Any thoughts on who might want to kill Romano?"

"Not really," I said.

"But . . . ?"

I shrugged. "I just didn't find him a likable guy, that's all. In fact, I thought he was quite obnoxious. Maybe somebody else reacted the same way."

"Like who?"

I shook my head. "If you killed everybody you didn't like, there wouldn't be many people left."

Vanderweigh smiled and sipped his coffee. "So," he said, "what brings you to Cortland?"

"I'm looking for Evie Banyon."

He nodded. I had the feeling that so far, at least, I hadn't told him anything he didn't already know. "Any luck?" he said.

"I haven't found her, no." It wasn't a lie, at least not technically. I hadn't found Evie. She had found me.

But if Vanderweigh knew that Evie was hiding in my motel room at that very moment, I doubted he'd be tolerant of a technicality.

It was wrong to deceive a state police homicide detective, especially with a murdered body sitting in a nearby car. But I'd said it, and I would stick with it.

"What made you think Ms. Banyon was in Cortland?" Vanderweigh asked.

"She wasn't home. She lived here before she moved to Concord. I figured she had friends here. Anyway, this is where Larry Scott lived, and since you guys seem to think she murdered him . . ."

"I never said that," said Vanderweigh.

I nodded. "But you think it. So anyway, I thought Evie might have an idea of who actually did kill Scott and came here to figure it out. Or maybe she just came here to get away from it all."

"To hide?"

"Whatever."

"Any idea if she actually did come here?"

"Like I said, I haven't found her. It was a dumb idea, me coming here. But I was worried, and I missed her. It made me feel better, doing something. Better than sitting around waiting for her to call."

"Did you know that Romano had a room here in this motel?"

"No. He never mentioned that."

"Both of you eating at the same diner, staying in the same motel, huh?"

"Here I am again," I said, "at the scene of the crime. Opportunity, means, and a damn good motive."

He shrugged. "You said it, not me."

"As far as I know, that diner and this motel are the only places to eat and sleep in this town."

"Did you tell Romano why you were here in Cortland?"

"No. I told him I was a lawyer and couldn't talk about it. So he told me a lawyer joke. You can't tell Polish jokes or blonde jokes anymore. But lawyer jokes are still supposed to be funny."

Vanderweigh smiled. "Did he think you were involved in buying the doctor's practice?"

"He might have thought that. It's more or less how it sounded, I guess."

He ran his hand over his bald head. "Well," he said, "here's the thing. First Larry Scott from Cortland is stabbed to death in Brewster on Cape Cod, and then a week later Dr. Paul Romano from New Jersey has his throat cut in Cortland." Vanderweigh arched his eyebrows at me.

"The Cortland connection," I said.

He shrugged.

"And I was present in these off-the-beaten-path places both times," I said.

"If Ms. Banyon happens to be in Cortland, as you think she is, then she was present both times, too."

"I guess so."

"Where were you around ten last night?" he said.

"Is that when it happened?"

"Give or take half an hour, according to the ME. One of the guests here spotted the body only about an hour ago."

I tried to think. When Evie came to my door, the Dirty Harry movie had ended. It had started at eight and probably ended sometime around ten. I'd been dozing. So Evie had appeared after ten. If she needed a ten o'clock alibi from me, I couldn't provide it.

That made two alibis I couldn't provide for her.

"I was alone in my motel room watching television," I said. "It was a Clint Eastwood movie on cable. I dozed off and missed the ending. That was probably around ten."

130

"So you can't account for your whereabouts last night between—what, eight in the evening and five this morning?"

"Oh, I can definitely account for my whereabouts. I was in my motel room."

"But you don't have a witness."

"I was all alone at ten o'clock. No witness. And I didn't kill that man, if that's what you're getting at."

"Well, of course it's what I'm getting at. Though damned if I can think of a single reason why you'd do it."

"He *was* boring."

"True," he said. "Not the worst motive I can think of." Vanderweigh pushed himself away from the car. "Let's go take a look at your room."

"Bloodstained clothing," I said. "Murder weapons."

"Sure," he said.

I hoped Evie had had the presence of mind to slip away. If she was still hiding in the bathroom, there wouldn't be much I could do.

As Vanderweigh and I skirted the crowd, I saw that Dr. Paul Romano's body had been bagged and strapped on a gurney. An ambulance sat nearby with its motor running and its back doors open, and a tow truck had backed up to the silver Oldsmobile.

Vanderweigh and I went around the corner of the building to my room. I made a point of rattling the doorknob to warn Evie—if she was still there—that we were coming in.

I unlocked the door and held it open for Vanderweigh. He stepped inside, and I followed him.

The bathroom door was still shut, the bed was still unmade, and Evie's soapy feminine scent still lingered in the air. I knew a forensics expert would have no problem coming up with a long strand of auburn hair on a pillow or on a damp bath towel or in the bathtub drain and deduce that it hadn't come from my head.

Well, if she was still hiding in the bathroom, even a rank amateur would notice her.

"Why are we here?" I said to Vanderweigh.

He was opening the bureau drawers. They were empty. "I'm looking for clues," he said, "like a good detective." He opened the closet door. Nothing in there, either. I had brought in only my overnight bag from my car. It sat on the floor at the foot of the bed. I hadn't bothered to empty it.

"Did you recover the murder weapon?" I said.

"Not yet."

I sat on the edge of the bed. Then I noticed Evie's sunglasses sitting on the bedside table where she'd left them. I casually picked them up and slipped them into my shirt pocket.

Her hat, which she'd left on top of the bureau, was gone. That, I assumed, meant Evie had gotten out.

I hoped she'd retrieved her panties from under the bed.

Vanderweigh opened the bathroom door, poked his head in and looked around, then came over to where I was sitting and looked down at me. "Where is she?"

"Who?"

"Ms. Banyon."

I shrugged. "I don't know."

He folded his arms. "She was here. Now she's gone."

"What makes you think that?"

"It's so obvious that even Sergeant Dwyer picked up on it. He mentioned it to me when he brought you over. Told me he smelled sex in your room." Vanderweigh smiled. I'd noticed he had a nice, cynical sense of humor, but there was no humor in this particular smile. "It's really important," he said, "that from now on, you tell me the truth."

I nodded. "Evie was here, yes."

He sat on the bed beside me and dangled his arms between his legs. "I'm going to overlook the fact that you've been lying

132

to me, Mr. Coyne," he said softly. "But I strongly advise you not to lie anymore."

"Actually, I didn't lie," I said. "I was quite precise. I told you I didn't find her. What happened was, Evie found me. She came here."

"I know the difference between the truth and a lie," he said. "You lied. Why?"

I shook my head and said nothing.

"You think she killed Paul Romano, right?" he said.

"No, of course not. Why would she?"

"You tell me."

"She wouldn't," I said. "Evie wouldn't kill anybody."

Vanderweigh blew out a quick breath. "Listen," he said. "The longer Ms. Banyon hides out and slinks around and keeps finding herself in places where people get killed with knives, the worse it looks for her. Whether she's innocent or not, the sooner she talks to us, the better off she'll be. Meanwhile, she's acting guilty as hell."

I nodded. I had told Evie the same thing.

"And you," he said, "are looking more and more like an accomplice. Maybe a killer. At least somebody who's obstructing justice."

"Oh, for Christ's sake, I'm a—"

"No, damn it. You listen to me." He took a deep breath and let it out slowly. "I don't give a shit whether you're a lawyer or the chief fucking justice of the Supreme Court, Mr. Coyne. I've got two vicious murders here, and you and Evelyn Banyon are right in the middle of both of them, and neither of you is cooperating. You're lying and she's hiding." He looked at me and shook his head. "I ought to arrest you, you know that?"

"What good would that do?"

"It would give me satisfaction," he said.

I smiled. "Please don't."

"So where is she, then?"

"Evie? I don't know."

"Listen—"

"I really don't know," I said. "I don't know where she's been staying down here, and I don't know where she went this morning. She ran into the bathroom when Dwyer knocked on the door. I guess she slipped away when I was over there talking with you. She didn't tell me anything. She just came here to tell me to go home."

"Like she doesn't want to get you involved."

"Not really. More like she wants to do whatever she's doing by herself. Evie is a very strong-willed person."

"But you arranged to meet her here, spend the night with her."

"I didn't arrange it. I didn't even know she was in Cortland. She came to my room last night when I was dozing. I didn't expect it."

"What time was that?"

"I didn't notice," I said. "Like I said, I was asleep."

"Before or after ten o'clock?"

"After, I guess."

"And she spent the night with you?"

I nodded.

"A safe place to hide, she figured."

"Certainly if she'd killed Romano, this motel where you found his body would hardly be a very safe place to hide."

"So she wanted your help."

"No, I told you—"

"What *is* she doing?"

I shrugged. "She came here to my room to tell me to go home. She wanted me *not* to try to help her. All I can tell you is that she's frightened. She thinks you've pegged her for Larry Scott's murder."

"Smart girl." Vanderweigh sighed and stood up. "Tell you what, Mr. Coyne. If you promise me you'll bring her to me next time you see her, I won't arrest you. Deal?"

"No deal."

"*No?*"

"If I see Evie again," I said, "I will once again suggest that she talk to you. I can promise you that much. But I won't force her, and I certainly won't rat her out."

" 'Rat her out'?" He laughed quickly. "Did you say that?"

I smiled. "I guess I did."

"You're not going to do what she wants, are you?"

"What do you mean?"

"Go home."

"No," I said. "I'm not going home. Not yet."

"Good." Vanderweigh went over to the door, put his hand on the knob, hesitated, then turned to face me. "You know," he said, "Roger Horowitz was right."

"What about Horowitz?"

"He said you were a pain in the ass."

"He was joking," I said.

"Horowitz," said Vanderweigh, "never jokes."

ELEVEN

After Vanderweigh left, I took a shower and then walked over to the motel office. An elderly man sat behind the counter reading a magazine. A radio sitting on a shelf behind him was tuned to a religious service.

"I'm in room ten," I told him. "I'd like to have it for another night."

He looked up at me. He wore thick black-rimmed glasses. Behind them, his magnified eyes looked startled. "We got plenty of rooms," he said. "You like number ten, it's yours. I'll need your credit card again."

I handed it to him, and he ran it through his machine and gave it back to me.

I thanked him and headed for the door.

"Hey, you hear about the excitement?" he said.

I turned. "What excitement is that?"

"Murder, right out back. Happened last night sometime. Some rich doctor got his throat cut in our parking lot. They found him sittin' in his car. They figure that woman who killed one of our local boys a week ago done it."

"Why?" I said.

"Huh?"

"Why did she do it?"

He shrugged. "Damned if I know. One of them sex things, I suppose."

I bought a Sunday *Globe* from the machine out front, then headed for the diner. I had gone less than a mile when I noticed the Cortland PD black-and-white in my rearview mirror. It stayed on my tail all the way, and when I parked in front of the diner, it pulled in two cars over from me.

I grabbed my newspaper, went over to the cruiser, and tapped on the window. It slid down. A female officer was sitting there grinning up at me.

"Why don't you come in, have breakfast with me," I said.

"I already ate," she said.

"Have some coffee, at least."

"I don't think I'm supposed to socialize with you."

"We don't have to talk," I said. "We can share my Sunday paper. You can have the front page. I got first dibs on the sports."

She smiled. "No, thanks. I'll just sit right here. Don't you go slipping out the back door on me, or they'll have my ass, okay?"

"Sure," I said. "I always cooperate with law enforcement officers."

The diner was mobbed at seven-thirty on this Sunday morning in August. They had two waitresses on duty, and they were working hard. They looked like high-school kids. Both of them were wearing green uniforms like the one Ruth had worn.

This would be my third straight meal here. Lunch, then supper, and now breakfast. A number of the patrons glanced up and squinted at me as I stood there looking around. None of them nodded or waved at me, but at least my arrival didn't bring conversations to a halt in midsentence. I was beginning to feel like a regular.

I found an empty stool at the end of the counter, propped the sports section up in front of me, and a minute later a mug of coffee appeared beside it. I looked up. One of the young waitresses stood there with her pencil poised.

I didn't bother looking at the blackboard. "Three eggs," I said, "over easy, on corned-beef hash, wheat toast, home fries, giant OJ. I like the whites cooked and the yolks runny. Keep the coffee coming."

She scribbled on her notepad, turned away, hesitated, then turned back to me. "You're that guy, aren't you?"

"What guy?"

"I thought they arrested you."

"Not me. I didn't do anything."

She shrugged. "Not what I heard."

"I guess you've got the wrong guy," I said.

She narrowed her eyes at me for a moment, then moved away. A couple of minutes later, I saw her down at the other end of the counter talking with a customer and jerking her head in my direction.

The eggs were perfectly cooked, the hash was crispy, everything was still hot, and the orange juice was freshly squeezed. Only at a truckers' diner.

It seemed unlikely that Dr. Paul Romano's murder was unrelated to Larry Scott's, although what that relationship was had to be pretty indirect. This second one, I knew, made it look worse for Evie. All the police had to do was come up with some plausible motive for her to cut Romano's throat and they'd have a terrific case.

Well, it didn't look that good for me, either. It's what happens when you're in the wrong place at the wrong time.

139

Could I come up with something the police couldn't find? Lieutenant Neil Vanderweigh didn't miss much. On the other hand, he seemed mainly interested in proving our guilt—Evie's and mine. My aim was to discover somebody else's guilt.

I had agreed to visit Dr. Winston St. Croix at eleven. He had dated Evie, and it was his retirement and the sale of his medical practice that had brought Paul Romano to Cortland. The doctor probably knew everyone in town. Maybe he'd have some insight.

And I remembered Larry Scott's mother. Mary was her name. According to Charlotte Matley, Evie and Mrs. Scott had been friends. It would be interesting to know if Mary Scott still considered Evie her friend.

I sopped up the last of the egg yolk with my last home fry, downed my orange juice, drained my coffee mug, and looked at my watch. Eight-fifteen. I had over two hours to kill before my appointment with Dr. St. Croix.

I put my newspaper under my arm, slid off the stool, left two dollar bills under my plate, and went down to the cash register at the end of the counter.

My waitress came over. "Was everything okay?"

"Perfect," I said. I gave her a twenty-dollar bill. "Give me two large coffees to go, please."

I took the coffees outside and went to the cruiser, which was still parked beside my car. The officer rolled down her window and looked out at me. "For me?" she said. I noticed that her nameplate read V. KERSHAW.

I handed one of the Styrofoam cups to her. "The least I could do. It looks like you've got a pretty boring day ahead of you. I brought cream and sugar, too."

She reached out and took the coffee. "Why, thank you. That's very sweet."

"What's the 'V.' for?"

She frowned. "Huh?"

"Your name." I pointed at her nameplate.

"Oh. Valerie. Val. I don't think we ought to be on a first-name basis, though. Do you?"

"Well," I said, "if you're going to tail me all day . . ."

She smiled.

"Seems like a waste of valuable person-power," I said.

"Nothing much ever happens in this town," she said. "Give us a homicide and we are mobilized."

"If the idea is that I'm going to lead you to Evie Banyon," I said, "I can assure you that she won't show her face around me as long as there's a cruiser up my butt. Maybe you should be more subtle about it."

"I appreciate the advice," she said. "But they told me to stick close to you. They didn't say anything about subtlety. I got the feeling if I tried to be subtle, you would, too. My job is to keep my eye on you, so that's what I guess I'll do. I hope you don't mind."

"The whole damn town has had its eye on me since I got here," I said. "I'm getting used to it."

"You're a marked man, Mr. Coyne. Driving that fancy BMW makes it easy for people to mark you."

I smiled. "Maybe you can do me a favor."

She nodded. She'd taken off her cap. It sat on the seat beside her. She had black hair and dark, vivacious eyes. "Fetch me coffee, then ask for a favor," she said. "There's always a catch, isn't there?"

"Can you tell me how to find Mary Scott's house?"

She frowned. "Scott?"

"She's Larry Scott's mother. She—"

"No," she said quickly, "I know who she is. I'm just not sure I should be, um, abetting you."

"I don't intend to murder her."

"I suppose not."

"If I do, you'll be right there to catch me. A feather in your cap."

"Yes," she said. "Good point." She took the top off her coffee, poured in some cream, dumped in a packet of sugar, and stirred it with the plastic straw I'd given her. "I can't have you follow me there," she said. "If you did, then I wouldn't be following you. I've got my orders."

"What if I promised not to slip away?"

"No," she said. "That's not good enough. I'm not supposed to trust you." She sipped her coffee, wrinkled her nose, and added more sugar. "Mrs. Scott's place isn't hard to find. Head north out of town and take the first right after the old drive-in movie theater. She lives about a mile down the road on the right. You can't miss it. Big old falling-down barn out back, a couple of car bodies rusting in the side yard."

"If I make a wrong turn or something," I said, "just flash your lights at me."

"Why, of course," she said. "Protect and serve."

I got into my car, pulled out of the parking lot, and turned north on Route 1. Valerie Kershaw's cruiser pulled out behind me and followed me back through town, past the village green and Charlotte Matley's office, past the road to Dr. St. Croix's place, past the garage where I had my valve stem replaced, and past the site of the old drive-in movie theater. Then I slowed down, and a couple hundred yards later I spotted a narrow roadway on the right. I turned onto it. Behind me, the cruiser's directional was blinking, and Officer Kershaw turned in behind me.

It was one of those winding two-lane country roads such as you find in rural parts of central Maine, with frost heaves and potholes and narrow sloping sandy shoulders and big old oaks arching overhead. On both sides it was bordered by stone walls and shaded by thick second-growth woods.

In any Massachusetts community more prosperous than Cortland, house-sized openings would've been bulldozed out of those woods, and more or less identical colonial-style houses would've been erected. The road would be widened and straightened and repaved, and GO SLOW CHILDREN and SCHOOL BUS STOPPING signs would pop up at every bend. But here in sleepy little Cortland, it was just a paved-over old dirt road, originally some nineteenth-century farmer's cart path, following the earth's contours through overgrown pastureland and uncut woodlot, and for nearly a mile there were no dwellings.

I rounded a bend and started down a long slope, and then I spotted a black mailbox beside the road. At that moment, Officer Kershaw flashed her cruiser's lights.

The name Scott was painted sloppily on the side of the mailbox. I pulled to the side of the road and stopped. The house was a nondescript square bungalow with a screened-in porch along the front. It was two stories tall, with a brick chimney on one end and a television antenna on the other. Its white paint was stained and flaking, and there were holes in the screening. The front lawn stood about a foot tall. A rotary lawnmower sat in the middle of it. To the right of the house, a gravel driveway led straight back from the road to a big weathered barn in back. Beside the driveway, knee-deep in weeds and half covered with vines, the skeletons of two ancient automobiles sat up on cinderblocks.

The red Ford Escort in the driveway appeared to be three or four years old. The pickup truck parked behind it looked much older. Its bed was half full of cordwood.

I got out of the car. Officer Kershaw had stopped ten or fifteen yards behind me. I waved in her direction, then headed down the driveway to the house.

When I got to the pickup truck, I noticed a pair of scuffed

143

workboots sticking out from under it. The boots appeared to be attached to a pair of legs, and the legs were wearing faded blue jeans.

"Excuse me," I said.

"Who's that?" came a growly voice from under the truck's chassis.

"I'm looking for Mrs. Scott. Is she home?"

The boots moved, and then a body slid out from under the truck.

His face and arms were streaked with grime, and he wore several days' worth of thick blond stubble. His squinty blue eyes were set too close together. He had a round, squished-in nose, a small mouth, and not much chin. His greasy straw-colored hair hung over his ears. He was, I guessed, in his early twenties.

He shaded his eyes with his hand and frowned up at me. He wore a gold hoop in his left ear.

I remembered Larry Scott from our encounters at the Cape. I wouldn't soon forget the image of his dead eyes staring up at the sky that morning by our cottage in Brewster. Larry had blue eyes and straw-colored hair and a compact, muscular body. He had been a handsome guy. This one, I guessed, was Larry's brother.

Larry had been the good-looking, quick one. This guy was the big, strong one. He had cut the arms off his T-shirt to show off his biceps. They were as big around as my thighs.

He sat up, pulled a rumpled pack of Marlboro reds from the pocket of his jeans, jammed one into the corner of his mouth, and lit it with a wooden match. He exhaled a big plume of smoke, then tilted his head and narrowed his eyes. "So whaddaya want with Mrs. Scott, anyway?" he said.

"I want to talk to her about her son."

"I'm her son."

"I mean Larry."

He turned his head and spit on the ground. "Larry ain't here."

"I know," I said. "That's what I want to talk to her about."

"There's been a million people talking to my mother. She's pretty sick of talking to people. I wish everybody would just leave her alone."

"What about you?" I said. "Have people been talking to you about what happened to Larry?"

He shrugged. "Me? What do I know?" He scratched his cheek. "Who are you, anyway?"

"I'm sorry. I didn't introduce myself. My name is Brady Coyne. I'm a lawyer." I held my hand down to him.

He looked at it for a moment, then wiped his hand on his T-shirt, reached up and gave mine a limp shake. "Lawyer, huh? So you gonna sue somebody, get my mother some money?"

I smiled. "No, I'm afraid not."

"Then what do you want?"

"Well, I'm a friend of Evie Banyon. You know Evie?"

"Sure I know her. She's Larry's friend."

"Have you see her lately?"

He took a long drag on his cigarette, then snapped the butt into the weeds. "Nope," he said. "Not for years."

"You think she killed Larry?"

"I don't know nothing about that." He jerked his head in the direction of the house. "My mother's in there. I gotta get this fixed." Then he lay on his back and pushed himself under the truck.

I turned and headed for the house. As I neared the front steps, I saw that a woman was standing behind the screen door. I wondered how long she had been there.

"Mrs. Scott?" I said.

"That's right." Her voice was soft and hesitant.

"My name is Brady Coyne," I said. "I'm a friend of Evie Banyon. I wonder if I could talk with you."

"Was Mel rude to you?"

"Not at all," I said.

She pulled the screen door open and held it for me. "Please come in."

I went up the three steps and into the porch. It was crammed with old patio furniture, cardboard boxes, rusted bicycles, and aluminum trash cans. Mary Scott was wearing a pair of baggy blue jeans and a man's white shirt with the tails hanging loose and the cuffs rolled to her elbows. She appeared to be in her mid-forties. She had the same straw-colored hair and blue eyes as Larry and Mel, although there were streaks of gray in her hair and creases at the corners of her eyes.

She had once been a pretty young woman, and now she was a handsome middle-aged woman.

She held out her hand. "I apologize for Mel. He hasn't been himself since . . ."

I took her hand. "I had no problem with Mel."

"Come in, please," she said.

I followed her into the living room. It was small and dark, but unlike the outside of the house, the inside appeared neat and clean. A big-screen television sat on a low table in the corner. A dozen or so framed photographs were lined up on top of it.

Mary Scott gestured to the sofa. I sat down.

"Can I get you something?" she said. "Coffee?"

"I don't want to bother you, Mrs. Scott."

"It's Mary," she said. "I just perked a fresh pot. How do you like it?"

"Black," I said. "Thank you."

She smiled quickly and left the room.

I stood up and went over to the television. Most of the

146

photos were Kmart portraits of the two boys at various ages. In the earliest one, Larry looked six or seven and Mel was a toddler. Even then you could see that Larry was the quick, bright, handsome one.

I picked up a wedding photo. Mary Scott looked like the high-school homecoming queen in her prom dress, although her smile struck me as hesitant and forced. The groom was barely an inch taller than her. He looked young and bewildered and awkward in his formal white jacket.

"That was Lee," said Mary Scott.

I put the photo back and turned around. "I'm sorry," I said. "I didn't mean to snoop."

"You leave photos out like that," she said, "it's because you want folks to look at 'em." She handed me a mug of coffee. "Lee ran off on me. Left me with two wild boys, and I haven't seen hide nor hair of the man in seventeen years." She smiled quickly. "Well, you didn't want to talk about my no-good husband, I guess." She sat on the end of the sofa, leaned forward so she could prop her elbows on her thighs, and held her mug in both hands.

I sat on the other end of the sofa. "I'm sorry about Larry," I said.

She nodded.

"I was there when it happened."

She turned and frowned at me. "You're Evie's friend, right?"

"Yes."

"Everyone thinks you two did it, you know."

"I know that," I said. "We didn't, of course. I'd like to figure out who did. That's why I'm here in Cortland. That's why I wanted to talk to you."

"I don't know you," she said, "but I know Evie. She didn't like Larry very much, and I don't blame her one single bit for that, the way my boy treated her. I would've felt like killing

147

him myself. But Evie never . . ." She shut her eyes and shook her head. When she opened her eyes, they were wet. She wiped them with the back of her wrist. "I got to stop this," she mumbled.

"You and Evie are friends," I said.

She smiled quickly. "Oh my, yes. I work in the cafeteria at the medical center, you see, and Evie worked there, too. Not in the cafeteria. She worked for Mr. Soderstrom. Evie's a very smart girl, and she had an important job. Anyway, we got to talking, you know, the way you do with folks you run into every day. Evie would time her coffee breaks with mine, and we'd sit together chatting just about every morning. She didn't mind hanging out with a lowly cafeteria worker. We hit it off, Evie and I. Folks're expecting me to be mad at her now, thinking she murdered my Larry. But I'm not mad, because I know Evie couldn't do anything like that."

"Have you and Evie kept in touch since she moved?"

"Oh, sure. We talk on the phone a lot, and we go out once in a while. I've been up to Boston a few times, and Evie takes me to the museum and we eat out. Sometimes she comes down from Concord to visit, and we drive to Providence the way we used to when she lived here. We like to go eat in a fancy restaurant. No fancy restaurants in Cortland, in case you haven't noticed."

I smiled. "You do have a good diner."

"Two bachelor ladies who like to dress up and eat out don't go to a diner, no matter how good the food is."

"Mrs. Scott," I said, "have you talked to Evie since Larry was killed?"

She turned away from me and said nothing.

"I know she's here in Cortland," I said. "The police are looking for her. I bet you know where she is."

"Maybe I do, maybe I don't" she said. "But I'm going to tell you what I keep telling the police. I don't know where

Evie is or what she's doing, but I do know that she didn't murder my son."

"Have you been lying to the police?"

She looked at me and smiled. "Part of it's a lie, yes, sir."

"I've tried lying to them, too," I said. "They're pretty good at figuring out what's a lie."

She shrugged. "Maybe I'm better at it than you."

I sipped my coffee. "This must be upsetting you," I said. "Talking about it."

She shook her head. "I'm plenty upset," she said. "But talking about it doesn't make it any worse. I wish they'd figure out who did it, that's all."

"I think they're pretty convinced it was Evie," I said. "Another man was killed here in Cortland last night, you know."

She nodded. "I must've got ten phone calls this morning, all my friends and neighbors spreading their gossip. Everyone thinks Evie did that, too."

"I guess they do, though nobody seems to have come up with any reason for it." I hesitated. "Mrs. Scott—"

"Mary, please," she said.

I nodded. "If it wasn't Evie, then who could have killed Larry?"

She gazed at the photos on the television for a minute, then turned to me. "I'll tell you the truth," she said. "When the police ask me that question, I tell them I have no idea. Larry was a good boy, I tell them. Not an enemy in the world. It's what I think a mother ought to be saying. But you know what, Mr. Coyne?"

"Brady," I said automatically.

She smiled. "The truth is, Brady, since Larry got home from that war, he was not a very nice person. He drank too much, and he bragged too much, and he lied too much, and except for Mel, who always worshiped his big brother, nobody much liked him anymore. Even me, God help me. I didn't like him

149

much, either. So I guess there's lots of folks who might not've wanted him around."

"What did he lie about?"

"He loved to talk about being in that war, how he killed people, how the bombs were going off right next to him, bullets flying around, tanks and missiles and airplanes, how he was a hero." She blew out a quick little breath. "The truth is, he was nowhere near where the fighting was. He ran a computer, was his job. That's what they taught him in the Marines. Computers. He copied press releases and sent 'em off on his computer. I guess those press releases were mostly lies. Maybe that's where he learned it." She smiled. "Running computers and telling lies. That's what Larry learned from the Marines. That's what he was good at."

"What about Evie?" I said. "Did she like him?"

"Evie tried to be nice to him," she said. "Because of me, I guess." She gazed over at the photographs on the television. "Larry was a handsome boy. Pretty smart, too. He could be charming. I think she liked him at first. Before she got to know him. And Larry, he mistook that for something else. Hell, it was Evie who got him that janitor job when no one else in town would give him a chance. She was doing me a favor. I sure wish I hadn't mentioned it to her. I should've just told her to steer clear of him. But I confess, I had it in the back of my mind that maybe they'd become friends. I thought she'd be good for him, calm him down, make him sweet like he used to be. I was a bad friend to Evie for not warning her about him." She lifted her hand, then let it fall to her lap. "My son drove my only real friend out of town. It wasn't her fault, what happened."

"Attacking him with scissors, you mean," I said.

She nodded. "They tried to make it like she wanted to kill him. All she was doing was trying to tell him he was driving her crazy and she couldn't take much more of it." She blinked several times. "They fired her because of it. What they should've done was lock up my son. If they had, maybe none of this would've happened, and he'd still be alive, and I'd still be having my morning coffee with my friend."

"Larry lived here with you, is that right?"

She nodded. "He couldn't afford to get a place of his own, that's for sure."

"I wonder if I could take a peek into his room."

"Oh, Lord," she said. "What in the world for?"

I waved my hand. "Just curious."

"Those policemen said the same thing. Just curious, they said. No, ma'am, they wouldn't touch anything. They just wanted to look around. Then they went trooping up there with their cameras."

I nodded. Of course the police would check out the murder victim's room. "I won't touch anything, either," I said.

"It's just a boy's room." Mary Scott shook her head. "I don't see what so interesting about it. But no harm, I guess. I keep the door shut, like he always did. He never wanted me in there, and since he died, I haven't had any spirit for going in and cleaning it up. Suppose I ought to one of these days." She pointed. "Up those stairs. Larry's room is the first one on the right. Mel's is down the end of the hall. You'd best not go into Mel's room."

"Thank you." I stood up. "I'll only be a minute."

I climbed the narrow stairs to the second floor. A cardboard sign identical to those you see nailed to trees along just about every country road in New England nowadays was tacked to the first door on the right. It read: POSTED. NO HUNTING, FISHING, OR TRAPPING WITHOUT LANDOWNER'S PERMISSION. I guessed Larry had ripped it off a tree somewhere.

Under those machine-printed words someone had scrawled in red crayon: TRESPASSERS WILL BE SHOT ON SIGHT.

I pushed open the door and stood in the doorway. It was

a small, dark, narrow room. There was an unmade single bed in the corner and a bureau under the only window. Dirty clothes and old magazines were scattered on the floor. A pump-action 12-gauge shotgun was propped up in one corner, and a bundle of spinning rods stood in another. A small bookcase held a twelve-inch television and a boom box and a few paperback books.

About two dozen snapshots were taped to the wall beside the bed.

I kneeled on the bed to look at them.

Evie. Every photograph showed Evie, and she was naked in most of them.

I blinked and looked up at the ceiling. Jesus.

I took a deep breath, turned back, and forced myself to look at them one at a time.

First a close-in headshot of Evie smiling her pretty, familiar smile.

Then Evie sticking out her tongue at the camera.

Evie with her hair falling over the side of her face like a curtain.

A head-and-shoulders shot of Evie with her eyes half-lidded and her tongue licking her lips.

Evie posing in a tank top and shorts with one hand on her hip and the other behind her head.

Evie kneeling on a bed peeling up the bottom of her tank top to show her flat belly and the undersides of her breasts.

Evie, topless, cupping her breasts in her hands.

Evie, bottomless as well as topless now, on her hands and knees on the bed—it was Larry Scott's bed, I realized, this same bed I was kneeling on—looking back over her shoulder into the camera.

Evie, lying on her back right here on this narrow bed in Larry Scott's room, completely naked, with her eyes closed and her fingers laced over her belly and her long, auburn hair fanned out over the pillow.

More photos of naked Evie. Evie lying on her belly with her chin propped up in her hands staring into the camera. Evie on hands and knees with her butt in the air. Evie sitting cross-legged yoga-style. Evie flat on her back gazing up at the ceiling smoking a cigarette.

There were twenty-four four-by-six color shots taped there on the wall beside Larry Scott's bed in four rows of six. All of them had been taken in this room, one right after the other.

This is what the police saw. Naked Evie, plastered all over Larry Scott's bedroom. I imagined Detective Vanderweigh and maybe Sergeant Dwyer up here, photographing Scott's display for evidence in Evie's trial, ogling her nakedness, creating X-rated scenarios to account for her killing him.

No wonder they thought she was a terrific suspect.

Oh, Evie.

I stood up, turned my back on the photos, and stared out the window at the big old barn out back and the thick summer woods beyond.

"I went out with him a few times," Evie had told me by way of explaining Larry when he followed us to the restaurant.

Posing for nude photographs?

"Went out with him"?

That, of course, was Evie's way of snubbing out a discussion before it got started. She hated to talk about her past. She always said that our lives before we met each other were irrelevant. She thought a little mystery was good for a relationship. It was better to preserve some secrets, she said.

I tended to agree with her. I'd made plenty of mistakes and done things I wasn't proud of in my life, and I didn't want anyone to judge me by them. We learn, and we change, and we are all continuously redefining ourselves.

Well, okay. So Evie had posed naked for Larry Scott. She'd probably had sex with him, too. It was none of my business. It had happened before I met her. She was a different person now.

I wished I hadn't come into this room.

I felt like ripping those photos off the wall and burning them.

I walked out of the room, closed the door behind me, and stood there in the hallway for a moment, taking deep breaths, trying to clear the buzzing out of my brain.

Just as I turned for the stairs, the sound of ragged breathing close behind me caused me to instinctively stop and jerk sideways, and that's when a big fist crashed against my shoulder.

I staggered, caught my balance, and pivoted around.

Mel. His face was red and his little eyes were blazing and his fist was coming at me again.

I ducked away from him as well as I could in the narrow hallway. But I had nowhere to go except down the stairs. Mel filled the space, and he was flailing away at me, grunting and throwing wild roundhouse rights and lefts.

With my arms up in front of my face I was able to block most of his blows. But he was inexorably backing me toward the steep stairway. It would take only one fist to the head or face to send me toppling backwards.

Low animal sounds came from Mel's throat, but he didn't say anything. His face was twisted in some insane combination of anger and hatred and fear, and his mouth was working, uttering silent words as if he was cursing to himself. His eyes were narrow glittering slits.

He was a strong, big-shouldered guy, but already he was panting and wheezing, and I figured if I could hold him off for another minute or two he'd exhaust himself and be too tired to lift his arms.

Then a heavy fist smashed against my ear. Lights exploded in my head, and I stumbled.

He came at me like a bull, with his head down and his fore-arms aimed at me, and it was obvious he intended to ram his head into my chest and drive me backwards down the stairs.

Just as his elbow was about to pound into my face, I dropped to my knees and threw my shoulder against his thighs. I tried to drive him onto his back, the way I'd been taught to tackle in high school.

The momentum of his upper body coming at me might have sent him sailing over my shoulder, and it would've been Mel, not I, who tumbled head over heels down the stairway. But I wrapped my arms around his legs and held on, and he collapsed on top of me.

I scrambled out from under him. He was sprawled on his belly, gasping and muttering and pounding his fists on the floor.

I climbed onto his back and grabbed a handful of his hair. He tried to buck me off. I slammed his face onto the floor. "Mel, goddamn it," I said, "cut it out. What the hell's the matter with you?"

"You leave my brother alone," he wheezed.

"Your brother's dead."

"Shut up. That's Larry's room. He don't want nobody there. He told me. 'Don't let nobody in there ever,' he said."

Mel had stopped bucking and heaving. Experimentally, I let go of his hair. He didn't move.

"Don't hit me anymore, okay?" I said.

"Oh, Jesus, I fucked up," he said. "Larry's gonna be pissed. He's gonna beat the shit out of me when he finds out. I'm s'pose to keep everybody outta his room. That's my job. He told me, when he ain't here, it's my responsibility to keep people out of his room. Even my mother."

I slid off him and leaned my back against the wall. "It doesn't matter anymore," I said. "Larry's dead. He's not coming back. He can't hurt you."

Mel rolled onto his back and pushed himself into a sitting position against the wall across from me. He slumped there, his chest heaving. Tears streamed down his cheeks, and a dribble of blood trickled from one nostril. "Don't say that," he mumbled. He wiped his mouth with the back of his hand, then looked at the blood on it.

"What about you?" I said. "Are you allowed in Larry's room?"

Mel shook his head. "Not me. Not my mother. Nobody. You hurt my nose."

"What about Evie?"

He looked up at me. "What about her?"

"Does Larry allow her in his room?"

He shrugged. "She's the only one."

"How do you like her pictures?"

He started to grin, then quickly shook his head. "I never looked at them pictures. I never even been in there. Larry don't allow it."

At that moment I heard the screen door slam. A moment later there were quick footsteps on the stairs, and then Valerie Kershaw appeared. She had her hand on her holstered revolver. "What's going on up there?" she said.

"Nothing," I said. "Mel and I are just having a chat."

"Mrs. Scott came running out for me," she said. "She thought Mel was killing you."

"Mel wouldn't want to hurt me. Right, Mel?"

Mel frowned for an instant, then shook his head. "Not me."

She looked from him to me, then shrugged. "You okay, then?"

"Sure," I said. "We're fine."

She smiled, then turned and disappeared down the stairs.

"You better get out of here before Larry sees you," said Mel. "He finds out you was in his room lookin' at his pictures, he'll kill you. He killed people in the war, you know. He don't mind killing people. He wouldn't mind killing me. He told me that."

I nodded and pushed myself to my feet. "Larry won't kill you," I said. "I promise." Then I started down the stairs.

Mary Scott was standing there looking up at me. "Are you all right?"

I smiled. "Sure. I'm fine."

"I should've warned you about Mel."

"Mel and I reached an understanding."

"I'm sure you did," she said. "He's never been right, you know. And since Larry . . ."

I nodded.

"I worry about Mel," she said.

"I'm sorry," was all I could think of to say.

"So did you find anything in Larry's room?"

"You haven't been in there?" I said.

"No. Never. Larry wouldn't allow it when—when he was here. Even when he was little. And now . . ."

"I understand," I said. "It would be painful for you." I shook my head. "It might be a good idea if you asked a friend, someone whose judgment you trust, to go in there, clean it up, pack away his belongings, throw out all the junk."

She smiled. "That's a good idea."

"You better be sure Mel understands."

She shook her head. "I apologize for Mel."

TWELVE

When I walked out of the house, Officer Valerie Kershaw was leaning against the side of her cruiser with her arms crossed over her chest. Although she was wearing sunglasses, I was pretty sure her eyes were smiling.

I went over to her and said, "You could've told me about Mel."

She pushed her sunglasses onto her head. "I didn't know you planned to scuffle with him."

I leaned beside her and lit a cigarette. "I didn't plan it. It was spontaneous."

She peered at my face, then touched her cheekbone. "You okay?"

I touched my own cheekbone where she'd touched hers. It was tender. "I don't even remember getting hit there," I said. "The heat of battle. I got him a couple good ones, too. He's a troubled young man."

"Harmless," she said. "That's the word the folks hereabouts

use. Everybody likes Mary. They feel sorry for her, with those two boys of hers, so everyone's pretty tolerant of them. Mel's mainly not very bright, and he's got a sudden temper, as I guess you noticed. Very handy with gasoline engines, though. Lawn mowers, chain saws, snow blowers, things like that. That's what he does. People drop off something that's busted, Mel fixes it. That barn is full of broken machines that he strips for parts."

"Harmless, maybe," I said. "But he tried to push me down the stairs. If he had, he might've done me some harm."

"Looks like you handled it."

"Good thing," I said. "If I'd waited for you to rescue me, I'd be running around with a broken neck."

"They told me to follow you," she said, "not rescue you. So what's your itinerary for the rest of the day?"

"So you can find me if I manage to elude you?"

"Exactly."

I glanced at my watch. It was quarter of eleven. "I've got an appointment with Dr. St. Croix in fifteen minutes. After that I don't know."

"You know how to find the doctor's place?"

"Yes. I better get going." I stamped out my cigarette and went over to my car.

It took about ten minutes to drive from Mary Scott's house to Dr. St. Croix's place. The same new blue Camry and old Jeep Cherokee that had been there the previous day were in the parking area when I got there. I went to the front porch. The inside door was open, and through the screen I heard the mumble of television voices coming from somewhere inside. I rapped my knuckle on the frame of the screen door.

A minute later Claudia Wells appeared on the other side of the screen. She was wearing white pants that stopped halfway down her calves, a blue-and-white-striped jersey, and sandals.

Her blond hair was tied back with a blue silk scarf that matched her eyes.

She smiled when she saw me. "Mr. Coyne," she said. "You made it."

"I hope it's okay."

"Oh, yes. The doctor's looking forward to seeing you." She pushed open the screen door, then lifted her chin and peered over my shoulder. "Oh, dear," she muttered.

I looked back. Valerie Kershaw's cruiser was parked in the street out front.

"Oh, don't worry about that," I said. "They're keeping an eye on me."

"Whatever for?"

"They think I might have murdered somebody."

"Aha," she said. "Dr. Romano."

"You've heard about that, then," I said.

"A state policeman was here earlier." She held the door wide for me and stepped back. "Please. Come on in. The doctor's out on the porch."

I stepped into the house and found myself in the living room. Braided rug, early-American furniture, built-in bookshelves, fieldstone fireplace. A big oil painting of a clipper ship hung over the mantel. The furnishings were unpretentious. They looked expensive to me.

Claudia put her hand on my arm. "What happened to you?" She reached up and touched my cheekbone.

"I bumped into a door," I said. "Has it ruined my flawless profile?"

She smiled. "It lends your appearance a rather endearing ruggedness. Does it hurt?"

"I'm bearing up quite stoically," I said. "So how's the doctor doing today?"

"He didn't have a very good night," she said softly, "and

his session with the police tired him out, I'm afraid. If I have to cut it short, please understand."

"Do you stay here with him?" I said.

"You mean do I live with him?" She smiled. "Heavens, no. I'm his employee, not his . . ." She waved her hand. "The doctor is very sensitive about scandal. In this town, if my car stayed in the driveway all night, it would be all over town by sunup the next morning."

"But you take care of him," I said.

She shrugged. "I'm a nurse. It's taken him awhile to acknowledge he needs taking care of. MS is an insidious disease."

"What's his prognosis?"

She looked away and shook her head. Then she said, "Come on. This way."

I followed her through the living room and dining room to a screened porch on the back of the house. It looked out over a small lawn bordered by flower gardens, with deep woods beyond. A sprinkler was going *tick-tick-tick*, and the water dripping off the plants glittered in the morning sunlight.

Winston St. Croix was sitting in an easy chair with his feet up on a hassock. He was wearing khaki pants and a blue shirt and a red bowtie. His wheelchair was parked in the corner.

A TV against the wall across from him showed several people sitting around a table. They seemed to be discussing the stock market.

When he saw me, the doctor smiled and waved me to the chair beside him. "Ah, Mr. Coyne," he said. "You made it. Good." He clicked the television off with a remote, then held out his hand to me.

I went over and shook it. His grip was feeble. "How are you this morning, Doctor?" I said.

He smiled. "My health. I can't think of a more boring topic." Then he frowned at me. "You've got a nasty contusion there. Bump into something?"

162

I nodded. "Clumsiness."

"You should put some ice on it." He looked over at Claudia Wells, who was standing in the doorway. "Bring us some coffee, my dear, would you please? And an icebag for Mr. Coyne."

She arched her eyebrows at me, and I nodded. "Black, please."

She left the room.

The doctor watched her go, then turned his head to me. "Remarkable woman," he said. "She should've been having babies years ago."

"She seems quite devoted," I said.

"Oh, indeed. Altogether too devoted. I keep telling her. Take a cruise. Meet men. Get married. Have children. Claudia loves children. She shouldn't be hanging around with an old invalid like me." He spread his hands. "She won't listen to me. Women. They just won't listen, will they?"

I thought of Evie and smiled. "The interesting ones don't seem to."

He reached over and touched my arm. "You heard about Dr. Romano?"

I nodded.

"You met him yesterday, am I right? In my office?"

"Yes."

"Terrible thing. The police were here earlier. Asked me all sorts of questions. As if I knew the poor man. I only met him yesterday. He was interested in buying my practice, you know."

I nodded.

"Seemed like a fine doctor," he said. "Unusual, these days, a young doctor who actually wants to help people. Most of them seem more interested in organs than people, if you know what I mean."

Claudia came back with a carafe of coffee and two mugs.

She put them on the table between the doctor and me, poured each mug full, and handed one to the doctor. I took the other one. Then she handed me an icebag. I thanked her and pressed it against my cheek.

St. Croix held his mug in both hands. "Thank you, my dear," he said to Claudia. "Now, Mr. Coyne and I want to talk."

She shrugged. "I'll be in the living room if you need me."

After Claudia left, I put the icebag on the table beside me and took a sip of my coffee. The doctor set his mug on the table, laid his head back, and closed his eyes. "I try not to let her know how I'm feeling. She worries too much." He sighed, opened his eyes, and looked at me. "So where were we yesterday, Mr. Coyne, when we were so rudely interrupted?"

"We were talking about Evie Banyon."

"Ah, yes. And you were telling me she had disappeared. Something to do with Larry Scott's unfortunate death."

"The police think she killed him."

"And you want to find the real culprit, is that it?"

I shrugged.

"Well," he said, "Evie Banyon wouldn't kill anybody. That's silly."

"I agree. But now they think she might've killed Dr. Romano, too."

"Why on earth would she do that?"

"She wouldn't," I said. "Do you know of any connection between Evie and Dr. Romano?"

"That Detective Vanderweigh was asking me the same questions just before you got here," he said. "He was giving me way more credit than I deserve. I don't know much about Evie, and I know even less about Dr. Romano. Evie honored me by letting me take her to dinner a few times. But that was several years ago. Dr. Romano came up from New Jersey to talk to me about buying my medical practice. I never saw him before yesterday. As delightful as Evie Banyon is, she is an unusually private person. I hardly feel that I know her. And I didn't know Dr. Romano at all." He blew out a breath. "I liked him, though. He reminded me of myself, oh, thirty years ago. Enthusiastic, idealistic, full of energy and ideas."

"Do you know of any connection between Romano and Larry Scott?"

Dr. St. Croix ran his fingers through his thinning white hair and stared out through the screen. "Just me, I guess."

"You?"

He shrugged. "Larry Scott was my patient, of course. Twenty years ago, when he was a child. Every child in Cortland was my patient back then. Oh, we were busy in those days, Claudia and I. Seven days a week, Mr. Coyne. Now they've got that new medical center. There's a pediatric group there, and some of the newer folks in town prefer to take their children there. We're still plenty busy, though. I'd love to just keep working, but . . ." He waved his hand.

I sipped my coffee and said nothing.

"I announced my retirement three months ago," he said after a minute. "There was a nice story in the local paper, and the Providence *Journal* and the *Globe* both picked it up. 'Old-time pediatrician who was actually still making house calls retires.' 'End of an era.' That sort of thing. They ran a picture of me from several years ago. You wouldn't recognize me, Mr. Coyne. I used to be a good-looking man, believe it or not."

"I believe it," I said automatically. "So is there a lot of interest in your practice?"

"I've had some feelers," he said. "But Dr. Romano was the first one who actually came to talk business with me. He seemed quite serious about it. He was going to come by today to go over my records with me. He was most insistent on seeing my records." He lifted his hand, then let it fall into his lap. "Well, I don't blame him for that, of course. We did have to decide what he would pay me."

"He was prepared to follow through with it?"

"Oh, yes. It was just a matter of arriving at a mutually agreeable arrangement."

"What about Claudia?"

"He said he hoped she'd stay on, work with him. I told her that after he left yesterday. She was pleased." He shook his head. "Well, that won't happen, of course. Not now."

"Could Evie have known Dr. Romano through her job at the medical center?" I said.

"I suppose it's possible." He frowned at me. "You're not thinking . . . ?"

"No," I said quickly. "Evie wouldn't harm anybody."

"She was very kind to me," he said softly. "You know, Mr. Coyne, when I graduated from medical school, I took an oath. The first principle was, never do harm to anyone. They attribute the oath to Hippocrates, although there's some doubt whether Hippocrates actually created it. Anyway, when you think about it, it's a good way to live your life, whether you're a doctor or a lawyer or an insurance salesman. You want to do some good while you're at it, too, of course. But it's not as easy as it sounds, just doing no harm. I think that's how Evie tries to live her life. She's a good-hearted girl who wants to do no harm, and she doesn't understand anyone who is willing to harm somebody else."

"Like Larry Scott," I said.

He shrugged. "Larry Scott seemed bent on doing Evie harm, all right. He made her life miserable. She stopped allowing me to squire her about because he was doing her considerable harm, and she feared he'd do me harm."

"Did Scott ever threaten you?"

"Not to my face," he said. "But Evie believed that he intended to harm me."

166

"If she kept seeing you," I said.

He nodded. "She thought we should stop having our dinners together. I agreed with her. I hoped that if she stopped seeing me, Larry would leave her alone. He was an unpredictable and dangerous young man."

"But he never did you any actual harm."

He smiled. "There was no reason why he should. Evie and I were friends. That's all."

"Yesterday you told me that you wished it was more."

"Oh, sure. Who wouldn't? But I knew better. I may be a decrepit old man, Mr. Coyne. But I am a realist."

"Doctor," I said, "when Evie and I—"

"It's Win," he said. "Please. If you insist on calling me 'Doctor,' I shall be obliged to call you 'Esquire.' "

I smiled. "Win it is, then," I said. "Anyway, when Evie and I were vacationing on Cape Cod a week ago, Larry Scott followed us and confronted us in a restaurant."

"Yes," he said. "I've heard all about that. Several highly imaginative versions of that story have circulated through this town, many of which involve Evie stabbing him with a kitchen knife."

"At one point," I said, "Scott mentioned you."

"Me?"

"He said to Evie, 'I know about your saint,' or words to that effect. I assume he was referring to you."

" 'Your saint.' That's flattering. I'm hardly a saint, and I don't think Evie ever thought of me as saintly." He smiled. "I'm sure she was fully aware of the devilish thoughts she inspired in me."

"I was thinking of your name."

He looked at me. "Oh, well, sure. Maybe. I didn't think of that."

"So if he was referring to you," I said, "what could he have known about you that he wanted to tell Evie?"

"How in the world would I know what was in that poor, obsessed boy's head?"

I shrugged. "I don't know. I thought maybe you'd have an idea."

St. Croix shook his head sadly. "Larry Scott wanted Evie and she didn't want him. It's a simple as that. She went out with me a few times, and he was blind jealous. He thought I was his competition. He made her life so miserable that he finally drove her out of town. I guess he thought if slandering me would win her back, he'd do it."

"But there was nothing he might have known—about you, I mean—that would have caused him to follow Evie to the Cape to tell her?"

He smiled at me. "You're cross-examining me, you know."

"I apologize," I said.

"What difference would it make, anyway?" he said. He tapped his legs. "I certainly didn't kill Larry Scott."

"I didn't think you did."

"Or Dr. Romano, either."

"Of course not."

"I'm not sure that Detective Vanderweigh is convinced," he said.

"Detective Vanderweigh suspects everybody," I said. "Even me."

Dr. St. Croix closed his eyes for a minute. "Multiple sclerosis is a terrible disease," he said quietly. "It cripples your body, but as far as I'm concerned, what's worse, it begins to eat away at your sanity. Depression, of course. But I've found that in the past several months I've also become increasingly short-tempered and distrustful. I have to monitor myself constantly against paranoia. I've yelled at poor, loyal Claudia, of all people, more than once. And now, I'm sitting here looking at these useless legs and these pitiful trembling hands, and I'm telling myself to stop thinking what I'm thinking, that I have no reason to distrust you." He blinked at me. "Do I?"

"No," I said. "No reason to distrust me at all."

"And I'm wondering if I should've distrusted Dr. Romano a bit more."

"Did you distrust him?"

"Yes, of course. As I said, nowadays I tend to distrust everybody. I admired his enthusiasm, his idealism. But at the same time, I couldn't quite believe that some bright, eager young doctor from New Jersey would really be interested in taking over this dead-end little small-town pediatric practice. You see? It's sick and reprehensible to have a part of your brain thinking the worst of people. I never used to be that way."

"Some people are always that way," I said.

"Never do harm to anyone," he said. "That starts with thinking well of people, giving them the benefit of the doubt."

"Well," I said, "Larry Scott—"

At that moment, Claudia Wells came into the room. She pointed at her wristwatch. "Excuse me, gentlemen," she said, "but it's time for your meds, Doctor."

"Leave us alone, woman," said St. Croix. "Brady and I are talking."

Claudia looked at me and rolled her eyes. "He's the world's most difficult patient." She turned to him. "I'm going to give you your shot, and I don't want any back talk."

I stood up. "I should get going anyway."

"Please stay," said St. Croix.

"No," said Claudia, "Mr. Coyne is right. He should leave now. He can come back."

"I told you," said the doctor to me, "she's a monster. She can't wait to haul down my pants and stick a needle into my bottom. You will come back?"

"I don't know how much longer I'll be in town," I said. "But if I get a chance, sure, I'll come back." I bent to St. Croix and held out my hand. "I've enjoyed talking with you."

He took my hand and held onto it. "Me too," he said. He glanced at Claudia. "It's good to talk to a man for a change."

I smiled and turned to leave. Claudia started to follow me. "I can find my way out," I said.

She nodded. "Do come back," she said softly. "He likes you."

"I like him, too."

I paused on the front steps to light a cigarette. As I started down the fieldstone pathway to the parking area beside the house, Valerie Kershaw pushed herself away from her cruiser and headed toward me.

She met me at my car. "You've got to follow me, Mr. Coyne."

"I thought you were supposed to follow me."

She shrugged. "We changed the rules."

"Why?"

"Detective Vanderweigh needs to talk with you."

THIRTEEN

I followed Valerie Kershaw's cruiser back into town. She pulled up in front of a cluster of new-looking, rectangular brick buildings. Town hall, library, police station, public works, firehouse, all lined up next to each together, directly across the village green from Charlotte Matley's office.

I parked my car, got out, and waited for Valerie to come over.

"You want to cuff me, bring me in?" I said.

She rolled her eyes. "Come on. This way."

She led me into the police station, past the front desk where a woman in civilian clothes said hello to her, and down a short corridor. She stopped at a door, peeked in through the glass, then opened it and held it for me.

I stepped in. Detective Vanderweigh and his partner, a young, blond guy—I'd met him in Brewster, but I couldn't recall his name—were sitting beside each other in leather chairs at a long oak conference table. They appeared to be studying the documents that were stacked in front of them.

Vanderweigh looked up over the tops of his reading glasses, smiled quickly, put the palms of both his hands on the tabletop, and pushed himself halfway into a standing position. "Mr. Coyne," he said. "Have a seat, please. Thanks for joining us."

I took a chair across the table from the two of them. "I wasn't given much choice," I said.

"What happened to your face?"

"Bumped into a door."

Vanderweigh shrugged. "You remember Sergeant Lipton."

I nodded at the other man. "Sure. You never forget your interrogator."

Lipton reached his hand across the table, and I shook it.

I looked around the room. The two big windows overlooking the village green had no wire mesh over them. The walls were paneled in knotty pine. There were two television sets with VCR hookups on one table, a coffee machine and a microwave oven on another, and a computer and a fax machine and two telephones on a desk. The chairs were comfortable, and there were no cigarette scars on the tabletop. "Not bad," I said, "for an inquisition room."

"This is a conference room," said Vanderweigh. "We want to confer with you."

"Does this mean I'm no longer a suspect?"

He smiled. "If you like." He cleared his throat. "Does the name Owen Ransom mean anything to you?"

I thought for a minute, then shook my head. "No."

"Ever been to Carlisle, Pennsylvania?"

"Actually," I said, "I have. There are some good trout streams in that part of Pennsylvania. Who's Owen Ransom?"

" 'Who *was* Owen Ransom,' " said Vanderweigh. "He's deceased."

I looked from Vanderweigh to Lipton. "You gentlemen being homicide detectives and all, I would surmise that this Owen Ransom did not die of natural causes."

"No," said Vanderweigh. "He got his throat cut."

"In an automobile behind a motel, by any chance? Sometime recently?"

He nodded.

"So Dr. Paul Romano's real name was Owen Ransom."

"Owen Ransom was not a doctor," he said. "Owen Ransom was a clerk at a hardware store."

"In Carlisle, Pennsylvania?"

"Yes," said Vanderweigh.

"Being well-trained detectives," I said, "you checked his wallet, looked at his driver's license and credit cards and other personal effects."

Vanderweigh nodded. "Sure. First thing we do with a homicide victim. Try to identify him."

"So Romano was using a fake name," I said. "You knew that when you talked to me this morning, I'll bet."

He smiled and shrugged.

"You're even more devious than I gave you credit for."

"We ran those Jersey plates on the Oldsmobile," said Lipton. "Turns out to be a rental. Came from Budget, at the Newark airport. Name on the paperwork they had was Owen Ransom, from Carlisle, Pennsylvania. We talked to the police in Carlisle. They confirm our identification."

"So," I said, "you want me to tell you why some hardware clerk in Pennsylvania would rent a car in New Jersey, drive to Cortland, Massachusetts, pose as a doctor, pretend to want to buy a small-town pediatric medical practice, and end up with his throat cut in a motel parking lot."

"Well," said Lipton, "yes. Do you know?"

"No, I don't."

"You encountered Mr. Ransom a couple of times yesterday," said Vanderweigh. "Can you remember anything he said, any offhand comment he might have made—"

"We've already been over this," I said. "I just thought he was a doctor."

"In light of this new information," said Vanderweigh, "any indication that he wasn't who he said he was?"

I thought for a minute, then said, "No. We didn't talk about medical things. Or hardware, for that matter. The only thing we talked about was women, and he did all the talking. He fooled me."

"You said you didn't like him."

I shrugged.

"We're trying to figure out who killed him, Mr. Coyne," said Lipton.

"He was boring and I didn't particularly like him," I said. "But I didn't kill him. I didn't kill him when I thought he was Dr. Paul Romano, and I still didn't kill him now that you've told me his name was Owen Ransom. What did the police in Pennsylvania tell you about him?"

Lipton shuffled through the sheaf of papers on the table in front of him. He picked one up, glanced at it, then looked up at me. "Owen Ransom, twenty-eight years old. Grew up in Carlisle, Pennsylvania. Ran cross-country for his high-school team. Average student, no trouble of any kind. Couple years of community college. Never married. Parents both deceased. Taught Sunday school at the Congregational church. Lived by himself in a one-bedroom condominium on the outskirts of town. Held the same job at the hardware store for five years."

"The profile of a madman," I said.

Vanderweigh smiled. "You'd be surprised."

"No," I said. "Actually I wouldn't. So what was he doing in Cortland if he wasn't interested in buying Dr. St. Croix's practice?"

"Well," said Vanderweigh, "that's the question, isn't it?"

"And what's this got to do with Larry Scott?" I stopped. "Wait a minute. Are you thinking . . . ?"

Vanderweigh shook his head. "If there's a connection between Ransom and Scott, damned if we can figure out what it is. Except, of course, for the fact that they were both murdered."

"Owen Ransom could've killed Larry Scott," I said.

"Why?"

"How would I know?"

"Say he did," said Lipton. "Then who killed Ransom?"

"Have you talked to Mel Scott?" I said.

"Who?"

"Larry's brother." I touched the bump on my cheekbone. "He loved his brother. He can be quite emphatic about it."

Lipton and Vanderweigh exchanged looks. Then Vanderweigh leaned across the table to me. "What about Evelyn Banyon?"

"What about her?" I said.

"Has she ever been to Carlisle, Pennsylvania?"

"Jesus," I said. "You guys are relentless." I shook my head. "I have no idea whether Evie was ever in Carlisle, or if she knew this Owen Ransom."

"You're not much help today, Mr. Coyne," said Vanderweigh.

"I'm sorry," I said. "So, how long are you planning to keep Officer Kershaw on my tail?"

"For as long as it takes."

"You think I'm going to lead you to Evie."

Vanderweigh nodded.

"Well," I said, "I don't know where she is."

Lipton shrugged, then gathered his papers into a stack,

tapped the edges on the table, shoved them into a manila folder, and looked up at me. "You can find your way out okay, Mr. Coyne?"

I stood up. "Evie didn't kill anybody."

"We'd sure like to talk with her about it," said Vanderweigh. "Have her tell us that in her own words."

"I'll pass along your message if I see her," I said. I headed for the door.

"Mr. Coyne," said Lipton.

I stopped and turned.

"If you think of something," he said, "come up with anything, even a wild theory, you just have Officer Kershaw give us a call, okay?"

"I'm an officer of the court," I said. "I know my duty."

I left the police station. Valerie Kershaw was standing beside her cruiser talking to a white-haired woman who was holding a large black dog on a leash. I went over to her. "I'm heading back to my motel now," I said. "I've got to make a couple of calls. Just wanted you to know, in case I inadvertently managed to elude you."

She looked at her watch. "It's about lunchtime."

"I'm not really hungry," I said. "Had a big breakfast. I'm just tired. They woke me up early."

"I was thinking about myself, not you," she said. "I'm hungry."

"Go get something to eat," I said. "Meet me at my motel."

She tilted her head and smiled at me. "I'm not allowed to trust you."

I sighed. "Okay. I believe in supporting our officers of the law. Let's go eat. Follow me."

We drove to the diner, and when Valerie and I went in together, heads turned and conversations momentarily stopped.

We sat at a booth by the front window where Valerie could keep an eye on her cruiser. Ruth was back on duty. She

176

seemed not the slightest bit surprised that I had a lunch date with a pretty uniformed police officer.

I had a turkey club sandwich and a glass of iced tea. Valerie had a cheeseburger and Coke. While we ate, she told me that she'd grown up in Gloucester, on the Massachusetts north shore, had gone to Williams College where she'd majored in history, and got her master's in law enforcement at Northeastern.

Her father was a stockbroker and her mother was a high-school math teacher. No one in her family had ever been a cop. She'd been on the job for a year and a half, and she was thinking of quitting and going to law school. She believed her talents were being wasted, following people around all day in Cortland, Massachusetts. She thought she'd make a good prosecutor.

I didn't try to talk her out of it.

When I asked her if she had a boyfriend, she rolled her eyes and looked away, which could have meant that she did but it wasn't working out, or that she used to but it hadn't worked out, or that she hadn't met anybody interesting yet, or that she preferred women.

Or, most likely, that it was a rude question for a murder suspect to ask, and none of anybody's business anyway.

After we finished eating, we drove back to the motel. Valerie parked her cruiser beside my car, and as I opened the door to my room, I saw that she was talking on her two-way.

The maid had come and made the bed and left me clean towels and given the room a squirt of Lysol. All traces of Evie were gone.

I stripped down, took a long steamy shower, then sprawled on the bed. I glanced at my watch. It was a little after two o'clock.

I picked up the phone beside the bed and dialed Julie's home phone. I hoped my secretary would be off to the pool with Megan, her daughter, on this sunny Sunday afternoon in August. Then I could leave a message on her answering machine and escape her lecture on an attorney's responsibilities to his clients and his secretary.

Edward, Julie's husband, answered.

"It's Brady," I said. "Julie's not there, is she?"

"No," he said. "She took Megan to a birthday party."

"Oh, good," I said.

He chuckled. "You called her, but you don't want to talk to her?"

"I was hoping just to leave her a message."

"Do you want me to deliver your message?"

"Just tell her," I said, "that I won't be in the office tomorrow. She knows what to do."

"Julie's not going to like it," said Edward. "You want me to convey your excuse, too?"

"Tell her that I'm down here in Cortland, looking for Evie. She might actually approve of that."

"She might," he said skeptically. "Anything else?"

"Tell her I'm sort of snooping around. There's been another murder."

Edward chuckled. "How do you do it?"

"What? Get into these situations?"

"No," he said. "Come up with these stories."

"Now you've hurt my feelings," I said. "It's not a story. It's true."

"Well, I'll pass it along. You got a number there if she needs to reach you?"

I gave Edward the motel number. "If you think she's tempted to call me," I told him, "you could do me a favor and remind your wife that I'm the lawyer and she's the secretary and her job is to do what I want."

"She knows better than that, Brady. But I'll do my best for you."

I thanked Edward, hung up the phone, smoked a cigarette, stared up at the ceiling, then picked it up again and dialed information.

It took awhile to convince the mechanical voice to connect me to an actual person, but finally I got the number for the local weekly newspaper in Carlisle, Pennsylvania, and even though it was a Sunday afternoon, when I rang that number, a raspy woman's voice answered.

"Are you the editor?" I said.

"Editor, reporter, sales rep, chief bottle-washer," she said. "Kate Burrows, at your service. Who's this?"

"My name is Brady Coyne. I'm calling from Cortland, Massachusetts." I paused, waiting for that to sink in.

She hesistated, then said, "Cortland . . . Oh. The Owen Ransom murder. Are you with the newspaper there?"

"No. I'm a lawyer. I have some information."

"I'm all ears, Mr. Coyne."

"Quid pro quo, Ms. Burrows."

She chuckled. "Lawyers. Okay. What've you got for me, and what do you want?"

"I want you to tell me about Owen Ransom."

"Do you know who killed him?"

"I'm afraid not. But I can tell you what he was doing here in Cortland. Fair?"

"Sure," she said. "I hope you have more to tell me than I have for you."

"You start," I said.

She cleared her throat. "Understand, before this morning I'd never even heard of Owen Ransom. He wasn't exactly famous around here. But a local boy gets himself murdered, I ask some questions, dig around in our archives, such as they are. The murder story will be front-page stuff, of course. I'm also trying to put together a sidebar about Mr. Ransom himself. You know, the human-interest piece of it. Mostly interviews with people who knew him. I haven't gotten very far with that. Owen Ransom was apparently a quiet young man, lived by himself, not many friends. I did talk with the owner of the hardware store where Ransom worked, a Mr. Gallatin. He's lived in Carlisle all his life. Knew Ransom's parents. Told me one interesting thing."

"What's that?" I said.

"He told me that Owen Ransom had a lot of money socked away. Inherited it from his parents, who died several years ago. Mr. Gallatin knew the parents. The father was a high-school teacher, the mother a homemaker. When the Ransoms moved to Carlisle, they paid cash for their house. They lived modestly, but they donated extravagantly to charities. Way more than could be accounted for by a teacher's salary, according to Mr. Gallatin. He told me that one time he'd casually asked Mr. Ransom—Owen's father—how he'd come by his wealth. Expected him to say it was old family money or something, but Mr. Ransom said—and I'm looking at my notes now, Mr. Coyne, and this is exactly how Mr. Gallatin remembers it: Mr. Ransom said it had cost him every drop of his soul's blood."

"What did he mean by that?"

"Mr. Gallatin didn't know. But obviously the phrase stuck with him."

I thought for a minute. "So Owen Ransom had money," I said. "Who stands to inherit it?"

"Sorry," she said. "I don't know. What I've learned so far, he had no living relatives. I suppose the police will be looking into that."

"What else can you tell me?"

"He attended the local schools. A decent student, never in trouble. Just a quiet, rather anonymous young man." She paused. "And that's about all I can tell you. Your turn."

I told Kate Burrows what I knew—that Owen Ransom had

come to Cortland using the name Paul Romano and posing as a doctor who wanted to buy the practice of a retiring local pediatrician and had been found in his rental car behind a motel with his throat cut. I told her that another young man, a native of Cortland, had been stabbed to death a week earlier down on Cape Cod.

She asked several clarifying questions, and I answered them as well as I could.

"And what," she said when I finished, "is your interest in all of this, Mr. Coyne?"

"I'm a lawyer, Ms. Burrows. I can't tell you."

"Of course you can't." She chuckled. "Well, I hope I may call you later for further enlightenment."

"Sure," I said. "My number's in the Boston book."

After I hung up with Kate Burrows, I yawned, turned out the light, slid in between the sheets, and stared up at ceiling, looking for insight.

None appeared, and I was too sleepy to look harder.

I closed my eyes.

The last time I'd been in this bed, Evie had been with me. I'd held her naked body while we slept, and remembering the scent of her hair in my face and the silky, electric feel of her skin against mine and the slow rise and fall of her chest under my arm eased me into a deep, hungry sleep.

The bleating of the telephone woke me up. For a minute I thought I was in my bedroom back in Boston. The phone rang several times before I blinked the disorienting afternoon sleep out of my head and picked it up.

I cleared my throat and grumbled, "Hlo?" I figured it was Julie, calling to bawl me out.

"Mr. Coyne?" A woman's voice. Not Julie's.

"Yes. Who's this?"

"It's Mary Scott, Mr. Coyne."

181

I hitched myself into a half-sitting position in the bed. Afternoon sunlight streamed in around the drapes in my little motel room. "What time is it?" I said.

"Beg your pardon?"

"Nothing. It doesn't matter. What's the matter, Mrs. Scott?"

"Oh, nothing," she said. "Nothing's the matter. I was just wondering if you might be able to drop by again. There's something I want you to see."

"Sure," I said. "What is it?"

"Just something of Larry's," she said. "It wasn't in his room, and I thought . . ."

"You're making this sound a little mysterious, you know."

She laughed quickly. "I guess I am, aren't I?"

"I can be there in about half an hour," I said. "Would that be all right?"

"That would be fine."

"Um, Mrs. Scott? Mary?"

"Yes?"

"How did you know where to find me?"

She hesitated for a moment. "I guess you must've mentioned you were staying at the motel."

"Right," I said. "I guess I must have. Well, I'll be right along."

I hung up the phone. I was pretty sure I had not mentioned that I was staying in a motel room, either to Mary Scott or to Mel.

Small town. Everybody knew everything.

FOURTEEN

I took a shower and let the cold water run over my face and chest for as long as I could stand it. It washed away the cobwebby blur of my afternoon nap, and by the time I'd dried myself and gotten dressed, I felt awake and reasonably alert.

I left my room, paid a dollar to the motel machine, and took a can of Coke to my car. I was alert enough to notice that Valerie Kershaw's cruiser was not parked there. I looked around the nearly empty lot in front of the motel and saw no cruisers whatsoever. Nothing that even looked like a plain-clothes cop car. No cars at all with anybody sitting in them.

Hmm.

I headed north on Route 1, past the diner, past the medical center, and past the village green, sipping my Coke and welcoming the little jolts of caffeine. I kept an eye on my rearview mirror. No cars of any description pulled in behind me.

I took the right after the old drive-in, followed the winding country road, and pulled up in front of her house on the edge of the woods.

The Ford Escort was still sitting in the driveway. So was Mel's pickup truck. No legs were sticking out from under it.

I went to the house, climbed the steps, rapped on the frame of the screen door, and a moment later Mary Scott came out onto the porch. "Come on in," she said.

I followed her into the house, through the living room, and into the kitchen. Mel was sitting at the table sipping from a can of Coors. An empty plate and a bottle of catsup sat in front of him. He'd washed his face and arms and slicked back his hair, but he was still wearing the same grimy T-shirt and blue jeans and workboots he'd had on in the morning.

He looked at me, touched his cheekbone with his fingertip, and said, "How you doin'?"

I nodded. "I'm fine. How about you?"

He pinched his nose gently between his thumb and forefinger and grinned. Then he held up his beer can. "Want one?"

"No, thanks." I turned to Mary. "What's up? What did you want to show me?"

She looked at Mel. He drained his beer, tossed the empty into the wastebasket beside the refrigerator, and stood up. "Come on. I'll show you."

"Wait," said Mary. She left the kitchen and headed for the front of the house. She was back a minute later. "It's okay," she said to Mel.

He led me through a pantry and out the back door. Mel held out his arm, and we stopped on the small wooden porch. A narrow dirt path led straight back to the big old barn. Another path angled off to the side where it met the driveway.

The back lawn needed mowing, and milkweed and goldenrod and brambles grew waist-high against the side of the barn. The rusty skeletons of harrows and reapers and plows, plus an ancient refrigerator and some old lawn furniture, were piled up against the barn, half-hidden in the weeds.

Mel put his hand on my arm. "I'm gonna look, make sure the coast is clear, okay? You stay here. When I give you the signal, you run into the barn. Go into the third stall on your left. You'll find a door. Go in there and take them steps down into the cellar."

"Then what?"

"You'll see," he said.

I shrugged. "Okay."

He moved to the driveway and peeked around the corner of the house to the front. Then he looked back at me, waved his hand, and pointed at the barn.

I took a deep breath, then sprinted down the path and through the big opening into the barn. I stood there in the middle of the wood-plank floor and looked around. It was dim and dank inside the barn, and it took a minute for my eyes to adjust.

A tractor and a flatbed truck were parked in the back. Along the entire length of the wall on the right was a workbench piled with power tools and hand tools and engine parts. Several bare, unlit lightbulbs hung down over the bench, dangling from long electrical cords attached to the beam overhead. An open stairway at the end of the bench near the front of the barn led up to the hayloft.

Horse stalls lined the entire wall on the left. I went into the third stall and looked for the door Mel had mentioned. In the dim light, it took me a minute to locate it. It looked like it had been cut out of the original wall. Its vertical sides matched up with the edges of the weathered wallboards. Only the thin horizontal saw-cut, about head-high, gave it away.

A hole the size of a quarter had been drilled into the door. A short length of thin rope hung out of the hole.

I pulled on the rope and felt a latch lift on the other side of the door. It swung open silently. I stepped through the doorway and found myself on a small landing at the top of a narrow, steep flight of wooden steps that descended into the darkness.

I pulled the rope back through the hole, and the door shut behind me. The latch snapped into place, and everything went completely black.

I stood there, hoping my eyes would make one more adjustment. But there was no light whatsoever in there. I felt around on the walls for a light switch but found none. Instead, my ears began to pick up faint sounds—the creak of old wooden beams and rafters, the chirp of crickets, the coo of pigeons, the scurry of mice in dry hay. After a minute, I thought I detected a faint, mechanical, clicking sound. I listened harder, and then I couldn't hear it anymore.

Standing there in the absolute darkness, I was more aware of the odors, too. Decomposed manure, axle grease, old leather . . . and something sweeter and fresher and cleaner that I couldn't identify.

I wished Mel had thought to give me a flashlight.

Take the steps down into the cellar, he had said.

He had not said what I'd find down there.

Was this stupid? Did I have any reason to trust Mel and Mary Scott? Mel had tried to kill me the last time I was here. I had no idea what Mary's agenda was.

For all I knew, both of them thought I'd killed Larry.

The rough walls were so close beside me that I could touch them by sticking out my elbows. There was no railing to hold on to. I put my hands out to guide myself and began slowly to descend the steps. I took them one at a time, pressing my hands against the walls for balance and feeling for the next step with my foot before shifting my weight onto it.

I counted fourteen steps, and then my forward foot felt a

dirt floor. I stepped down onto it, reached out my hand, and touched a rough wooden wall in front of me.

I groped on the wall until my hand brushed against a latch. I lifted it with the crook of my forefinger, pushed the door open, and stepped through the doorway.

I had to squeeze my eyes shut against the sudden glare of light. Before I could open them, something hard jabbed into my ribs.

"Put your hands behind your neck and take two steps forward," growled a voice from behind me. "Try something stupid and I'll blow a hole in you."

I did as I was told, then slowly turned my head.

Evie stood there, holding a double-barreled shotgun at her hip. She was wearing shorts and a man-sized T-shirt. She'd ditched the felt hat. Her auburn hair hung in a long braid down the middle of her back.

"Well, here we are again," she said.

I let out the breath I didn't realize I'd been holding. "So this is where you've been holing up."

She lowered the barrel of the shotgun so that it was pointing at the plywood floor. "Be it ever so humble."

I looked around. A couple of fluorescent bulbs on the ceiling filled the room with harsh white light. A door laid across a pair of file cabinets made a worktable. On the table were a computer with an external modem and a printer and a scanner, along with a telephone, a fax machine, a twelve-inch television set, a portable CD player, and an electric fan.

On one wall was a small dirty window with no curtains. A door beside it stood ajar. It opened to the outdoors, where the dark woods loomed close. This room, I realized, was at ground level on the rear wall of the barn.

A narrow cot with an unrolled sleeping bag on it sat along one wall. Shelves hanging on another held paperback books and stacks of magazines and newspapers and reams of paper.

Evie propped the shotgun in the corner, sat on the cot, and looked at me without smiling. "I understand you were in Larry's room this morning," she said.

I nodded. She was thinking of the photo display.

She shrugged. "What can I say?"

"You don't have to say anything, honey," I said. "You didn't even know me then." I waved my hand around the room. "What is this place?"

"Larry's hideaway," she said. "He practically lived here. Him and his beloved computer."

"And this is where you came, after . . ."

She nodded. "After we got back from the Cape."

"Why?"

She shrugged.

"I know you tried to call Charlotte Matley," I said. "How come?"

"After finding Larry, and then those policemen, accusing me . . ." She took a deep breath and blew it out quickly. "I needed advice. Advice from someone . . . objective. Someone I could trust."

I started to speak, to tell her she could've trusted me, but she held up her hand. "Charlotte wasn't there," she said, "and I guess I panicked. I just had to get the hell away from there. So I grabbed my backpack and came here. I knew Mary would take care of me."

I went over, sat beside her on the cot, and put my arm around her shoulders. "So now what are you doing, honey?"

She leaned against me. "What do you mean?"

"You can't live forever in this—this hole."

"I sneak out," she said. "Mary and Mel are watching out for me. Anyway, it's not forever. Just until they catch whoever's killing people."

"As near as I can tell," I said, "their only suspects are you and me. I think the only reason they haven't arrested me is because they think I'll lead them to you."

She was quiet for a minute. Then she pressed her cheek against my shoulder and said, "I do love you, you know."

I turned and kissed her neck. "I wasn't sure," I said. "I love you, too."

"There's a 'but' coming at you," she said.

I smiled. "Isn't there always?"

"Here's the 'but,' " she said. "But—I don't think we should see each other anymore."

"Meeting like this?" I said. "Sneaking into motel rooms? Clandestine rendezvous in hidden rooms under barns? It's actually kind of romantic, if you ask me."

"I'm not kidding," she said.

"No, I didn't think you were. Things'll be different after this is over with."

"They'll be different, all right," she said. "They'll never be the same."

"If it's those photos—"

"I told you I wanted you to go home, stay away from me."

I shrugged.

She nodded. "I mean it. I wish you hadn't come to this town."

"You think I'm bad for you," I said.

"No," she said, "I think I'm bad for you."

"Well, you're stuck with me."

She looked at me for a minute, then rolled her eyes and stood up. "Well, I want to show you something."

She went over to the table with the computer on it. "I've been sleeping down here for a week," she said. "This morning I started poking around Larry's stuff. I found this." She picked up a piece of paper.

I went over and she handed it to me. It was a page that had

been torn from the "Living" section of the *Boston Globe* dated June 12, about two months earlier. The headline read, "End of an Era in Cortland." The subhead read, "Illness Forces Small-Town Children's Doctor to Announce Retirement." It took me a moment to recognize Dr. Winston St. Croix's photo. It had obviously been taken before he became ill. He had a rugged face, a head of thick, silvery hair, a dark, neatly trimmed mustache, twinkling, humorous eyes. He wore a white jacket over a light-colored shirt with a polka-dotted bowtie. In the photo he was holding a tongue depressor in the mouth of a boy who looked about eight years old. They were looking at each other with wide eyes and arched eyebrows. The doctor's mouth was open, too, and you could almost hear both of them saying "Ahh" at the same time.

I looked at Evie. "What's the significance of this?"

"I don't know," she said. "I found it stashed under some old maps." She pointed her thumb at the bookshelves. "I assume Larry tore it out of the paper."

"Why would he do that?"

"Well, of course, I used to go out with Winston St. Croix. This"—she tapped the newspaper photograph—"is how he looked before he got sick."

"A good-looking man. Probably too old for you."

She smiled. "Point is, Larry was jealous of him. Always called him 'your saint.' "

"I remember that." I skimmed through the article. The first several paragraphs described St. Croix's old-fashioned way of practicing pediatric medicine—answering his own phone, making house calls, advising parents on child-rearing issues, donating his services to local schools. He received hundreds of Christmas cards every year from former patients who'd grown into adults. There were quotes from Cortland folks telling stories about Dr. St. Croix braving blizzards to tend to babies with fevers and ear infections, Dr. St. Croix diagnosing rare illnesses, Dr. St. Croix holding office hours on Sunday afternoons, Dr. St. Croix sponsoring Little League teams.

He was a veritable candidate for sainthood.

According to the article, there weren't any left like him. He was the last of the old-time caregivers. In these days of managed health care and malpractice insurance and assembly-line medicine, the retirement of Dr. Winston St. Croix was, indeed, the end of an era.

I noticed that a few lines about two-thirds of the way through the article had been underlined in pencil. They read: "Dr. St. Croix opened his first office in the little town of Gorham, Minnesota, in 1968. He moved his practice to Cortland in 1980."

I looked up at Evie and pointed to those lines. "Is this significant?"

"Larry apparently thought so. He underlined them."

"Why?"

"That's what I've been trying to figure out." She shuffled among some papers on the desk, then handed one to me. "Here. I found this, too."

It had been printed off the Internet from the archives of the *Philadelphia Inquirer*. The date was November 13, 1987. The headline read, "Carlisle Teen Suicide Baffles School, Church Leaders."

I looked up at her. "Carlisle, Pennsylvania," I said. "That's where Owen Ransom was from."

"Who's Owen Ransom?"

"When the police came knocking on my door this morning? When you scooted into the bathroom?"

She nodded.

"That was Owen Ransom. They found him in the parking lot out back of our motel. His throat had been cut." I filled her in on my encounters with the man who had called himself Dr. Paul Romano, his murder, the fact that he was an impostor, and my conversation with Kate Burrows, the editor of the Carlisle newspaper.

"You've been busy," said Evie.

"It hasn't produced much."

She tapped the printout I was holding. "Owen Ransom would've been a teenager in 1987."

"Well, Owen Ransom didn't commit suicide in 1987," I said. "I talked with him yesterday."

I skimmed the article. A high-school freshman, a boy, had hanged himself in the basement of his home on a Saturday night. His parents found him when they got up on Sunday morning. He had left no note.

He had been a popular kid, a member of the basketball team, an honor-roll student. Teachers and friends were shocked. He'd seemed to be a happy, well-adjusted boy.

The article quoted some statistics on teen suicide. The rate had been rising alarmingly in that part of Pennsylvania. Oftentimes the victims were, like this one in Carlisle, apparently happy and well-adjusted youngsters.

The Carlisle school board was directing the administration of the school to develop a plan to identify depressed and potentially suicidal students. Local churches were expanding their counseling and outreach programs for troubled teens.

The article discreetly neglected to mention the name of the suicide victim.

I looked at Evie and shrugged. "I don't get it."

She shook her head. "Me neither. But it must've meant something to Larry. Here. Read this." She handed another piece of paper to me. "This was the other thing I found."

This one, too, had been printed out from the archives of the *Inquirer*. It was dated August 7, 1990. "Carlisle Couple Dead in Boating Accident," was the headline.

I skimmed the article. The victims were a married couple named Margaret and Robert Ransom. They'd taken a canoe onto a local lake one summer evening. Their bodies and the capsized canoe were found by fishermen the next day. There had been no storm or wind that night. The couple were survived by a teenage son, unnamed in the article.

"Owen Ransom's parents," I said.

Evie nodded. "What do you make of it?"

"I don't know," I said. "But it all revolves around your doctor friend. Your saint. Something about his retirement. Ransom showing up and getting murdered. That canoe accident. The suicide. They're connected. Or at least Larry Scott thought they were." I hesitated. "And, of course, the fact that Larry was gathering this material, and that Larry himself got killed. That's another connection. Did you find anything else?"

"No, but—"

At that moment the telephone rang.

Evie looked at it, then she arched her eyebrows at me.

I shrugged.

It rang again. Evie picked it up, put it to her ear, but said nothing. Her eyes shifted from the ceiling to me. Then she said, "Yes, okay," and hung up.

"That was Mary," she said. "You've got to get back up into the barn right away."

"Why?"

"Just go," she said. "She said make it quick."

Evie grabbed my arm, opened the door I had come in through, and pushed me to it.

She gave me a quick hug, then I started up the stairs. She left the door open so I could see where I was going.

When I reached the top, she closed the door. In the sudden darkness, I found the latch and pushed the door that opened into the horse stall on the main floor of the barn. I made sure the latch rope was not hanging on the outside of the door. Then I stepped into the stall and pushed the door shut.

I walked out of the stall. The inside of the barn was now brightly lit by the bulbs over the workbench. Mel Scott was sitting there with his back to me, working on a small engine.

He turned, beckoned me over, and pointed at the stool beside him.

I crossed the barn floor and sat on the stool. "What's going on?" I said.

"Just watch what I'm doing," he said. "This here is the motor from a snowmobile. I'm showing you how to replace the fuel pump, okay? You're interested in this stuff, right?"

I shrugged. "Sure." I leaned on my elbows to watch him.

Less than a minute later, two silhouettes appeared in the entrance to the barn. They stood there for a minute. Then one of them said, "Hello, Mr. Coyne."

It was Detective Neil Vanderweigh.

I waved to him. "Hello."

The two of them came over, and in the light from the bulbs over Mel's workbench, I saw that the other one was Sergeant Dwyer, the Cortland cop.

Dwyer nodded to me and said, "How you doin'?" to Mel.

"Workin' on it," said Mel.

Vanderweigh jerked his head at Dwyer, who started wandering around the barn.

"What brings you here?" I said to Vanderweigh.

"I'm the cop," he said. "I get to ask the questions. That was my question."

"Mrs. Scott invited me over," I said. "I accepted. There's not a helluva lot to do in this town. Watching a mechanical genius repair a snowmobile engine is pretty entertaining stuff. I'm learning a lot. That's the fuel pump he's working on."

From the corner of my eye, I watched Dwyer. He was poking around the tractor and the flatbed truck that were parked in the back of the barn.

Vanderweigh pulled a stool up beside me and hitched himself onto it. "I wondered what you'd do if you found yourself without an escort."

"So you tracked me down. I'm flattered."

"Oh, we care deeply," he said.

Dwyer returned from the rear of the barn and was looking up the stairs that led to the hayloft.

Mel had some small engine parts spread out on the newspaper in front of him. "See this?" he said, poking at something with the tip of a tiny Phillips screwdriver. "See how it's worn here?"

I leaned over to look, then nodded. "Sure enough."

"So," said Vanderweigh. "Any new thoughts since last time we talked?"

I thought quickly. If I told him about the suicide and the boating accident that had happened in Carlisle, Pennsylvania, over a decade ago, he'd want to know how I'd heard about them, and that would force me either to lie or to tell him where Evie was hiding. I did not want to lie, and I would never tell him where Evie was.

I could have told him about talking with Kate Burrows down in Carlisle. But that hadn't given me any new thoughts.

I had accumulated a few new facts, but no new thoughts to go along with them.

"If I had any new thoughts," I said, "I'd've sought you out immediately so I could share them with you."

Okay, maybe that was a lie of sorts. I preferred to think of it as a slick evasion.

Dwyer had gone up into the hayloft.

"What about Ms. Banyon?" said Vanderweigh.

"What about her?"

"Any new thoughts about her?"

I shook my head. "Same old thoughts. I miss her. She didn't kill anybody. You're wasting your time, worrying about Evie."

"No idea where she might be hiding?"

I shook my head. "No."

That was a straightforward lie. I'd just have to try to live with the shame of it.

Dwyer came down the stairs from the hayloft, glanced around the barn, then went over to the horse stalls.

I tried not to watch him. I was afraid I'd give something away if he looked into the third one. I turned to Mel. "So you're telling me that this little doohickey prevented the thing from running?"

"It's worn," he said. "See here? So the engine kept flooding."

"Interesting," I said. "And you figured that out from the way the guy described his problem?"

"It could've been three things," said Mel. "This was one of 'em."

I shifted my weight on the stool, and as I did, I glanced over toward Dwyer. He was coming out of the second stall. He moved to the third, went up on tiptoes, and looked over the shoulder-high wall.

I turned to Vanderweigh. "You find out anything more about Owen Ransom?"

He shook his head.

"Find the murder weapon?"

"Nope."

"Any suspects?"

He shrugged.

I watched Mel reassemble the engine.

Vanderweigh, sitting beside me, watched him too.

Dwyer finished peering into the horse stalls, wandered outside, and after a while he came back inside.

Vanderweigh turned to him. "Well?"

Dwyer shook his head.

Vanderweigh blew out a breath, then turned to me. "You enjoying Cortland?"

"Pleasant little town," I said. "Friendly folks, plenty of open spaces, nice diner."

"Planning to stick around for a while?"

"I've got my room for another night."

"Good," he said. "Make it easy to keep an eye on you."

FIFTEEN

After Vanderweigh and Dwyer left, I let out a long breath. "Too close," I said to Mel.

"That Dwyer," he said. "He's a friend of Larry's. They hunt deer together."

He was still thinking about his brother in the present tense.

"Does Dwyer know about that room down there where Evie's hiding?" I said.

He shrugged. "I don't know. Larry's real private about that place. Anyways, Evie ain't down there now. Dwyer wouldn't've found nothing but an empty room."

"Where'd she go?"

He looked at me, shrugged, and turned back to his pile of engine parts.

I smiled. Mel and Mary weren't taking any chances with Evie, and that was fine by me.

"What about Evie's car?" I said. "I know she's got it with her, because she came to my motel last night."

"It's hid good," he said. "Don't worry about that."

"She's been holing up in that little room all week?"

He shrugged. "Sleeping there is about it. She and my mother hang out, drinking ice tea, talkin' all the time, the way women do. Mostly about my brother, I guess. They don't want me around."

"That bald-headed man," I said to him. "He's a state police detective. He's very smart."

"Johnny Dwyer ain't no dummy himself," said Mel.

"Evie's going to have to be careful," I said. "As long as the detective is around, she better not take any chances. He's looking for her. That's why he followed me here. He thinks she killed Larry."

Mel looked at me and smiled. "I know that," he said. "I'm not as dumb as you think. Don't you worry about Evie."

"I don't think you're dumb."

He returned his attention to his engine parts. "I acted pretty dumb this morning," he mumbled.

"We both did," I said. I slid off the stool. "Guess I'll be on my way. I'm staying in the motel if anybody wants to find me."

"Gotcha," said Mel.

I walked out of the barn and followed the driveway to the front of the house.

As I started to get into my car, Mary Scott called to me from the screen porch. I went over, and she came out and stood on the front steps. "Everything okay?" she said.

I nodded. "They didn't find her."

"She showed you what she found?"

"Yes."

"Make any sense to you?"

I shook my head. "Your son had been doing some searching on the Internet. I'm sure it all means something, but I don't know what."

"You'll find out, won't you?"

"I'll try," I said.

She offered me some iced tea, but I declined. I wanted to talk to Dr. Winston St. Croix again.

One of those big square family vans with sliding doors was parked alongside the Camry and the Jeep in Dr. St. Croix's driveway. I pulled up and stopped beside it, and when I got out, I saw that a couple of children's car seats were strapped in the back.

Claudia Wells came to the door when I rang the bell. She smiled at me through the screen door and said, "Mr. Coyne. How nice. Come on in. The doctor has company, but I know he'll be glad to see you."

She held the door for me, and I followed her out onto the screened porch.

Winston St. Croix was seated in the same chair he'd been in when I was there in the morning. On the sofa beside him was Thomas Soderstrom, the administrator of the medical center. They were sipping what looked like iced tea and watching a baseball game on the television.

Soderstrom jumped up and held out his hand to me. "Mr. Coyne. How are you?"

I shook his hand. "I'm fine," I said. "How about you? Got things under control at your office?"

He smiled. "Hardly. Win and I were just complaining about how much we missed Evie."

I turned to St. Croix. "How're you feeling?"

"A little better," he said. He winked. "The Sox just got a run, and if the bullpen can hold on, we'll pull this one out. That would make my day."

I took the chair on the other side of the doctor, so that he was bracketed by me and Soderstrom.

"Can I get you something?" Claudia said to me. "Beer? Coke? Iced tea?"

"Iced tea would be fine," I said, and she left the room.

We watched the game in silence for a couple of minutes, then Claudia came back, handed me a glass of iced tea, and sat on the sofa next to Soderstrom.

When the inning ended and a commercial came on, St. Croix turned to me and said, "I thought you'd be headed back to Boston by now, Brady. How long do you expect to be around?"

I shrugged. "I've got my room at the motel for another night."

"Enjoying Cortland?" said Soderstrom.

I smiled. "I like the diner. Wish I'd brought my fly rod, though. There's not a lot to do around here."

"The lake has good fishing, I hear," said St. Croix.

"They don't think Evie had something to do with that murder this morning, do they?" said Soderstrom.

I shrugged. "I guess they do."

He shook his head. "Ridiculous."

The commercials ended, and the game resumed. We watched the Red Sox set down the Tigers in the ninth. When the last batter flied out to left field, the doctor clapped his hands. Then he fumbled for the remote and turned off the television.

"I do love baseball," he said. "I played third base in college, you know."

"Where was that?" I said.

"University of Minnesota. I batted leadoff, believe it or not. I didn't have much power, but I could run."

"Did you go to medical school there, too?"

He nodded. "It's where I got started." He gazed up at the ceiling and smiled. "Opened my first office in a little farm community in Minnesota. I was the only pediatrician in a radius of about a hundred miles. Made a lot of house calls in those days."

"That's where he picked up all his bad habits," said Claudia.

"So what brought you to Cortland?" I said.

St. Croix turned to me. "There's a television reporter coming down to interview me this week," he said. "She saw that story about me in the *Globe*, and I guess she thinks she'll get some juicy human-interest stuff out of me. You know, the beloved old doctor, now wheelchair-bound, dying slowly of some insidious disease." He reached over and patted my arm. "She'll probably ask me these same questions. I must remember to tell her about playing third base."

"So why *did* you come to Cortland, of all places?" said Soderstrom.

St. Croix lifted his hand and let it fall into his lap. "The usual reason, I guess. Ambition. They needed a pediatrician here, and Boston is the medical mecca of the world. I figured with a base in Cortland, I might be able to hook up with Mass General or Beth Israel or one of those other great hospitals. Maybe get an appointment at the Harvard Medical School." He shrugged. "I was young and full of myself. In the end, I just kept doing what I'd always done."

"Taking care of children," said Claudia. "The old fool even refused an affiliation with the new medical center."

"In spite of my best efforts," added Soderstrom.

"Did you ever practice medicine in Pennsylvania?" I said to the doctor.

He looked at me. "Huh? Pennsylvania?"

"Around Carlisle?"

He looked at Claudia. She shrugged.

"I'm not sure I even know where Carlisle, Pennsylvania, is," he said to me. "Whatever made you think I might've worked in Pennsylvania?"

"Carlisle is near Harrisburg," I said. "Did you ever know a couple named Margaret and Robert Ransom?"

He frowned and shook his head. "No . . . Wait. That name is familiar. Ransom?" He looked at Claudia.

"That detective this morning," she said to him. "He told us that Dr. Romano's real name was Ransom, remember?"

He rolled his eyes. "Yes, now that you mention it, of course I remember. My mind is rapidly turning to mush." He turned back to me and smiled—a bit sadly, I thought. "You seem to be cross-examining me again, Brady."

I waved my hand. "I apologize. I guess my concern for Evie has made me forget my manners."

"Well, your questioning is good practice for when that reporter comes. I do hope she doesn't spring questions like yours on me, though. I'd like to be prepared. I still don't understand where you came up with Carlisle, Pennsylvania."

"Dr. Romano—Owen Ransom—was from there."

"He told me he was from New Jersey."

"Right," I said. "Why do you think he lied to you about his name and where he was from?"

"What difference could it possibly make?" said Claudia.

"Well," I said, "he tried to disguise his identity. He wasn't even a doctor. And somebody cut his throat. Those facts would seem to be connected in some way."

Soderstrom leaned forward. "You think he was worried that if people knew who he really was, he'd be in danger?"

"Something like that, maybe," I said.

"And," said Soderstrom, "somebody *did* figure out who he was, and they killed him."

"The police didn't say anything like that to us this morning," said Claudia.

"Well, my dear," said St. Croix, "you know the police. They don't tell you anything."

"The rumor that's going around," she said, "is that Dr. Romano, or whatever his name was, got involved with a married woman or a prostitute or something."

"So," I said to St. Croix, "the names Margaret and Robert Ransom don't ring any bells with you?"

He shrugged. "I'm afraid not. I don't believe I've ever even been in Carlisle, Pennsylvania." He looked at Claudia. "Have I?"

She smiled at him. "No. You've always been right here with your patients."

"Owen Ransom's parents died in a boating accident about ten years ago," I said.

"That's tragic," said St. Croix. "But I don't understand why you're telling me these things about a person I only met for the first time yesterday."

"He came here specifically to see you."

"Well, all he told me was that he was a doctor who wanted to buy my practice."

"But that was a lie," I said.

St. Croix narrowed his eyes at me. "If I didn't know better, Brady, I'd think you were accusing me of something."

"No, sir," I said quickly. "I'm sorry if it sounds that way."

"As if you think I killed that young man," he said.

"Sorry. I don't think that at all. Sometimes I can be too direct. Lawyer training, I guess."

"I wouldn't say you were especially direct," he said. "But you certainly do sound like a lawyer."

"Whenever I sound like a lawyer," I said, "I feel like I should apologize. Nobody wants to sound like a lawyer. Especially a lawyer."

St. Croix smiled. Then he let out a long sigh, slumped back in his chair, and looked up at Claudia with his eyebrows arched.

She nodded to him, then stood up. "Well," she said, "it's been lovely, but . . ."

Soderstrom pushed himself out of his chair. "We've overstayed our welcome," he said.

"Not at all," said St. Croix. "But I am tired. I hope you'll both come back."

I stood up, too. "Please forgive me for being rude," I said.

He waved his hand. "You weren't rude. A bit lawyerly, perhaps." He smiled. "I do mean it. I'd enjoy visiting with you again."

Soderstrom and I both shook hands with St. Croix and then followed Claudia to the front door. When I apologized to her for upsetting the doctor, she shook her head. "It's good for him to have his mind stimulated. He's grown noticeably more forgetful in the past few months. I know he meant it. He'd enjoy seeing you again."

"Well, I don't know how much longer I'll be here, but it looks like it'll be for at least another day. If so, I'll be back."

She put her hand on my shoulder and smiled. "I'd enjoy it, too."

When I went out to my car, Soderstrom was there leaning against the side of his van. "You were kind of rough on him," he said.

I lit a cigarette. "I didn't think so. I just asked him a couple questions."

"It sounded like you knew something, had a theory or suspicion or something."

"Me?" I laughed. "I don't know anything. I just know that the police think Evie killed two people, and she didn't, and it upsets me."

"You think the doctor had something to do with those murders?"

"Well," I said, "somebody did, and it wasn't Evie Banyon."

"He's in a wheelchair, for heaven's sake," said Soderstrom. "You can't possibly think . . ."

"I don't know what to think," I said. "What about you? What do you think?"

"Oh," he said, "I agree with you. It couldn't possibly be Evie. Or Dr. St. Croix, either. Beyond that, I haven't really given it much thought." He glanced at his watch. "Well, it's getting around to suppertime. My wife and kids should be back from the lake by now. Time for Daddy to hustle home and cook some hamburgers on the grill." He held out his hand to me. "Good to see you again. I hope everything works out with Evie."

I shook his hand. "I'll give her your regards if—when I see her."

He nodded. "Please do that. Tell her I miss her."

"That makes two of us," I said.

After I left Winston St. Croix's place, I went back to my motel and decided I better try to talk to Julie. This time she answered the phone, and she was none too pleased to hear that I'd be playing hooky on Monday. I let her rant about my responsibilities to my clients, the importance of accruing billable hours, the need to attend to paperwork on a daily basis, and my general cavalier attitude toward our business, but when I reminded her that I was in Cortland to help Evie, that mine was a mission of love, and that I hadn't even brought my fishing gear with me, she was quiet for a minute.

"Is she really in trouble?" she said finally.

"They like her for the Larry Scott thing, and they want to question her on this other murder."

"You've talked to her?"

"Yes. She's here in Cortland."

"Is she okay?"

"She's got a place to hide out. She's handling it better than I ever could."

"Well, you do what you've got to do," Julie said. "I'll take care of everything on this end."

"Thank you."

She hesitated. "You really didn't even bring your fishing pole?"

"It's called a rod," I said. "How many times to I have to tell you? No. I didn't bring it."

"Hard to believe."

After I hung up from Julie, I called Kate Burrows in Carlisle, Pennsylvania. When she answered, I said, "Do you work all day on Sundays?"

"Who is this?"

"It's Brady Coyne again."

"Oh, yes," she said. "Well, the answer is, our paper hits the newsstands on Tuesdays, so Sunday is a busy day for me. But that's not why you called. Do you have anything for me?"

"Possibly."

"Good. Shoot."

"Questions, really," I said. "First, a teenage boy committed suicide in Carlisle in 1987. It might be interesting to know who that boy was. Second, Owen Ransom's parents died in a boating accident in August of 1990. I'm wondering if there was anything suspicious about it. Third, a doctor named Winston St. Croix. He's the one Ransom came here to Cortland to see."

Kate Burrows laughed. "You want me to do some research for you, is that it?"

"There might be a story in it for you," I said.

"I'll see what I can find out. I suppose you want me to call you."

"I'd appreciate it." I gave her the motel number. "If I've checked out, try my office." I gave her that number, too.

I took what I hadn't yet read of the Sunday paper to the diner. My arrival stopped no conversations, nor did it even raise any eyebrows, that I noticed.

I was getting to be a fixture in the place.

A waitress I hadn't seen before took my order. I splurged on the sirloin tips, medium rare, with french fries and fresh broccoli and a slab of blueberry pie for dessert.

Back at the motel, I watched Mel Gibson and Danny Glover smash up cars, shoot people, and bleed a lot. When the movie was over, I took a shower and crawled into bed.

I lay awake for a long time. Usually I read *Moby Dick* after I go to bed. I've been reading that book for years. I've learned a lot about the whaling industry, and Melville's stolid prose usually takes my mind off whatever it's been on and puts me to sleep.

Without *Moby Dick*, I tend to stare up at the ceiling at bedtime. I'm not sure if that would gratify Melville.

So I stared at the ceiling, my mind churning around Owen Ransom posing as a pediatrician, boating accidents and suicides in Carlisle, Pennsylvania, and Larry Scott following Evie down to the Cape, and I thought about all the folks I'd met in Cortland, and, of course, I thought about Evie, how the previous night she'd come creeping into my room, how nice it would be if she decided to do it again, and how easy it always was to fall asleep with Evie's head on my shoulder.

But she didn't come creeping into my room.

Eventually, I fell asleep anyway.

When the phone woke me up, there was no light sifting in around the curtains. I fumbled for it in the dark, got it pressed to my ear, and mumbled, "Hello?"

"Hi, honey. Sorry to wake you up." It was Evie.

I pushed my pillow up and wormed my way into a half-sitting position. "Where are you? What time is it?"

"It's a few minutes after three, and I'm still here in Larry's little room in the barn."

"I wish you were here."

"Yes," she said. "Me too. But it's not safe."

"I miss you."

"I know."

I found my cigarettes and got one lit. "What's up, honey?"

"I found out some things."

"About Larry?"

"Yes."

"First," I said, "say something sweet."

She laughed softly. "I *do* wish I was there with you."

"Me too."

"Sleeping in your arms."

"Yes."

"It was nice last night," she said.

"It sure was."

"I'm sorry you got dragged into this mess."

"I didn't get dragged," I said. "It was my choice."

She cleared her throat. "Brady, listen," she said. "I've been on the Internet on Larry's computer. I don't quite know what to make of it, but it all seems to involve Winston St. Croix."

"Are you okay, honey?" I said.

"Oh, sure," she said.

"Those cops—Detective Vanderweigh and Sergeant Dwyer— they came prowling around the barn when I was there this afternoon. I was worried they'd find you."

She laughed quietly. "They didn't."

"Dwyer was a friend of Larry's," I said. "I was afraid he might know about your little hideout."

"Well, if he checked it out, he wouldn't've found me or any sign of me there. I was out in the woods."

I took a drag off my cigarette and blew it up at the ceiling. "So what about St. Croix?" I said. "Or did you call because you miss me?"

"No," she said. "I do miss you, but that's not why I called."

She paused for a moment. "Remember that teenage suicide in 1987? His name was Edgar Ransom."

"Aha," I said. "A relative of Owen Ransom, no doubt."

"His brother. He was two years older than Owen."

"You sure? How'd you learn that?"

"I went on Larry's computer and checked the obituaries from Carlisle, Pennsylvania, for November 1987," she said. "The name Edgar Ransom jumped right out at me. The obit didn't mention the cause of death. It just said 'suddenly.' It listed his surviving relatives. Two parents—Margaret and Robert—and a brother, Owen."

"The obits," I said. "That's brilliant." I thought for a minute. "So Owen Ransom's brother Edgar commits suicide in 1987 in Carlisle, Pennsylvania, and in 1990 their parents drown, and then eleven years later Owen, a hardware-store clerk, comes to Cortland. Owen's using a false name and posing as a doctor who wants to buy Winston St. Croix's pediatric practice, and next thing you know, he gets his throat cut in back of a motel. It's pretty interesting, but I don't get the connection."

"Well," she said, "I found one other thing that might shed some light on the subject." She hesitated. "I checked the obits for Margaret and Robert Ransom, who died in that boating accident in 1990. According to the paper, they had moved to Carlisle in 1984. Guess where they lived before that?"

"Come on, honey. It's three A.M. I just woke up, and I haven't had any coffee. I'm not good at guessing."

She chuckled. "Sorry. I should know better." She cleared her throat. "Before the Ransom family moved to Pennsylvania, Robert Ransom was a schoolteacher at a regional high school in Gorham, Minnesota."

"Wait a minute," I said. "That's where Winston St. Croix had his medical practice before he came to Cortland, right?"

"Bingo."

"So," I said, "it's likely that the Ransoms and Dr. St. Croix knew each other."

"In fact," said Evie, "it's likely that both Edgar and Owen Ransom were Winston St. Croix's patients. Their ages would be about right."

"I talked with St. Croix this afternoon after I saw you," I said. "He didn't seem to recognize the name Ransom."

"It was a long time ago," she said. "He's had thousands of patients."

"So what does all this have to do with Larry Scott?"

"I don't know yet," she said. "I'm still working on it. But I wouldn't be surprised if Larry knew all of this. And maybe more."

"You're thinking about those printouts you found, and that newspaper article. They were Larry's."

"Yes," she said. "He'd bookmarked the *Philadelphia Inquirer*'s Web address on his computer. He probably found out more than I have so far."

"Like what?"

"Well, obviously I don't know yet. But I'm not done. I'll let you know if I find out anything else."

"Let me know if you don't, too."

"Sure." She paused. "Maybe."

"Or just let me know that you're okay," I said. "I worry about you."

"I know. That's sweet. But please don't try to see me again or contact me. Okay?"

"Listen, honey—"

"I mean it, Brady. It's dangerous for both of us."

"Okay. I guess you're right."

"I wish you'd just go back to Boston," she said.

"When I'm ready."

"I worry about you, too, you know."

"I know."

She hesitated. "There's something else," she said slowly. "I don't know what to make out of it."

"What is it?"

"I remembered one time Larry mentioning that he had a secret place where he hid his special treasures. He called it his safe. I—I was worried that he might be keeping some, um, personal things in it."

I wondered what Larry might've had besides those photographs taped beside his bed that would worry Evie. "So," I said, "did you find Larry's hidey-hole?"

"Yes. There's a loose floorboard under the cot here in this room. He had a lot of money in there."

"What's a lot?"

"Exactly thirty thousand dollars. All in hundred-dollar bills. They were in a plastic bag in a shoebox."

I thought for a minute. "Remember that night down the Cape?" I said. "He said something about money."

"Yes," she said. "He said he had money. Larry never had money, which gave him a gigantic inferiority complex. He only made minimum wage at the medical center. He thought a hundred dollars was a fortune. The Scotts were always dirt-poor. Mary never got any help from her ex-husband. She's always struggled to make ends meet."

"So what are you thinking?" I said. "Was Larry stealing money or something?"

"I don't know," she said. "I guess he might have been. He was certainly capable of it. No matter what I told him, he was always convinced that I stopped seeing him because he was poor, and that I went out with Win because he was rich. Maybe he thought if he had money I'd be more . . ." She let her voice trail off.

"Speaking for myself," I said, "I'd lie, cheat, and steal if I thought it would win your heart."

213

"No you wouldn't. But Larry certainly might." She paused. "Anyway, I don't know what Larry's money has got to do with anything."

"Me neither."

"Brady?" she said after a moment.

"What, honey?"

"I'm going to try to sleep now."

"Okay."

"You sleep, too."

"Sure," I said.

"I hope this is all over soon."

"So do I. I miss you."

"Yes," she said. "Me too. But I meant what I said this afternoon."

"What was that?"

"I'm not good for you."

"Now, listen to me—"

"Sleep tight, dear man," she said. Then she hung up.

SIXTEEN

I lay there in the darkness for a long time mulling over what Evie had told me. My poor, sleep-deprived, middle-of-the-night brain refused to operate logically. All sorts of wild and random scenarios ricocheted around up there, and after a while they morphed into a series of wild and random dreams that made no sense, either.

I woke up in a tangle of wet sheets. My heart was drumming, and sweat drenched my body, and even as I lay there in my little motel room with my eyes open, the weird terror of my dream was still palpable.

I'd been naked, trapped in a dark cavernous room that was vaguely Mary Scott's barn, except ten times bigger. Evie was stalking me with a knife, except it wasn't Evie. She wore a man's felt hat and sunglasses and a long auburn braid, and in my dream I knew that she was some stranger disguised in Evie's body. She'd backed me into a corner, and the rough plank walls were puncturing and shredding my bare skin. Billy and Joey, my two sons, were hunched over a workbench way over on the other side of the big room. A single lightbulb over their heads lit them up like a spotlight in the darkness. They were poking through a pile of body parts—hunks of wet flesh, shiny organs, bloody fingers and toes. One of my boys would pick up something slimy and drippy, hold it up to the light, and both of them would laugh. I kept trying to scream to them to help me. My throat ached from the effort, but no words came out of my mouth.

I sat up in bed, took several deep breaths, and finally managed to blink away the awful, vivid reality of my dream.

Sunlight was streaming in around the shades. I checked my wristwatch. It was nearly nine in the morning.

I stumbled into the shower and waited for it to wash away the lingering fragments of my dream. Then I got dressed, went out to my car, and headed for the diner.

As I drove, I pondered what Evie had told me. The person most likely to be able to fill in the blanks was Winston St. Croix. It was a Monday morning, and I figured he'd probably be seeing patients. I decided to get some coffee circulating in my system, have a leisurely breakfast, then go sit in the doctor's waiting room until he had time to talk to me.

I found an empty stool in the diner, and a minute later Ruth set a mug of coffee in front of me. I looked up at her. "Good morning," I said.

"Is it?" she said. "You look like you rassled sheep all night. You're just supposed to count 'em, you know."

"That bad, huh?" I smiled. "There were way too many of them to count, and they all had horns."

I ordered a mushroom omelette with home fries, Canadian bacon, wheat toast, and orange juice, then spotted a newspaper on the seat of an empty booth. I snagged it, took it back to my stool, and skimmed through the sports section while I sipped my coffee.

My omelette arrived before I finished my first mug of coffee, and I'd just about cleaned my plate when four men came stomping into the diner. All four of them looked to be somewhere in their thirties. They were wearing calf-high black rubber boots, blue jeans, and T-shirts. Their faces and arms and shirts were smudged and stained with what looked like a combination of sweat and soot. They were all talking and gesturing and laughing at the same time, full of adrenaline, or testosterone, as if they'd just played a big ball game. Their eyes were red, and none of them had shaved.

They settled into an empty booth, and although I couldn't make out their words, I caught the tone of jazzed-up excitement in their voices.

A couple of people got up from where they were sitting and went over to talk to the four guys, and then a few others joined them, and pretty soon a crowd had gathered around their booth.

When Ruth came over to clear away my plate and refill my coffee mug, I jerked my head in the direction of the four men and said, "What's all the excitement about?"

"Oh," she said, "those boys are volunteer firemen. They're comin' from a big one."

"A fire?"

She rolled her eyes. "No, they won the lottery."

I smiled. "Sorry. I've only had one cup of coffee today."

"Barn fire," said Ruth. "Them old barns, you know? Dried timbers, full of hay." She made an exploding motion with her hands. "They just go up."

"They couldn't save it?"

She shrugged. "Nobody hurt, no livestock to worry about, and they saved the house. They did their job."

217

"Where was the fire?"

She gestured vaguely. "North of town. Mary Scott's place."

"Oh, shit," I said. I dropped a twenty-dollar bill on the counter and got the hell out of there.

If there had been a cop on my tail, he'd have pulled me over for speeding. But I didn't care. I drove fast.

Evie had been in that barn.

When I got to Mary Scott's place, there was a Cortland PD cruiser in the driveway and a red Subaru wagon out front. I recognized the Subaru. Charlotte Matley, Evie's lawyer, drove it. I pulled up in front of the Subaru, got out, and walked halfway down the driveway.

Out back beyond the house, I could see what was left of the barn. The front wall was still standing, but most of the roof had either burned or been torn off, leaving the charred beams and rafters of the old building's skeleton exposed. Slabs of black wood lay scattered around the backyard. It smelled like a campfire that someone had pissed on.

As I started toward the front porch, the screen door opened and Sergeant John Dwyer stepped out. He paused there on the steps, looking back inside and talking to somebody on the other side of the door. Then he glanced my way, lifted his chin at me, waved at the person on the porch, and came over to where I was standing.

"This a social call, Mr. Coyne?" he said.

"I heard about the fire," I said. "Wanted to be sure everybody was okay."

"Well," he said, "that's right neighborly of you. Old Mel got himself some burns, trying to salvage his junk. Mrs. Scott just got herself scared. That's about the extent of it. Of course, between the smoke and the fire and the water, everything in that old barn was ruined."

"There was nobody in there, then?"

"Mel and Mrs. Scott were sleeping when it went up."

"The firemen looked all through it?"

"Sure. Of course."

I let out a little breath of relief. "When did it happen?"

"Mrs. Scott called it in sometime after five." He shrugged. "Guess by then it was going pretty good. The firemen left about an hour ago."

"Any idea what started it?"

He shook his head. "Big old wood barn full of hay and paint cans, oily rags, gasoline and turpentine, and who-knows-what-else. Mel and Larry did the wiring themselves, never got it inspected. Mrs. Scott's going to have herself a time collecting insurance on it, I suspect. Damn shame is what it is."

"I was wondering about arson."

Dwyer smiled. "Why would you wonder that?"

"Well," I said, "somebody killed Larry. Maybe they have a grudge against the family or something."

"Like who?"

"I don't know."

"Well," he said, "Cortland isn't exactly Boston, you know. We've got an all-volunteer fire department. They're pretty damn good at putting out fires, but not a one of 'em's any kind of arson expert. Nothing valuable in there, nobody hurt. It's just an old barn." He shrugged. "Maybe they'll call in one of the state fire marshals, I don't know."

At that moment, the radio on Dwyer's belt squawked. He took it from its holster, turned away, mumbled something, listened for a minute, then said, "Jesus Christ."

He turned back to me. "I gotta go," he said, and he jogged over to his cruiser, climbed in, and backed out of the drive-way. Then he switched on his flashing lights, and his tires spewed up gravel as he took off up the dirt road.

I watched until he disappeared, and a minute later I heard the wail of his siren.

I turned and went to the front of the house. Just as I put my foot on the first step, the screen door pulled open and Mary Scott was standing there.

She was looking up the road where Dwyer had left a cloud of dust. His siren had faded away. "What was that all about?" she said.

"I don't know. He got a call, and he took off."

She shook her head. "If it ain't one thing, it's another." She sighed. "Well, it's nice to see you."

"I heard about the fire," I said to her. "I was worried about—"

Mary quickly put her finger to her lips and rolled her eyes back toward the inside of the house. "Everybody's okay," she said.

I arched my eyebrows and mouthed the question, "Evie?"

She smiled quickly and nodded. "She got out," she whispered. Then in a normal voice she said, "Please, come on in, join us for coffee."

I followed her through the house to the kitchen. Mel and Charlotte Matley were sitting across from each other at the table. Mel had no shirt on. There were scratches and red marks on his bulky chest and shoulders, and his right hand and forearm were wrapped in white gauze.

Charlotte smiled and stood up when she saw me. She was wearing a gray pinstriped lawyer suit with a white blouse buttoned to her throat. She held out her hand to me.

I took it. "Chasing fire engines, are we, Counselor?"

She shook her head. "Of course not."

"I was joking."

"It's hardly a joking matter," she said.

"You're right," I said. I looked at Mel. "What happened? You okay?"

"Me?" He blew out a breath. "Oh, yeah. I'm okay. Lost a

220

lot of good stuff, though. Couldn't rescue it in time." He held up his bandaged hand. "Barely got out of there before the roof came down."

"He got a bad burn," said Charlotte. "I wanted to drive him to the medical center, but he's a stubborn boy."

Mel shrugged. "Insurance," he said, which I took to mean that he didn't have any. "Charlotte patched me up."

Mary handed me a mug of coffee. "Black, right?"

I nodded. "Thank you."

"Won't you sit down?" she said.

I looked at Mel. "I was wondering if you'd show me around outside."

"It's a mess," said Mary.

Mel stood up. "Let me get a shirt."

I sipped my coffee, and a couple of minutes later Mel showed up wearing a clean T-shirt. "Okay," he said. "Let's go."

As soon as we got outside, I grabbed his arm. "What about Evie?"

"She got out." He held up his bandaged hand. "How do you think I got this?"

"You tried to save her?"

He nodded. "She was already gone. She wasn't there."

"You sure?"

"Yes, sir."

"Where is she?"

He shook his head. "I don't know."

We were walking around the side of the barn, and looking at it close-up, I could see that the back and one side wall had mostly burned down, and the inside had been gutted. The stench of wet burned wood was overpowering. Nobody inside could have survived.

"So what do you think happened?" I said.

"Oh, man," he said. "Larry and me did the wiring. We

221

might not've done it up to code, you know? Charlotte's sayin' that my mother's house insurance might not pay her when they figure that out."

"You think it was electrical?"

"What else could it be?"

I thought it could be arson, but I didn't see any reason to say that to Mel. "Who discovered it?"

"Me," he said. "My room's on the back of the house. Something woke me up. I think it was the smell of smoke. I looked out my window and saw the flames comin' out under the edges of the roof."

"So you called it in?"

"I yelled to my mother and she did," he said. "I ran out to get Evie."

"But you didn't see her?"

He shook his head. "I went around the back to Larry's room. Burned my damn hand pullin' open the door. She wasn't there. Her car's gone, so I guess she got out. Don't ask me where she went to."

We continued around to the back of the barn, and I saw that the door to Larry's little hidden room was standing ajar. I looked inside. The floor was ankle-deep in water, and the inside walls were charred. Larry's computer and other equipment were scorched, and the papers and books on his shelves were big lumps of soggy ashes.

I didn't know much about how fire worked, but I knew it burned up, not down. It appeared to me that this one had started at the bottom of the barn in the rear. If not in Evie's room, then close to it. I figured it would have been going strong before anyone in the house or driving past, looking at the front of the barn, would've been able to detect it.

"I talked to Evie on the phone a little before three this morning," I said. "What time did you notice the fire?"

Mel looked up at the sky. "Five? Around then sometime. It was still dark. I tell you, man, seein' them flames in the nighttime right next to our house . . ."

"It must have been scary."

He nodded. "Especially thinkin' Evie was in there."

"Well," I said, "I'm sorry about your workbench and your tools and everything."

He blew out a breath. "That's another damn thing. Charlotte says the people who gave me stuff to fix might come after me for the cost of it. Hell, I had about twenty things in there to repair."

I touched his arm. "I'm sorry."

"Well," he said, "fuck 'em, you know? They can't get outta me what I haven't got, and I ain't got their machines and I ain't got any money, either."

"Maybe the insurance will work out."

He shrugged. "Yeah, maybe."

As we continued around the barn, I noticed that an old rutted roadway led off into the woods out back. "Where does that go?" I asked Mel.

"It's about a mile down to the pond. Old tote road. The farmer who lived here before us used to cut wood out there. I do that some, too, and haul it out with the tractor. Larry's hunting cabin's down there."

"Does Evie know about it?"

"I guess so. Larry don't keep anything from her."

"Maybe she's there."

"At the cabin?" He shrugged. "Doubt it. She hid her car down that road. There's other ways out besides through here."

"What do you mean?"

"You haul wood, you gotta have lots of roads. This here's the main one, comes back to the farmyard. But there's others."

"So there are several roads Evie could've taken out of the woods."

"Well," he said, "there's a couple of 'em, at least, good enough to drive that little Volkswagen of hers on."

"She might've gone to that cabin, though," I said.

Mel shrugged.

"I'm going to take a look." I started down the roadway.

Mel held back for a moment, then came along beside me. "I better go with you," he said. "You take a wrong turn in these woods, you'll be lost for a month."

As we walked along the rutted old tote road, I was aware of the fact that just two days earlier Mel Scott had tried to throw me down the stairs. Now he was striding along beside me in the middle of the woods, and I was very aware of how big and strong and young and fine-tuned he was.

The midsummer forest—a mixture of mature oak and pine, with a few patches of younger birch and poplar—was fragrant and overripe, and it pressed in on both sides of us. The big old oaks arched overhead, shading us from the midmorning sun. Tumbledown stone walls ran along both sides of the roadway, and here and there a break in the wall marked another ancient tote road leading off to one side or the other. A couple of those old roadways looked navigable by a non–four-wheel-drive vehicle.

There were several forks in the road, and Mel and I trudged along for ten or fifteen minutes before it began to slope down a steep hillside. Then through the trees I spotted the glitter of sunlight on water.

The road ended at a long, skinny pond. I could see where a little stream fed into it up at the end. I estimated it covered no more than two or three acres. "Beavers?" I said to Mel.

He shook his head. "Farmer dammed it up a hundred years ago. Me and Larry used to catch pickerel out of here when we were kids."

The cabin was off to the left, half-hidden by a screen of pines. I walked over to it. It was small and square, maybe twenty by twenty, with a tin roof and dark, weathered plank sides. There were two small windows in front and no lock on the door.

I peeked in through one of the windows, and by cupping my hands around my eyes I could make out a rectangular table with five or six wooden chairs around it, a woodstove with an aluminum chimney pipe leading up through the roof, a ratty old sofa, and two sets of bunk beds. An old-fashioned kerosene lantern, a deck of cards, a cribbage board, and four or five beer cans all sat on the table, and a couple of mounted deer heads hung on the wall. It looked dark and musty and unlived-in.

"I didn't think she'd be here," said Mel.

I went around to the back of the cabin. There was no rear door, no other windows, no outhouse, no electrical wiring, no propane tank.

There was, however, a pile of old beer cans and empty bottles and semi-decomposed cardboard boxes. An old wooden rowboat sat with its bow pulled up on the bank of the pond and its stern sunk in the water.

"Doesn't look like the place gets much use," I said to Mel.

"Just deer season. Larry and his buddies like to sleep here, drink and play cards and get up early to go hunting."

Again I noticed Mel's use of the present tense whenever he referred to Larry. "What about you?" I said to him.

He shook his head. "I don't shoot animals. That's Larry's thing. I never use this place."

Evie wasn't here, and I saw no evidence that she—or anybody else—had been recently.

I nodded to Mel. "Thanks for bringing me here. It's a nice cabin and a beautiful spot. Guess we might as well head back."

We started walking back up the road.

225

"You better not tell nobody about our cabin," Mel said after a few minutes. "Larry will be some pissed at me if he finds out I brought you here."

He was frowning at me, and I saw that in some dark corner of Mel's muddled brain, Larry Scott was still alive and bossing his baby brother around.

SEVENTEEN

When we got back to the house, Mel said he wanted to poke around in the barn and see if anything was salvageable. He invited me to join him, but I took one look at the soggy, charred, and twisted wreckage of the fire and declined. "I'll just say good-bye to your mother and be on my way," I said.

He shrugged and headed into the barn.

I went up the back steps, tapped on the door, and when Mary Scott called, "Come on in," I went inside.

She was sitting at the kitchen table staring down into the empty coffee mug she was cradling in both hands. When she looked up at me, I saw that her eyes were red and her cheeks were damp.

"Did Charlotte leave?" I said.

Mary nodded.

I sat down across from her, reached over, and took both of her hands in mine. "It could have been worse," I said.

She tried to smile. "I know. That's what Charlotte was saying. I don't care about that old barn. I feel bad for Mel, though. He don't have much going for him, but he does love those tools and machines of his." She shook her head. "It was scary, thinking Evie was in there . . ."

"She got out."

She nodded. "I forget my manners. The coffee's still hot."

"Thank you," I said. "I'd like some."

She got up and poured a mugful from the electric pot on the counter. She put it in front of me, then sat down again.

"I been feeling awful bad," she said softly, "lying to you about Evie the way I did."

I waved that thought away with the back of my hand.

"It's how she wanted it," she said. "She said just don't let on to anybody. I don't guess she expected you to show up, but I figured I better play it the way she wanted, even with you."

"Where do you think she went?" I said. "Anybody she might go to?"

"Lord, I don't know. Evie's awfully sweet, but she doesn't have a lot of real friends, if you know what I mean. You and I are about it. Evie doesn't trust many people. I guess she's got good reasons."

"Nobody you can think of here in Cortland?"

She shook her head. "I've been thinking about that all morning."

"What about Thomas Soderstrom? Or Charlotte Matley?"

"They weren't Evie's friends, Brady. Not like you and me. Not so she could trust them to hide her away."

"Dr. St. Croix, maybe?"

She smiled. "Maybe if he wasn't sick and if that nurse of his wasn't around all the time."

"Evie doesn't like Claudia Wells?"

"Oh, I think she likes her okay. It's just, Claudia's kind of possessive about the doctor."

"Was Claudia jealous of Evie when she was going out with the doctor?"

"Evie thought she might've been, a little." Mary glanced down into her coffee mug, then looked up at me. "My bet is that she's miles and miles from this town, Brady, and she isn't coming back. She was set on figuring out who killed my Larry, clearing her own name, but now, that other murder, then the fire . . ."

"Did they tell you what caused it?"

"The fire?" She shrugged. "Johnny Dwyer said he guessed it could've been the wires. Larry and Mel hooked 'em up. Those boys were pretty good at things like that, but . . ."

I wanted to ask her if she could think of anybody who might have torched her barn. But if the idea of arson hadn't occurred to her, I figured it would be better not to mention it. No reason to upset her any more than she already was.

"What makes you think Evie's miles from here?" I said.

Mary looked up at me and smiled. "We did a lot of talking these past several days, Evie and me."

"What did she say?"

She looked down at the table and shrugged.

"Did she give a hint where she might have gone?"

"If Evie wants you to find her," she said, "she'll let you know. It's not up to me."

"You're right, of course," I said.

I finished my coffee, stood up, thanked Mary, and then gave her one of my business cards. "If you ever need anything, or if you think of anything, give me a call," I said. "Anything at all. I know you've got Charlotte. But I'm a lawyer, too."

"You're heading home, then?"

I smiled. "Soon."

She stood up, came over to me, hesitated, then put her arms around me and gave me a hug. "I can see why Evie loves you," she murmured against my shoulder.

"Sometimes I'm not sure I do," I said.

She laughed and stepped away from me. "You be sure to say good-bye before you head back to Boston," she said.

"I will."

"I hope you and Evie find each other again."

"I hope so, too." I turned for the back door. "I'm going to say good-bye to Mel."

"He'll appreciate that, I know," she said.

I went outside and looked in through the entrance to the barn. Mel had a rake, and he was using it to scrape around in the rubble near what was left of his workbench. I called to him, and he looked up.

"Come here for a minute," I said.

He shrugged and came over.

"Have you been in Larry's little room downstairs where Evie was hiding?" I said.

He shook his head. "That's Larry's room. He don't let me go in there."

"Mel," I said, "Larry's dead."

He turned away from me and looked up at the sky.

I touched his shoulder. "Listen to me for a minute."

He shrugged my hand away. "I gotta get back in there, find my stuff."

"You've never been in that room?"

He looked down at his feet. "Maybe I peeked in a couple times."

"You went in there this morning looking for Evie, didn't you?"

"That was different."

"I want you do to me a favor, okay?"

He shrugged.

230

"I want you to go into Larry's room. Look under the cot. There's a loose floorboard. Lift it up and see if there's anything there."

"Something of Larry's?"

"I don't know. It might not belong to Larry."

"What if I find something?"

"Leave it there, at least for the time being. Maybe it was Larry's, and maybe it wasn't. I just want to be sure you know about it."

"Under the cot, huh?"

"Yes."

He narrowed his eyes at me. "How do you know about it?"

"Evie told me."

He nodded. "I guess if there's something there, it won't go nowhere. Maybe I'll look. Right now, I gotta go back and find my stuff." Mel gave me a nod, then turned and trudged into the old barn's charred corpse and resumed raking around in the rubble.

I watched him for a minute, then went out to my car.

Les Katz, a private investigator I used to know, once described his job to me as "thrashing around in the underbrush until you scare something up."

As I drove away from Mary Scott's place, I thought about what I should do next, and I remembered Les's words. I'd come to Cortland hoping to track down Evie, and I'd done some thrashing around, and eventually I'd found her—or rather, she'd found me. But now she was gone again, and this time I had no idea what underbrush I should resume thrashing around in.

Les also used to say, "Detecting is pretty good work, provided you've got a high tolerance for boredom and you're getting paid by the hour."

Les was good at his job, and when he thrashed around, it

231

was always with a purpose. His specialty was confronting people, sometimes to antagonize them and sometimes to charm them, just to see how they'd react. Every once in a while, somebody would give away something that Les hadn't known was there.

The other thing about Les Katz was that the last time he thrashed around, somebody ran him down with a truck and killed him.

Les Katz was a good guy, but he was a poor role model. I didn't have a very high tolerance for boredom, and the only people who paid me by the hour were my clients back in Boston—who were paying me nothing as long as I was thrashing around in Cortland.

Anyway, I didn't care for the way Les's thrashing around had ended up.

Evie was gone, and solving Larry Scott's murder seemed less important than it had. It was time for me to go home. First I figured I'd better tell Detective Vanderweigh what I knew about the Ransom family history, not that I understood its significance.

At the end of the dirt road, I turned south on Route 1, heading for the police station in the center of town. If Vanderweigh wasn't there, they'd be able to find him.

I'd have to try to tell him what I knew without dragging Mary Scott into it. She was Evie's friend, and she had enough problems. She had been harboring a suspected murderer, and I assumed that at some point or other she had lied to the police about it, and even if it was out of love and loyalty, they probably wouldn't be sympathetic.

I'd just driven past the old drive-in movie theater when a police cruiser passed me heading in the opposite direction. I watched in my rearview mirror as it made a U-turn behind me. Then its blue flashers went on, then its siren, and it closed the distance between us quickly.

I flipped on my directional signal and pulled to the side of the road. The cruiser stopped behind me, and Valerie Kershaw got out and came to my window.

"I was just thinking," I said to her, "there's never a cop around when you want one, and here you are."

"Here I am," she said. "Will you follow me, please?"

"Sure. Where to?"

"Just follow me."

She went back to her cruiser and pulled out in front of me, and I followed her. Five minutes later, we ended up at Dr. St. Croix's place. Half a dozen vehicles, including another Cortland PD cruiser, were parked in the gravel turnaround and along the side of the road.

Valerie pulled off the road and got out of her cruiser. I stopped behind her and slid out of my car.

"What's going on?" I said to her.

She shook her head. "They want to talk to you inside."

We went up the path to the doctor's office. Sergeant Dwyer was standing guard outside the door. He nodded to us, stepped aside, and we went in.

There were half a dozen people in the waiting room. Sergeant Lipton was in the corner by the window talking quietly with a small Asian woman who had two cameras around her neck. An overstuffed middle-aged man in a dark suit stood with them, listening. Claudia Wells and Charlotte Matley were sitting close to each other on the sofa. Claudia was staring down at her hands, which were tugging at a handkerchief. Charlotte was leaning toward her, whispering intently. If they noticed me, they chose to ignore me.

Thomas Soderstrom was sitting stiffly in a chair on the other side of the room. He looked up when I walked in, blinked at me through his thick glasses, and nodded without smiling.

In fact, nobody was smiling.

The one person who was conspicuously absent from the room was Dr. St. Croix.

I thought I got the picture.

"What's going on?" I whispered to Valerie.

She shook her head.

"It's the doctor, right?"

She didn't answer me.

A moment later, Sergeant Lipton looked up, nodded to me, said something to the Asian woman, and came over. He held out his hand. "Mr. Coyne," he said. "Thanks for coming."

I shook his hand. "I wasn't given much choice."

"Detective Vanderweigh wants to talk with you. You can sit down if you want to. It might be a few minutes."

"Is anybody going to tell me what's going on?"

"Detective Vanderweigh will fill you in."

Lipton went back to the Asian woman and the overstuffed man. I started for the sofa, where there was room to sit beside Charlotte Matley, but Valerie held my arm. "They don't want you talking to anybody until Detective Vanderweigh sees you."

"The doctor died, didn't he?"

She looked away.

"If he had died of natural causes," I persisted, "there wouldn't be a bunch of cops here."

"Please, Mr. Coyne," she said.

"Well," I said, "do you think it would be all right if I went outside, had a cigarette? Sergeant Dwyer can keep an eye on me out there. I promise not to flee."

She shrugged. "I guess that would be all right."

She went to the door and spoke to Dwyer, then nodded to me.

I went outside and lit a cigarette. "This was that call you got at the Scotts' house, huh?" I said to Dwyer.

He nodded

"Something happened to Dr. St. Croix?"

"Vanderweigh talk to you yet?"

"No."

"Then I can't."

So I stood there on the stoop, and I didn't talk to Dwyer, and he didn't talk to me.

I finished my cigarette, watched a chipmunk prowl through the flower garden, shifted my weight from one leg to the other, listened to some crows arguing in the distance.

After a while, Valerie Kershaw came out, got into her cruiser, and drove away.

A few minutes later, Sergeant Lipton came to the door and said, "Mr. Coyne, you want to come in here now?"

I followed him into the waiting room. I noticed that another man, this one tall and white-haired, had joined the Asian woman and the overstuffed man in the corner.

Lipton pointed to Dr. St. Croix's office. "In there."

The door was ajar. I pushed it open and went in.

Detective Neil Vanderweigh was standing there with his back to me, looking out the window. "Close the door," he said without turning around.

I closed the door.

He turned to face me. "Have a seat, Mr. Coyne." He gestured at the same chair I had sat in the first time I talked with Dr. St. Croix.

Vanderweigh looked at me for a minute. I couldn't read his expression. Then he sighed, sat down on the other side of the desk, and picked up a sheet of paper. He glanced at it, then handed it to me.

"What's this?" I said as I reached for it.

"Take a look, tell me what you make out of it."

It was a piece of white, legal-sized paper with writing

scrawled on it, obviously a photocopy. I could make out the faint lines that indicated the original had been written on a legal pad. I guessed the handwriting was in pencil, although on the photocopy I couldn't be sure.

The writing itself was shaky. It appeared to be a list. It read:

> *Can't continue anymore*
> *Early days in Gorham—good times*
> *All those children—loved them all*
> *Never do harm to anyone*
> *MS—pain—losing my mind?*
> *End it on my own terms*
> *Tired all the time*
> *Third base—ran like the wind*
> *Dizziness, double vision*

Something else was scratched on the next line, but I couldn't decipher it.

I looked up at Vanderweigh. "Did St. Croix write this?"

He nodded.

"Suicide?"

"Evidently." He gestured at the sheet of paper I was holding. "How does that strike you?"

"It's not your conventional suicide note, but . . ." I shrugged.

"The ME thinks he died of an overdose of the medication he was taking," said Vanderweigh. "At this point, our guess is that he wrote that"—he pointed at the paper I was holding—"after he injected himself. He died in bed. The notepad was on the floor beside him, along with a pencil and a hypodermic needle. His nurse, Ms. Wells, found him this morning." He put his forearms on the desk and leaned toward me. "I understand you've visited the doctor several times since you've been here. Did he strike you as suicidal?"

"Do you question it?" I said.

"Unattended death," he said. "A medical examiner's case, as you know. He has questions about it. You got any thoughts?"

"I'm not sure what the questions are," I said, "but I do know some things." So I told Vanderweigh about the suicide of Owen Ransom's teenage brother, Edgar, in Carlisle, Pennsylvania, in 1987, and I told him that the Ransom family had moved to Carlisle from Gorham, Minnesota, in 1984, and I told him that the Ransom parents had died in a boating accident a few years after Edgar's suicide. I also told him that Dr. Winston St. Croix had opened his first pediatric practice in Gorham, and before he could ask me, I told him that I had talked with the newspaper editor in Carlisle, Pennsylvania, but hadn't learned much except that the Ransoms seemed to have a lot of money which Owen inherited, and that the other things I'd learned had come from Evie Banyon, and that Evie had discovered them from newspaper clippings and computer printouts she'd found in Larry Scott's room in the cellar of his barn where she'd been hiding, and which had burned down just that morning.

"Scott had this information?" said Vanderweigh.

I nodded.

"And you've had it for how long?"

"Some of it yesterday, some just this morning."

"You got it from Ms. Banyon."

"Yes."

"When you were here yesterday afternoon," he said, "you were asking St. Croix some questions." He stated this as a fact, not a question. I figured he'd already talked to Thomas Soderstrom and Claudia Wells. They would have told him about our conversation.

"Yes," I said.

"Questions about these things you've just told me." Again, a statement, not a question.

"Some of these things. I didn't know all of them then."

"How did he react?"

"He accused me of cross-examining him. But he seemed to be treating it lightly, like he was was making a lawyer joke out of it."

"He didn't seem upset?"

I shrugged. "Not really. He was tired. We didn't stay that long."

" 'We'?"

"Thomas Soderstrom was there, too. And Claudia Wells, of course. They were watching the ball game when I got there, as I'm sure you know."

Vanderweigh smiled. "You knew where Ms. Banyon was all along, didn't you?"

"Not until yesterday."

"But when Sergeant Dwyer and I found you there in the barn, you knew then."

I nodded.

"And you lied to us."

"Well, technically . . ."

He shook his head. "I could make things very uncomfortable for you, you know."

"You already have."

"You know what I'm talking about."

"Listen," I said, "I've been trying to tell you that you're wasting your time and the taxpayers' money focusing your investigation on Evie. She was trying to get at the truth, and she might have, too, if somebody hadn't burned down that barn."

"There's no evidence that anybody set fire to that barn."

"Well," I said, "think about it."

"Sure," he said. "Thanks for the advice." He leaned back in

238

his chair, laced his fingers behind his head, and looked at me. "Let's see. Larry Scott, citizen of Cortland, is murdered down in Brewster. Then a week later, Owen Ransom, hardware clerk from Pennsylvania posing as a doctor from New Jersey, is murdered in Cortland. Then Dr. Winston St. Croix, originally from Gorham, Minnesota, commits suicide. Oh, and Larry Scott's barn burns down and Evelyn Banyon, who was hiding there, disappears. And let's not overlook the interesting fact that you have not been far removed from any of these events. So tell me, Mr. Coyne. How does it all fit together?"

"I don't know. It doesn't seem to. Something's missing."

"Something Ms. Banyon might have?"

"If she does, she didn't share it with me."

"She should share it with me," he said.

"Well, I have no idea where she is."

He shrugged. "Why should I believe you?"

"Because I'm an officer of the court. I know my duty."

He smiled. "In view of your recent behavior, Mr. Coyne, I'm hardly convinced."

"I've told you everything I know."

"Maybe. Still, I hope you've reserved that motel room for another night."

"Actually, I was planning on going home," I said.

"Do me a favor," he said. "Stick around another day. I'll want to consult with you some more."

"You can consult with me in Boston," I said. "I've got a law practice to take care of."

"And I've got a murder case to take care of." He blew out an exasperated breath, then smiled at me. "Please?"

I laughed. "How can I refuse?"

"Good." He waved the back of his hand at me. "Now get out of here. After what you've told me, I've got to talk to those people out there all over again."

When I walked out of the doctor's office, Claudia and

Charlotte and Soderstrom and Lipton and the others all turned their heads and looked at me expectantly, as if I might have some answers for them.

I stopped in front of Claudia. She looked up at me with wet eyes.

"I'm very sorry," I said.

She tried to smile. "Thank you."

When I went outside, Dwyer was still there guarding the door. "How'd it go?" he said.

"Fine, thank you." I started for my car.

"Hang on there," said Dwyer.

I stopped. "What's the problem, Officer?"

He held up his hand at me and spoke into his radio. He listened for a minute, then looked at me and nodded. "Okay," he said. "You have a good day, sir."

"It's off to one helluva start," I said.

EIGHTEEN

I slid into the front seat of my car, let out a big breath, and looked at my watch. To my surprise, it was after four o'clock in the afternoon.

Time sure does fly when you're having fun.

When I got to my motel room, I slipped off my shoes, flopped on the bed, and called the front desk to extend my stay for one more night.

Then I called my office in Boston. When Julie answered, I told her it looked like I'd be away for at least one more day. Fortunately, she was on another line with a client and couldn't interrogate me.

I heard the frustrated disappointment in her voice. She wanted to hear all about it, I knew. But I was relieved. I was in no mood for rehashing everything with her, and if she hadn't been busy, she'd have given me no choice. Julie burns with curiosity, especially about matters of the heart, and most especially about matters of *my* heart. She considers it an important part of her job as my secretary to monitor the health of my love life and to prescribe remedies when she diagnoses an ailment.

For many years after my divorce, Julie had been convinced that I was destined to reunite with Gloria, my ex-wife, and she looked upon any new woman in my life as the enemy of my ultimate happiness. It took her a long time to resign herself to the fact that Gloria didn't want to remarry me any more than I wanted to get back together with her.

Julie had a good marriage with her Edward. She believed in marriage, and when I met Alexandria Shaw, Julie thought I should marry her. She might have been right, but it didn't happen. Alex moved to Maine, and eventually we discovered that absence made our hearts grow less fond. At the time, this convinced Julie that I was destined for a life of solitary misery.

Now she believed that Evie was my absolute last shot at happiness. She never came right out and said it, but I knew what she was thinking: *You're not getting any younger, you know.*

Actually, I thought she might be right. I'd loved and lost some good women who had seemed to love me and who had accepted my countless imperfections. I didn't think there could be many more of them around.

Evie, where are you?

I bunched the pillow under my head and stared up at the water-stained ceiling of my grungy little motel room. I hadn't had any lunch. Now it was nearly suppertime, and I thought I should be hungry. But I wasn't. I felt like I'd swallowed a bottle of Drano.

Mainly, I was depressed. I'd been thrashing around in this little town for three days—it felt like three weeks—all with the simple and selfish purpose of finding Evie and clearing things up so she and I could resume our tranquil life together. Evie was the reason I cared who'd murdered Larry Scott and

242

Owen Ransom, and who'd burned down Mary Scott's barn, and why Winston St. Clair had killed himself.

For me, it was all about Evie.

Now she was gone again, and this time I had no idea where she was.

Well, I'd promised Vanderweigh I'd stick around for one more night, and I would. Tomorrow morning I'd go home.

Meanwhile I had a night to kill.

I thought of calling Kate Burrows in Carlisle, but I didn't have anything new to tell her, and she'd promised to call me if she came up with anything.

As I stared at the ceiling, questions about Dr. St. Croix flitted through my mind. *Did* he commit suicide? Why wouldn't he? He knew how to do it. And he was a doctor. He knew what was in store for him.

Still, that was a strange suicide note.

Two murders and one suicide. They had to be connected.

I remembered that Owen Ransom and Winston St. Croix had both lived in Gorham, Minnesota. That was the only connection between them that I knew of. It was an old connection. According to Evie, St. Croix left Gorham in 1980. The Ransom family moved away a few years later.

I picked up the phone, got information for Gorham, and learned that the town didn't have a newspaper. I thought of asking the operator to connect me with the oldest living resident of the town, but she didn't seem to have much patience. So I asked for the local police.

A male voice answered. "Gorham Police."

"I'm an attorney in Boston," I said, "and I hope you'll bear with me, because I have an unusual request."

"Fire away."

"Who's got the most seniority on your force?"

"Seniority?"

"Who's been there the longest?"

"I know what seniority means, sir," said the officer. "I was just agreeing that this is an unusual request. It would be Chief Proctor. He's been on the force for . . . I guess he's coming up on twenty-five years."

"So he was there in 1980."

"Unless my math is worse than I thought."

"I wonder if I could speak to him."

"You probably ought to tell me what you want to speak to him about," he said. "Then I can ask him if he wants to speak to you."

"I just want to know if he remembers a man who used to practice pediatric medicine in Gorham. His name was Winston St. Croix."

"St. Croix?"

"That's right."

"Hang on."

I waited nearly five minutes before a different male voice, this one older and raspier, said, "This is Chief Proctor."

"Chief," I said, "my name is Brady Coyne, and I—"

"You're asking about Winston St. Croix."

"That's right. Did you know him?"

"Yes, I did. Why?"

"He died today, and—"

"You're calling to tell me he died? He hasn't been near this town for over twenty years."

"I'm wondering why he left Gorham in the first place."

Chief Proctor cleared his throat. "Far as I know, he went looking for greener pastures. It happened kind of sudden, as I recall. Folks weren't happy about it. Fact is, we don't keep good doctors around here for very long. Good lawyers, either, come to think of it. Not that you run into many of them."

"What do you mean, 'sudden'?"

"Well," he said, "it was a long time ago, but I do remember Dr. St. Croix didn't give any notice. Just up and left, practically overnight. The town was without a pediatrician for a couple years. That didn't set well with people."

"But he was a good doctor?"

"I guess he was. Never heard anything to the contrary."

"Does the name Ransom ring any bells with you?"

"Ransom?" He paused. "You want to give me a hint?"

"High-school teacher and his wife. They had two boys. Edgar and Owen. They moved away in 1984."

"You know more about it than I do, I guess. People come and go. I don't recall any Ransoms. Why?"

"I was wondering if the Ransom boys were Dr. St. Croix's patients."

"These were young boys?"

"Yes. They would've both been under ten at the time."

"No doubt they were his patients, then. He was the only pediatrician in town."

"How well did you know the doctor?"

"Look," he said. "I don't know what you're after here, but you're talking about ancient history, and my memory of those days is pretty fuzzy. I knew Dr. St. Croix. Gorham was a small town back then. It's still small, but it was quite a bit smaller then. Dr. St. Croix practiced medicine here for a while, then he moved on. People liked him. Far as I know, he was a good doctor. Beyond that . . ."

"Owen Ransom was murdered two days ago," I said. "He'd come to a town here in Massachusetts posing as a doctor. He sought out Dr. St. Croix, pretending he wanted to buy his practice. Then he got his throat cut."

"You think St. Croix did it?"

"No. Dr. St. Croix had multiple sclerosis. He was in a wheelchair."

"Well," he said, "if you're suggesting there was bad blood between the Ransom boy and Dr. St. Croix, you're asking the wrong man."

"Who should I ask?"

"You could've asked my predecessor, but he died six years ago."

"The previous chief?"

"That's right. He and St. Croix were close friends. When the doctor left town, the chief refused talk about it. Wouldn't even allow St. Croix's name to be mentioned around him. Mad as hell about it."

"Why would he be mad?"

"Damned if I know."

"Is there anybody in town who might know more about it than you?" I asked.

"It was a long time ago," he said. "Sorry. And I don't mean to be rude, but . . ."

"I appreciate your time," I said.

"Give me a number," he said. "If I think of anything, I'll get back to you."

After I hung up from talking with Police Chief Proctor in Gorham, Minnesota, I realized I was feeling hungry. So I splashed some water on my face, put on my shoes, and drove to the Cortland diner for what I hoped would be the last time in my entire life.

This time I got there before they ran out of meatloaf. It was moist on the inside and crispy on the outside, just like I remembered my mother made it. They served it with two strips of bacon, a twice-baked potato, and candied carrots. It reinforced my faith in diner meatloaf.

The hot apple pie and coffee afterwards left me feeling replete and happy.

When I walked out of the diner, it was still light. So I drove north past the village green, turned down the road that led to the old Victorian where Evie had lived when she worked in Cortland, and continued past it to the lake. I kept glancing in my rearview mirror. As far as I could tell, Vanderweigh hadn't attached a tail to me.

I pulled into a dirt parking area beside the lake and walked down to a sand beach, where a few young women wearing bathing suits and wide-brimmed straw hats sat on blankets watching toddlers splash in the shallows.

If I had my topography right, the stream that the old farmer had dammed to make the pond behind Mary Scott's house emptied into this lake across the way from where I was standing.

At the left end of the beach, there was a jumble of furniture-sized boulders. I went over and sat on one of them, lit a cigarette, and gazed upon the water.

A freshwater pond around sunset at the end of a summer's day offers endlessly fascinating entertainment. Swallows and purple martins swooped and darted barely inches over the surface, chasing insects. Here and there their wingtips ticked the glassy water, leaving rings like feeding fish do. Bats and nighthawks had emerged from the shadowy woods along the shore to snag mosquitoes, and a string of half-grown mallards paddled single-file behind their mother among the reeds. A blue heron stood knee-deep in the water, still as a stump with its neck arched like a half-drawn bow, poised to strike a hapless bluegill. Bullfrogs grumped and grumbled in the lily pads, and now and then a bass or a pickerel swirled in the shallows trying to catch one.

While I sat there, I thought about Winston St. Croix and Owen Ransom and Larry Scott, and I thought about Evie, and I thought about the people I'd met in Cortland, and I pondered scenarios that might link them all together. I had no flashes of insight.

Still, sitting on a rock watching the water around dusk on a summer evening never fails to soothe my soul and restore my perspective.

By the time I stood up and headed back to the car, the stars were popping out overhead and mist was rising from the surface of the lake and the young mothers had taken their children home for bed.

Back at the motel I watched a seventies movie in which Robert Mitchum played a small-time Boston hood who was ratting out his friends to the feds in hope of saving himself from prison. In the end, Mitchum's friends killed him.

The credits were scrolling when somebody knocked on my door.

My heart thumped. Evie?

More likely it was Vanderweigh, coming to grill me.

I got off the bed and pulled the door open.

I hadn't expected anybody to knock on my motel-room door, but if I had thought about it, the last person to come to mind would have been Claudia Wells.

She stood there rubbing her hands up and down on the tops of her thighs and looking at me with big solemn eyes. She smiled quickly. "I'm sorry," she said. "This was stupid."

"It's nice to see you, Claudia," I said. "Do you want to come in?"

She shrugged. "I guess so. Sure. Thank you."

I held the door for her. She brushed past me and stood uncertainly in the middle of my little motel room. She was wearing a dark blue Providence College sweatshirt, snug-fitting white jeans, and white canvas sneakers. A little purse hung on a strap over her shoulder. Her blond hair was tied back with a scarf that matched the sweatshirt. She wore pink lipstick.

It looked like she'd tried, but her makeup failed to hide the redness and swelling and sadness around her eyes. They looked like they'd seen too much.

I closed the door and waved my hand around. "It's not

much," I said. "But it's what I've been calling home lately." I gestured at the only chair in the room, in the corner beside the television set.

She put her purse on top of the TV and sat down. "I should've called," she said.

"No problem."

"I was hoping to talk to you."

I sat on the foot of the bed facing her. "Why me?"

"I'm sorry," she said. "I really shouldn't've—"

"Please stop saying you're sorry. I'm happy to have some company."

She looked at me for a moment. "Why you?" She shrugged. "I couldn't think of anybody else, I guess."

"Well, that's flattering."

She leaned toward me and put her hand on my knee. "I didn't mean it that way. All I meant was, there's nobody in this little town I feel like I can talk to. Sometimes it's better to talk to somebody you don't know so well. Know what I mean?"

I nodded.

"I mean, you seem like somebody you can talk to. Somebody you can trust. Who won't judge a person or spread gossip all over town."

"Well," I said, "I am a lawyer. Did you want to talk to a lawyer?"

She shrugged. "Not necessarily. It's not that you're a lawyer. It's that . . . you seem like a nice guy."

"Claudia," I said, "are you in some kind of trouble?"

"No. It's nothing like that."

Her hand was still resting on my knee. I patted it, then picked it up, gave it a quick squeeze, and let her take it back.

She slumped in her chair and folded her arms across her chest. "It's about Win," she said. "The doctor. I didn't see it coming, and I feel like I should have. I didn't have a clue. I

249

can't get my mind around it. It's like somebody punched me in the stomach." She shook her head. "Do you realize what it's like, working side by side with the same man for twenty-one years, seeing him practically every day, taking care of him when he's sick, scheduling his activities, thinking you know everything about him, and then something happens and you realize you didn't know him at all?"

I nodded but didn't say anything. All I could think of were glib platitudes, and I didn't think Claudia wanted platitudes from me.

"I feel so alone," she said softly. "It's worse than when my parents died. I—I gave that man half of my life, and then he turns around and leaves me like that."

"Maybe he wanted to make it easier for you."

"He should have known me better than that. He should've known I'd want him to talk to me about it."

I shrugged. "He was sick and depressed. He probably thought you'd try to talk him out of it."

"Well, maybe I would have." She tried to smile, then shook her head. "You know something, Brady?"

"What, Claudia?"

"This has been an awful day. The worst day of my life. There were people around all day. Friends of mine. Of ours. Me and Win. They knew how—how close we were. But not one of them even thought I might need a hug." She gave a little shrug, then turned her head away. I realized she was crying.

After a minute, she got up, went into the bathroom, and came back with a tissue. She wiped her eyes and blew her nose, then balled up the tissue and tossed it into the wastebasket.

"You seemed to know a lot about him," she said.

"The doctor?"

"Yes. Yesterday, when you came over, I had the feeling you knew something you weren't saying."

"Not really."

"That Detective Vanderweigh," she said. "The state police-man. After you left, he was asking strange questions."

"Like what?"

"Oh, about Win's work before he came to Cortland, about that Dr. Romano—Ransom, I guess his name was, who was murdered. About Larry Scott, and . . . I don't know. It was like he thought there were secrets that I should know."

It occurred to me that Vanderweigh would have told Clau-dia and the others whatever he wanted them to know. It was likewise safe to assume that what he hadn't told them, he didn't want them to know. "I don't know what Vanderweigh was after," I said.

"Yesterday when you were talking with Win," said Claudia, "it seemed like you had something on your mind. He sud-denly got all defensive and said he was too tired to talk. Didn't you notice?"

I nodded. "I guess I did."

"It was like you had some kind of suspicion."

"I didn't really. I just wondered if there was some old con-nection between him and Ransom."

"Like what?"

"I don't know."

"Well," she said, "whatever it was, you hit a nerve. He sud-denly got all upset. Maybe you didn't notice it, but I did. And then that same night he kills himself? That doesn't seem like a coincidence."

"Are you blaming me for his suicide?" I said.

"Not at all. I'm just trying to understand it." She sighed. "Well, I guess I should probably get going?" She made it a question.

I answered it with a nod. "I'm afraid I haven't helped you much."

"No, I feel better. I like talking to you." She cleared her

throat and looked down at her lap. "I could stay for a while," she said softly.

"That probably wouldn't be a good idea," I said.

She looked up at me and laughed softly. "Not many men would turn down an invitation like that." She stood up and smiled. "Oh, well." She went over to the single window, parted the curtain, and gazed outside for a moment. Then she turned to face me. "Sometimes I hate this crappy little town, you know?"

I nodded.

"I think I gotta get away from here," she said, "start over again. Get myself a life."

"That's probably a good idea. Maybe—"

At that moment, a beeping noise came from the direction of the television.

"Oh, shit," said Claudia. "My cell phone." She glanced at her watch. "I better get it."

She reached into her purse and pulled out her phone. She flipped it open, held it to her ear, and said, "Yes?"

I didn't try to listen, but it was hard not to hear Claudia's end of the conversation. It consisted of a series of monosyllables: "Yes . . . No, it doesn't look like it . . . I don't know . . . Nothing . . . I doubt it . . . Okay, right."

She snapped the phone shut and shoved it back into her purse. "Sorry. I really hate those things, but nowadays . . ."

"I refuse to get one," I said. "Drives my secretary nuts. She likes to be able to keep in touch with me, and she doesn't understand that sometimes I don't want her to be in touch with me. Julie is—"

There was a loud knock on the door.

"Now what?" I said. I looked at Claudia and raised my eyebrows.

She shrugged.

"Whoever it is," I said, "I'll get rid of him. You want to go in the bathroom or something?"

The knocking became more insistent.

Claudia nodded. "That's a good idea." She went over to the TV, picked up her purse, and took it into the bathroom. She pushed the door shut but didn't latch it.

I went to the door and cracked it open.

Sergeant John Dwyer of the Cortland PD stood there scowling at me. He was out of uniform. He wore blue jeans and a dark windbreaker over a white T-shirt. "May I come in?" he said.

I pulled the door all the way open. "I guess so."

He came in, looked around, and wrinkled his nose. "You got company? Am I interrupting something?"

"If I did," I said, "that would be my business. Is that why you came here? To see if I had company?"

"Vanderweigh sent me," he said. He looked around the room, then went to the bathroom and put his hand on the door.

I grabbed his shoulder. "This is my room," I said, "and unless you've got a warrant—"

I didn't see it coming. In one sudden motion, he pivoted and clubbed me on the side of my head with his elbow. It sent me sprawling backwards onto the bed.

"Don't you ever touch a police officer," said Dwyer.

"Get out of my room," I mumbled. My vision was blurry. I wondered if he'd broken my jaw.

"You invited me in. I don't need a warrant. You're a lawyer. You should know that." He pushed the bathroom door open. "Okay," he said. "You can come out now."

Claudia came out. She looked at me. "Are you all right?"

I shrugged.

She turned to Dwyer. "Did you have to hit him?"

"Didn't have to. I wanted to."

She touched his cheek. "You're a bad boy."

Dwyer was smiling at me.

"Better cuff him," she said.

He nodded and came over to the bed. "On your belly," he said.

"There's no need for that," I said. "I'm happy to talk to Vanderweigh. You can—"

He punched me in the stomach.

I doubled up and gasped for breath, and Dwyer grabbed my shoulder and turned me onto my belly. I felt the handcuffs click around my wrists. Then Dwyer spun me around and hauled me into a sitting position.

Claudia came over and sat beside me. She touched my face. "If you cooperate, he won't hit you anymore."

"What're you two up to?" I said.

She shook her head. "Please cooperate, Brady. That will make it a lot easier for all of us." She turned to Dwyer. "We better get going."

"Stand up," said Dwyer to me.

With my hands cuffed behind my back, it was a struggle to get to my feet, and when I did, a wave of dizziness made me stagger. Claudia grabbed my arm before I fell and held me upright.

After a minute my head cleared. "I'm okay now," I said. "So are you going to tell me—?"

"Shut up," said Dwyer. To Claudia he said, "Get his car keys."

Claudia wormed her hand into my pants pocket and came out with my keys. She held them up for Dwyer to see.

He nodded, then went to the door, pulled it half-open, and glanced around outside. "Okay," he said. "Let's go."

He went out and Claudia steered me out behind him. A black SUV was parked directly in front of my motel room.

Dwyer was holding the passenger door open. Claudia led me to it, and the two of them shoved me in and snapped the seatbelt across my chest. Then Claudia got in the backseat behind me, and Dwyer went around and slid in behind the wheel.

"Do it now," he said over his shoulder.

Suddenly Claudia's forearm went around my throat and she levered my head back. Her wrist pressed against my windpipe cutting off my air, and I struggled to drag in a breath.

"Hold still," she said. "It'll be quicker that way."

Then I felt a prick in my right shoulder, followed by the unmistakable burning of a hypodermic needle sliding into my muscle.

I thought I could actually feel the drug enter my bloodstream and seep up into my brain. When it got there, it radiated warmth and peace throughout my body, and I felt better almost instantly.

In fact, I felt *really* good. Relaxed, carefree, happy, calm.

Not a care in the world.

Everything was going to be just fine . . .

NINETEEN

After Claudia hit my shoulder with the needle, she leaned forward, stroked my cheek with the palm of her hand, and murmured, "There, now. Isn't that better?"

I wanted to tell her it *was* better. In fact, it was terrific.

But I couldn't seem to find any words.

Sometime later, she got out of the back seat, and when she slammed the door, it sounded like a bomb going off inside the car.

I was aware of her talking to Dwyer through his window, and I heard her say, "See you there."

Then Dwyer and I were riding through the night, and I closed my eyes and let myself enjoy the sensation of movement.

I didn't entirely lose consciousness. I drifted on a hazy fog in some gray, dreamy never-never land. Vague thoughts and foggy images and odd, disconnected memory fragments floated around in my head, but as hard as I tried to pin them down and make sense of them, I couldn't seem to latch on to a single one of them.

But that was okay. I didn't care. I didn't care about anything.

After a while—a few seconds? hours? days?—the movement changed. We seemed to be going much slower, and we were bumping and rocking and swaying. Now and then I heard scraping sounds on the sides of Dwyer's truck.

The bumps and jerks aroused me a little, although it took an exhausting amount of concentration and willpower to open my eyes. It seemed as if I had to send specific directions to my eyelids to make them move.

There wasn't much to see. Just varying shades of darkness. Here and there a lighter patch appeared, and there were shadowy shapes blurring and morphing right outside the window.

At one point we stopped moving and Claudia got in the backseat. She reached around and touched my cheek. "You okay?" she said.

I don't think I answered her.

Then we started moving again. Beside me, Dwyer was humming and drumming his fingers on the steering wheel. I might have asked him where we were—the question had formed in my mind, though I wasn't aware of actually saying anything— because he said, "Almost there. Just relax."

I think I told him that I was as relaxed as I could possibly be.

After a while, we stopped moving, and Claudia and Dwyer wrestled me out of the car and started half dragging me through the darkness. I wanted to cooperate, but I couldn't seem to summon up the energy or the concentration to instruct my legs to move. I was awfully tired, and whatever they wanted to do with me was fine.

After a while, I guess I went to sleep.

*   *   *

When I woke up, I found that the fuzziness in my brain had been replaced with a sharp, throbbing ache. I blinked my eyes open, then shut them quickly. The light stabbed at my eyeballs like a fusillade of darts.

"I think he's awake," I heard Dwyer say.

"It's been about two hours. It should've worn off." That was Claudia's voice.

I was aware of an achy tingling in my arms and legs. When I tried to move them, I discovered that I couldn't.

I cracked open my eyelids. There was a bright light burning right in front of me. When my eyes focused, I saw that it was the flame in a glass-covered lantern. Dwyer and Claudia were sitting in the shadows beyond the lantern, looking at me.

I glanced down at myself. Duct tape had been wrapped around my arms, chest, thighs, and ankles. It felt like my wrists were still cuffed behind me. They'd taped me to a hard, straight-backed chair that was pulled up to a rectangular wooden table. A deck of cards and a cribbage board and a few beer cans were scattered on the table.

If I wasn't mistaken, we were in Larry Scott's hunting cabin deep in the woods by the pond. Dwyer had been here before. He'd been one of Scott's deer-hunting partners.

"Good morning, sleepyhead," said Claudia. "How are we feeling?"

I tried to speak. My throat felt as if a Brillo pad was caught in it. "Thirsty," I croaked.

Claudia got up, and a minute later she was holding a plastic bottle to my lips. "Take it slow," she said. "We don't want you vomiting all over yourself."

She squeezed water into my mouth, and I held it there for a moment to savor the soothing moisture on my tongue before I let it slide down my parched throat.

"More," I whispered.

Claudia gave the bottle another squeeze and then took it

away. "That's all for now," she said. "You be a good boy and you can have some more." She patted my cheek, then went back and took the chair beside Dwyer.

He was lounging back with his arms folded over his chest. Claudia had her elbows on the table and her chin in her hands. The two of them were looking at me. I tried to read their expressions.

Amusement?

Curiosity?

Expectation?

"What do you want?" I said.

"Just a little information," said Claudia.

"You could've tried asking nicely."

"I did," she said. "I thought I was terribly nice."

"So that's what that—that seduction act—was all about? You wanted information?"

She smiled. "It would've been more fun than this."

"I don't know anything you don't know."

"That's not what your friend Detective Vanderweigh says," she said. "He says you know a lot of things that you're not sharing."

"Like what?"

"Like what Larry Scott and Owen Ransom knew about Dr. St. Croix."

"I have no idea what they knew."

"But Evie knows," she said. "Right?"

"Evie doesn't know anything," I said.

"That's bullshit," growled Dwyer.

Claudia frowned at him, and he shrugged. Then she looked at me again. "So where is she?"

I shook my head.

"Brady," she said, "we need to know where Evie is."

"I don't know where she is, but—"

Dwyer's fist slammed down on the table. "Bullshit!"

"—but if I did know," I continued, "I wouldn't tell you."

Dwyer pushed himself away from the table and came around so that he was standing beside me. "Where is she?" he said.

"I don't know. Vanderweigh—"

Dwyer's fist slammed into my solar plexus. It drove the breath out of me and released an explosion of pain. I wanted to double over, but the tape around my chest held me upright. I gasped and gagged, and just when I finally managed to drag in a breath, he slugged me again in exactly the same place.

"Where the fuck is she?" he said.

My chest felt as if a grenade had gone off in it. I could only shake my head and gasp desperately for air. Tears were running down my cheeks, and my entire body was soaked in sweat. I figured if he hit me one more time, I'd never breathe again.

I sat there gasping and sweating and trying to make my lungs work. Dwyer loomed in front of me, glaring down at me, pounding his fists against his thighs.

"Wait," said Claudia. She got up, came around the table, and took Dwyer's hands in hers. "You're being cruel," she said to him. "I think Brady would like to cooperate." She looked at me. "Wouldn't you?"

"No," I managed to whisper.

She frowned. "I'm afraid Johnny's going to kill you if you don't."

"He'll kill me anyway."

"Don't be silly," she said.

"He killed Larry Scott and Owen Ransom."

She glanced at Dwyer. "Did you do that?"

Dwyer grinned. "Me?"

"He burned down the barn," I said. "Probably killed the doctor, too."

"Now why would he do a thing like that?" said Claudia.

"I don't know."

She stroked my forehead with her fingertips. "Sure you do."

I shook my head.

"So where's Evie?"

"I don't know."

She shrugged, then turned to Dwyer and said, "Johnny, honey, maybe you should ask him."

Dwyer smiled and showed me his fist.

"Wait a minute," I said. "Don't hit me."

"Where's Evie?" said Claudia.

"I'll make a deal with you," I said. "You tell me what you two are up to, and I'll tell you where Evie is."

"I told you he knew," she said to Dwyer. She patted my cheek. "It's a deal. You tell us first."

"You gonna let me go?"

"Of course," she said.

I looked at her for a minute, then dropped my eyes. "Arizona," I mumbled.

"What?"

"Arizona," I said. "Evie's headed for Arizona."

She turned to Dwyer and arched her eyebrows.

"He's lying," he said.

"Are you lying, Brady?" said Claudia.

"No," I lied.

"Where in Arizona?"

"Scottsdale."

"Be specific."

"With a friend."

"Got a name for us?"

"Peters," I said. "Barbara Peters. She owns a bookstore there."

"How do you know this?"

"Evie told me."

"When?"

"I don't remember," I said. "My brain's fuzzy from your damn drug."

"No, it's not," she said. "That's not how it works. You've probably got a headache, and you might be feeling a bit nauseated. But your brain is not fuzzy. What else did Evie tell you?"

"That's all. She told me where she was going. Then she left."

"No," said Claudia, "there's more. Tell us what you know about Dr. St. Croix."

"Give me more water."

Claudia held the water bottle to my mouth and gave me a squirt.

I swallowed it a little bit at a time and tried to think clearly. The fact was, I didn't understand what was going on, but it occurred to me that if I told them what I knew, they might decide not to go after Evie. So cleared my throat and said, "This is all I know, and it's all Evie knows, too." Then I told them about Owen Ransom's brother Edgar committing suicide, about the Ransom parents dying in a boating accident in Carlisle, Pennsylvania, about how the Ransoms had once lived in the same Minnesota town where Winston St. Croix had his first pediatric practice, and how Owen and Edgar had most likely been St. Croix's patients.

When I was done, Dwyer said, "Yeah? And what else?"

I shook my head. "That's it."

"Not according to Vanderweigh, it's not."

"Vanderweigh may know something else," I said, "but I don't. And neither does Evie."

Claudia put her hands on my shoulders and bent to me so that her face was close to mine. "What's the significance of all this?" she said.

I shook my head. "I don't know."

She stared into my eyes for a moment, then straightened up. "I don't think we're going to get anything else out of him," she said to Dwyer.

"Maybe," he said. "I'm gonna hit him again anyway, see if he changes his mind."

She nodded. "Worth a try."

This time I saw it coming, and I managed to tighten my stomach muscles. Still the blow left me gagging, and the almost unbearable pain made me wonder if he'd ruptured some important internal organ, like maybe my heart.

I let my chin slump onto my chest and pretended I'd lost consciousness.

"Did you kill him?" I heard Claudia say.

"Nah," said Dwyer.

"Well," she said, "let's get it over with."

"Give him the needle," said Dwyer.

"Let's get him over to the bunk first," she said.

Then their hands were on me, and they were tearing the tape off my wrists and legs and chest. When they were done, they grabbed me under my armpits and hauled me to my feet.

Claudia was right. I wasn't going anywhere. I had no strength, and my wrists were still cuffed behind me, and my arms and legs were numb. I was also dizzy, and the sharp, deep pain in my stomach and chest made me gasp when they moved me.

They dragged me across the room, laid me on the bunk, and Dwyer took off my handcuffs.

Then Claudia knelt beside me and showed me a hypodermic needle. "It's not going to hurt at all," she said.

"That how you killed the doctor?"

She smiled. "This much isn't going to kill you," she said. "It'll just make you nice and relaxed."

"You're not going to kill me?"

"I didn't say that," she said.

She jabbed the needle through my shirt and into my upper arm, then bent so close to me that I could smell her perfume. "It would've been so much more fun if you'd done it my way," she whispered.

"Let's get going," said Dwyer.

I waited for the drug to hit me. It seemed to come more slowly this time.

Claudia stood up and moved toward the door, and then Dwyer picked up the lighted lantern from the table. He brought it over beside me, unscrewed the bottom, and tipped it on its side. The kerosene poured out of it and splashed on the wooden floor next to the bunk where I lay.

I tried to push myself up, but the dizziness hit me and I fell back. The room began to spin, and in its slow whirl I saw Dwyer drop the still-lighted lantern onto the floor in the pool of spilled kerosene. The glass mantle shattered, and an instant later there was a sudden whoosh of fire. It seemed to fill the room, a spinning explosion of flame right beside me.

I tried to move. I had to get the hell out of there. But I couldn't. My brain wasn't getting through to the rest of my body. I couldn't wiggle a finger.

The smoke burned in my nostrils, and the flames leapt all around me, bright in my eyes, roaring in my ears, fiery on my skin.

I had to get out of there...

But then I felt Claudia's drug. It began as a kind of soft, wet blackness somewhere in my belly. It filled my chest, and began slowly to ooze its way up into my head, and I realized that it really didn't matter after all.

Nothing mattered.

I just wanted to sleep. Sleep would be nice.

I closed my eyes and relaxed.

TWENTY

I lay there on that bunk surrounded by flames and smoke and blistering heat, and even Claudia's tranquilizing drug couldn't lull me into ignoring the fact that I was about to die.

There was nothing I could do about it. My body was limp and unresponsive to the halfhearted commands I sent to it.

Anyway, it just didn't seem terribly important.

Over the roar and crackle of the fire, I gradually became aware of other sounds—distant explosions, muffled shouts, faraway thumps and bumps and crashes. And then someone was beside me, grabbing at me, hauling on my arm, yelling at me to stand up, to get going, to hurry.

I tried to tell whoever it was that I couldn't move, but not to worry. What was the rush, anyway?

Then I felt myself being dragged through the flames and the smoke, and suddenly we were out of it, and the air tasted sweet and clean.

I lay on my back staring up at the star-filled sky, vaguely aware of people around me and hands prowling over my body.

Then a bright light shone in my face. "He's breathing," somebody said. It was a female voice.

"Hey, Brady," said somebody else, a man. "How're you feeling? You all right?"

I tried to smile and nod and say the word, "Drug." It came out as a croak.

"Give him some water," said the male voice.

I felt arms around my shoulders, helping me lift my head and prop it up in somebody's lap. Cool, wet water on my face and lips and in my mouth. A damp rag wiping my forehead, neck, and throat.

I squinted against the bright light and turned my face. The light moved away, and then I saw Detective Neil Vanderweigh squatting beside me.

"Did you catch them?" I said.

He nodded.

"Claudia and Dwyer?"

"We got 'em."

"They killed Larry Scott and Owen Ransom and Dr. St. Croix," I said, "and they burned down Mary Scott's barn."

"Did they tell you that?"

"Not exactly."

"What did they say?"

"Can't you let him rest for a minute?" said the female voice.

I turned my head and looked up into Valerie Kershaw's face. It was sweat-stained and streaked with soot. She was cradling my head in her lap and holding that cool wet rag on my forehead.

I smiled up at her. "Was that you who saved my life?"

"I hauled you out of there, yes," she said.

I let my head fall back on her lap. "Thank you."

"My pleasure."

I closed my eyes. "Claudia gave me a drug, and Dwyer kept hitting me in the stomach," I said. "I'm awfully tired. Can we talk later?"

"Okay, so what *did* those two tell you?" said Detective Neil Vanderweigh.

We were sitting at the conference table in the Cortland police station. Outside the window, the sky was just beginning to grow light. I was on my third mug of coffee. Caffeine seemed to be an effective antidote to the drug Claudia had shot into my arm, and the three aspirins Valerie gave me had taken the edge off the various aches and pains John Dwyer had left on my stomach and chest, although it hurt like hell when I tried to take a deep breath.

"They didn't tell me anything," I said. "They asked me questions. Mainly they wanted to know where Evie was."

"What'd you tell them?"

"Arizona."

He smiled. "She's not in Arizona, is she?"

"I don't think so."

"Well," he said, "it doesn't matter. We know what we need to know."

"Did they talk?"

He smiled. "Got them separated, mentioned the penalties for murder, arson, and kidnapping, and they were more than willing to blame each other."

"So you don't need me, then."

"Oh," he said, "You were a big help."

"You set me up, didn't you?" I said.

He shrugged. "Kind of. Sorry about that."

"I was your fucking decoy, huh?"

"We had you covered. You were never in danger."

"Oh, yeah?" I said. "Dwyer kept slugging me in the stomach. He could've killed me. Then that drug, and the fire—"

269

"I said I was sorry," he said. "Point is, you're okay, and we got the bad guys."

"So yesterday at Dr. St. Croix's house," I said, "after you talked with me, you interviewed everybody all over again, asked them new questions, fed them some tidbits about Ransom and Gorham, Minnesota, implying that I had the answers, and then you waited to see who'd take the bait. Right?"

He smiled. "Something like that."

"You watched my motel room to see who'd show up."

"Officer Kershaw was hiding in the parking lot."

"You suspected Dwyer?"

"No," he said. "Dwyer was a surprise. Claudia Wells wasn't, though. I thought she might've given the doctor an overdose."

"I didn't quite buy that suicide note," I said.

"It wasn't a suicide note," he said. "It was just some scribbles he'd made, thinking about an interview he was going to do. She took it from his desk and left it beside his bed."

"So Claudia put the poor guy out of his misery, huh? Mercy killing, you think?"

"Nope. Greed. He left everything to her."

I shook my head. "I was convinced she really cared about him."

"Oh," he said, "I believe she did. She's quite emotional about it."

"So why didn't she just let him finish out his life? He had a disease that was going to kill him. She'd get her money soon enough."

"It could've taken years," said Vanderweigh. "By then, the doctor might've been broke."

"Broke? Why?"

"Larry Scott was blackmailing him."

I nodded. "And when Claudia found out about it, she killed Scott."

"She didn't," said Vanderweigh. "Dwyer killed Scott."

"Before Scott could bleed the doctor dry."

"Right. Scott was hitting him for ten grand a month, and the doctor was paying."

"So Dwyer followed him down the Cape . . ."

"And saw the perfect opportunity to deflect suspicion onto you and Ms. Banyon."

I pointed my finger at Vanderweigh. "He did a damn good job of it, too. You bought it."

He shrugged.

"So," I said, "Dwyer and Claudia . . . ?"

He nodded. "They were in it together. When she found out Larry Scott was blackmailing the doctor, she seduced Dwyer, promised to split her inheritance with him, got him to do the dirty work."

"So where did Owen Ransom fit into it?"

"Ms. Wells was afraid Ransom was going to blackmail the doctor, too. She arranged to meet him that night—the night he annoyed you at the diner. Led him to believe that she was a lonely, small-town girl eager to fuck a studly out-of-town doctor. She's a good-looking woman."

"Yes," I said. "I noticed."

"So she seduced him into telling her his real intention."

"He was going to blackmail St. Croix, too?"

"It's not clear. Maybe. According to Ms. Wells, he never exactly said. But he had something on the doctor, and he was going to make him pay. She said those were his words: 'Make him pay.' "

I thought about that. "Revenge, maybe?"

Vanderweigh nodded. "Could be. For what, though?"

"For something that happened back in Gorham, Minnesota, when they were both living there."

He shrugged.

"So Claudia cut Ransom's throat."

271

"Dwyer did that," said Vanderweigh.

"Didn't Claudia say what these guys had on St. Croix, that they were blackmailing him for?"

"No," he said. "I don't think she knows. All she knows is that the doctor was paying Scott, so it had to be something real. It started with Scott shortly after the announcement of St. Croix's retirement hit the newspapers. Then along came Ransom. The only solution was to get rid of those two, and then get rid of the doctor before somebody else came along."

"Nobody could blackmail him if he was dead," I said.

"Nope."

"Be nice to know what they had on him, though."

"Your friend Ms. Banyon might know."

"She might," I said. "Wherever she is."

Vanderweigh bought me breakfast at the diner, which seemed to me to be the least he could do, then drove me back to the Cortland Motor Inn, where my car was waiting for me outside my room. They'd fetched it for me from where Claudia had left it in the woods. She'd followed behind Dwyer when he drove me to the cabin. Their plan was to make it look like I'd decided to spend the night there in Larry's cabin. There were plenty of people who'd heard me complain about my claustrophobic motel room. If Vanderweigh and Valerie Kershaw hadn't rescued me, it would've appeared that I'd had a few beers, flopped down on the bunk, and then knocked over the kerosene lantern. Tragic accident.

I slid out of Vanderweigh's car, and he did, too. It was eight-thirty on a Tuesday morning in mid-August, and already the sun was steaming off the pavement of the motel parking lot.

We leaned side by side against his car.

Vanderweigh squinted up at the cloudless sky. "Gonna be another hot one."

"Looks like."

"Guess you'll be heading back to the city, huh?"

"In the blink of an eye," I said.

"I hope you don't expect an apology from me."

"You owe me one," I said, "but I don't expect to get it."

He turned his head, looked at me for a minute, then smiled. "We'll be in touch with you."

"The DA will want to depose me."

"I expect so. Ms. Banyon, too."

"If you can find her."

"Oh," he said, "we'll find her."

"I hope so," I said.

I cleaned out my room, paid my bill at the motel office, and a little over an hour later I was in my apartment on Lewis Wharf on the Boston waterfront.

Cortland, Massachusetts suddenly seemed far away and long ago.

I loaded up my electric coffee pot, soaked in the shower, slipped into a pair of shorts and a T-shirt, and took a mug of coffee and my portable phone out onto my balcony, where there was always a cool, salty breeze coming in off the water, even on a scorching August day.

I called Julie at the office and told her I was home but not feeling well, so I was taking the rest of the day off. She wanted to know all about it, of course. I told her I was too tired to talk and it would have to wait until tomorrow.

Then I tried Evie's number at home.

Her machine answered, as I'd expected. "It's Evie. I can't come to the phone right now, but your call is important to me, so please leave a message and I'll get back to you, I promise."

I wasn't at all sure she'd get back to me, but I left a message anyway: "It's Tuesday. A lot has happened since I talked to you, even though that was just yesterday. Seems like a year ago. I want to tell you all about it. Preferably in person. Anyhow, it's all over. Detective Vanderweigh arrested Claudia Wells and Officer John Dwyer this morning for the murders of Larry Scott and Owen Ransom and Dr. Winston St. Croix. Maybe you didn't know about the doctor. I assume you were long gone by the time that happened. The good news is, you and I are no longer suspects, and the people who wanted to hurt us are safely locked up. So wherever you are, honey, you can come home. Will you? I hope you will." I cleared my throat. "I sure do miss you."

After that, I called Marcus Bluestein, Evie's boss at Emerson Hospital. I told him that I'd found Evie and then lost her again.

He hadn't heard from her.

Then I hobbled into my bedroom, dropped my clothes on the floor, and crawled in between the cool sheets.

When I woke up, the day had passed and it was dark outside.

The following Friday afternoon I was at my desk still trying to catch up on all the paperwork that had accumulated in the few days I'd been gone when Julie buzzed me.

Marcus Bluestein was on the phone. "I just talked to her," he said.

"Evie?"

"Yes."

"Is she all right?"

"Well," he said, "she said she was fine."

"But?"

Bluestein blew out a breath. "But she told me she wanted to quit."

"Quit her job with you?"

"Yes."

"Why? Where is she?"

"She didn't say. She didn't say much of anything, Brady, and I didn't push her. She was full of apologies, but it was pretty clear she'd made up her mind." He chuckled. "You know Evie."

"Nobody really knows Evie," I said.

"I told her I wouldn't allow her to quit," he said. "I told her I was giving her an indefinite leave of absence. Her job will be waiting for her whenever she wants it."

"What did she say to that?"

"She said thank you."

"Do you think that means . . . ?"

"That she'll come back?" He paused. "I don't know, Brady. Maybe. She knows I'll have to train temporary help, and it wouldn't be like Evie to let me do that unless she was at least considering coming back."

"Well," I said, "that's good news."

"I assume she hasn't been in touch with you."

"No" I said. "She called you, not me."

The next day was Saturday, exactly a week after I'd driven down to Cortland, and two weeks from the day that Evie had found Larry Scott's dead body in the driveway in Brewster.

A lot had happened in those two weeks.

Normally Evie and I would play on a weekend. On a summer Saturday, we might drive to Rockport or Tanglewood, or we'd just stroll through the Common and down Newbury Street and maybe end up in Fenway Park, or if it was raining we'd go to a museum. We'd cook and eat and make love and play Trivial Pursuit and watch a movie on television and make love some more, and we'd shower together and sleep together, and on Sunday we'd do the same things again.

Now Evie was gone—maybe for good—and I figured I might have to work out a different definition of a "normal" weekend for myself.

I was tempted to mope around my apartment, pondering my many sins and missing Evie. Instead I drove to the Swift River out near Amherst and went trout fishing.

The Swift is one of the most heavily fished rivers in the world, but I know a stretch downstream from the Route 9 bridge where I can usually find some solitude as well as trout, even on a summer weekend.

I spent a lot of time sitting on the bank, smoking and daydreaming and looking at the water. There was a big aching hole in my chest where Evie used to be, and even trout fishing couldn't fill it up. I didn't want to believe that she was gone. But I knew I better get used to the idea.

I caught a few small, easy trout, and then I spotted a bigger one rising irregularly just off the tip of a fallen tree against the opposite bank. He was a rainbow of sixteen or seventeen inches, and I guessed that he was eating the occasional tiny blue-winged olive mayflies that I saw drifting on the river's surface. I watched that fish feed until I thought I had gauged his rhythm, and the first time I managed to float my little bluish gray dry fly over him, his nose poked out of the water and he ate it.

He pulled hard and jumped once, and after he tired himself out, I steered him in beside me, reached down, and tweaked the hook from his lip without lifting him from the water.

He stayed right there by my feet for a minute, working his gills and slowly waving his tail in the soft current. When I touched him with the toe of my boot, he darted away.

And so for a while, at least, I didn't think about Evie.

The next day I called Mary Scott in Cortland. She told me that stories about Claudia Wells and John Dwyer and Dr. St.

Croix were flying around town, and she made it clear she wanted me to tell her my version.

I told her that as a witness I couldn't say anything about it, and that I'd just called to see how she and Mel were making out.

She said she was doing as well as could be expected, thank you, and if I'd like to talk to Mel, he was out in the yard working on his truck.

I said I would. She said she'd get him for me.

A couple of minutes later, he picked up the phone. "How you doin', Mr. Coyne?"

"I'm fine," I said. "You?"

"They burned down Larry's cabin, you know. He's gonna be some pissed."

He was still thinking about his brother in the present tense.

"Mel," I said, "remember I told you about that hidey-hole under Larry's cot in the cellar of the barn?"

"Yup. I remember."

"Did you look there?"

"Yes, sir."

"And?"

"There was a box of money."

"It didn't get burned in the fire?"

"Nope. The box was all soggy, but the money was in a plastic bag."

"What did you do with it?"

"I put it back like you tole me."

"Did you count it?"

"Nope. I just seen what it was and put it right back. Looked like a lot."

"That was Larry's money," I said. "Now it's yours. Yours and your mother's. You should use it. Maybe repair your barn, get your workshop up and running again."

"That's Larry's money," he said.

"No," I said, "it *was* Larry's money. Past tense. He can't use it now. He'd want you to have it."

"You think?"

"Yes, I do."

"But—"

"Mel, goddamn it, get that money. Do what I tell you."

"Well, okay."

"Your brother's dead," I said.

"Yes, sir," said Mel softly. "I know that."

TWENTY-ONE

In the middle of the morning on the Thursday after Labor Day, Julie came into my office with the day's mail. I was on the phone with Frances Dawkins, who had finally decided to leave her husband after ignoring his infidelities for twenty-seven years. She wanted to talk about what a prick he was. I wanted to talk about her credit-card debts and her husband's 401K and their summer house on Martha's Vineyard.

Julie stood in front of my desk with her hands on her hips. I rolled my eyes at her.

She pointed at the stack of mail and mouthed the words: *Look at it.*

I shrugged. Julie always opens the mail and keeps the interesting stuff—the bills and checks and assorted legal papers— leaving the catalogs and bulk mailings for me to toss.

She pointed again, and I nodded and waved my hand. She gave me a hard look, then left my office.

"Listen, Frances," I said into the phone. "Whether he's a

prick or not is irrelevant. You want a divorce, you can have a divorce. The only thing the judge will care about is whether the settlement is equitable. We're just trying to get the best deal for you, okay?"

Frances said that as far as she was concerned, the best deal would involve fixing up the philandering bastard with Lorena Bobbitt and letting nature take its course.

I told her the best revenge was taking the bastard to the cleaners.

It was exhausting work, and it didn't much resemble what I'd envisioned for my career when I was in law school. Back then, I aspired to argue important constitutional issues before the Supreme Court.

But as Julie kept reminding me, phone conversations with clients added up in billable hours, even if all they really amounted to was amateur therapy.

After I finally soothed Frances Dawkins and convinced her to switch over to Julie to set up another appointment, I lit a cigarette and picked up the mail.

On top of the pile was a postcard. Julie had left it facedown, so that the picture on the back was showing. It was the Golden Gate Bridge, with its orange towers poking up through a cottony layer of fog.

I flipped the postcard over and recognized the handwriting instantly.

Evie.

It had been two and a half weeks since I'd returned from Cortland. In that time, I had not heard from her. I had not reconciled myself to the fact that she was gone for good. But I had begun to believe it.

She didn't even sign the postcard. It held no message of love or regret or wish-you-were-here. All she had written were a name and a phone number.

The number had a 404 area code.

If I remembered correctly, 404 was in Georgia.

The name Evie had written was Shirley St. Croix Flagg.

St. Croix. Hmm.

I held the postcard in my hand, flipping it over and back, hoping, maybe, that some secret message would rub off on my fingers.

The only message, I concluded, was that Evie wanted me to call Shirley Flagg.

So I dialed the number on the postcard.

After two rings, a woman's voice said, "Yes?"

"Is this Mrs. Flagg?"

"Yes it is. Who's this?"

"My name is Brady Coyne. You don't know me. I'm a lawyer here in Boston."

"Oh," she said. "A lawyer."

"This isn't about any legal matter," I said. "It concerns Dr. Winston St. Croix."

There was a long pause on the other end of the line. Then she said, "Why all the sudden interest in him?"

"I beg your pardon?"

"You, sir, are the third person in the past couple of months to call me out of the clear blue sky asking about Dr. Winston St. Croix. After all these years, I'd stopped even thinking about that man. I've got my husband and my children and my home and my . . . my life, and suddenly everybody wants to know about what happened back in Gorham, Minnesota, over twenty years ago."

"What do you mean, 'everybody wants to know'?"

"Well," she said, "first there was that young man."

"What young man was that?"

"His name was Mr. Scott. He was very polite. Working on a newspaper article, he said. He called, oh, back in May or June, I believe."

"Who else called?"

"A young woman. I don't recall her name, I'm afraid."

"Was that about two weeks ago?"

"Why, yes. Yes, it was."

"Was her name Evelyn Banyon?"

"I don't think she actually told me her name."

"And both of these people were asking you the same questions?"

"Yes, sir."

"About what happened in Gorham, Minnesota, twenty years ago?"

"That's right."

"And did you answer their questions?"

"I certainly did. As far as I'm concerned, the more people who know, the better this world will be."

"Mrs. Flagg," I said, "would you tell me what you told those others?"

"Of course I would." She cleared her throat. "I told them that Winston St. Clair was a dirty child molester. He was a pervert and a predator, sir, and if there was any justice in this world he would have spent these past twenty years rotting in prison."

Shirley Flagg didn't need any encouragement to tell her story. She'd been a young nurse when she married the handsome resident. After his residency, the couple moved to the little town of Gorham, where the doctor established a thriving pediatric practice.

She never had a clue, she said, that his fondness for children went beyond caring about their health and well-being.

But then a young boy said something to his third-grade teacher, and the teacher spoke to the principal, and the principal passed along the boy's story to the local police chief—who happened to be one of Dr. St. Croix's golfing partners.

The police chief interviewed the boy and his parents. Then one evening he came knocking at the door of Shirley and Winston St. Croix. The chief and the doctor spent over two hours holed up in the doctor's study, and when they emerged, they shook hands at the door.

That same night, the doctor told his wife that he'd decided to shut down his practice in Gorham. They were heading east, where there were better opportunities to advance in the profession.

She didn't understand it. He'd never talked about advancing in the profession or moving before.

She asked him what the police chief had wanted. He said it was nothing, just man talk.

The next day, she went to the police chief's office and demanded to know what he and her husband had been talking about, that he would all of a sudden decide to close down his practice and head east.

The chief didn't want to talk about it, but she told him she wouldn't leave until he did.

Finally he told her to go talk to the parents of the young boy who had spoken to his teacher.

The parents were more than eager to tell her what their boy had told them.

That very day, while Dr. Winston St. Croix was still at his office, Shirley St. Croix went home, packed up a few clothes, took the Greyhound to St. Paul, and made an appointment with a lawyer.

"Mrs. Flagg," I said, "do you remember the name of that boy?"

"I certainly do," she said. "It was Edgar Ransom. He was a sweet little boy. He had a younger brother. Owen was his name. I guess those boys would be in their twenties or early thirties now."

"And nothing happened to the doctor? He just left town?"

"That's right," she said. "He gave Mr. and Mrs. Ransom a lot of money so they wouldn't press charges against him, and

283

he left. That was the deal the police chief arranged. Nobody in that town wanted any scandal."

"Have you been in touch with any of your friends in Gorham since then?" I said.

"Lord, no. I was too embarrassed."

"So you don't know what happened to the Ransom family."

"No, sir, I don't. But I have thought about them. I imagine those parents have been struggling with their guilt ever since, knowing that Winston St. Croix has probably been preying on young boys all this time because they allowed themselves to be bought off."

"The doctor died a few weeks ago," I told her.

"Well, thank the Lord," she said. "I hope it was slow and painful, and I hope the faces of those innocent children flashed before his eyes as he contemplated eternal damnation."

"He knew he had a terminal disease," I said. "I expect he had plenty of time to think about everything he did."

"Thank the Lord," she said again.

"Did you ever talk to the doctor after you left him?" I said.

"No," she said. "He tried to call several times, but I refused to talk to him." She hesitated. "He did send me a letter a couple of years later. He apologized to me, told me that he'd made just that one mistake with the Ransom boy, that he'd learned his lesson, and that he'd vowed to devote his life to taking care of children." She paused. "I didn't quite believe him, but I've often wondered if he was telling me the truth. What do you think?"

"Perhaps he was," I said.

I did not tell her that soon after Dr. St. Croix left Gorham, the Ransoms moved to Carlisle, Pennsylvania, or that the distance wasn't great enough to allow Edgar to forget what had happened to him, or that he'd finally hanged himself.

Nor did I tell her that a few years later Edgar Ransom's parents had died in a boating accident—which, now that I

284

thought about it, might have also been suicide. They had, after all, accepted money in exchange for their silence. I couldn't imagine the guilt they would have felt for allowing themselves to be bought off, especially after their son took his own life. What was it that the newspaper editor in Carlisle had told me? Ransom's father said his wealth had cost him his soul's blood.

That was a heavy price to pay.

I didn't tell Shirley St. Croix Flagg about the recent events in Cortland, Massachusetts, where all of Winston St. Croix's sins finally came home to roost, either.

I saw no point in upsetting her further.

After I hung up with Mrs. Flagg, I lit a cigarette, swiveled my chair around, and gazed out my office window. It was one of those crystal-clear late-summer lunch hours in Boston. Autumn was in the air, and the secretaries and coeds who were striding across the plaza in Copley Square were wearing jackets or light sweaters over their blouses and short skirts.

After a few minutes, I turned back to my desk and called state police Detective Neil Vanderweigh.

When I told him what Shirley Flagg had told me, he said, "So there's our motive. That's what Scott and Ransom had on him. I figured it had to be something like that."

"I didn't," I said. "He seemed like an okay guy to me."

"You don't see the evil that I see every day."

"Thank God for that," I said.

A little while later, Julie came into my office. "Did you look at the mail?" she said.

I nodded.

"Well?"

"I called that number. It cleared up a lot of things."

She frowned. "That's not what I meant."

"What did you mean?"

"The postcard," she said. "It was from Evie, right?"

"Yes."

"So what do you think?"

"I think she had information she wanted to share with me."

"God, Brady!" Julie shook her head. "Did you look at the postmark?"

I picked up the postcard. It was postmarked San Francisco. "Okay," I said, "so it's got a picture of the Golden Gate Bridge and it's postmarked San Francisco. So Evie's out there somewhere. About as far from me as she can get. What about it?"

"Did it ever occur to you that she could've conveyed this information to you in some other way that would not reveal where she was?"

I shrugged.

"Or," she continued, "that maybe she was using this information as an excuse to get in touch with you?"

"If Evie wanted to get in touch with me—"

"You can be *so* dense sometimes," said Julie. "She doesn't want to make it easy for you."

"Why not?"

"Because she doesn't know how much you love her."

"I've told her a million times."

"She's a woman," said Julie. "She needs reassurance."

"I'd be thrilled to tell her again. But I don't know how to reach her."

"Exactly!"

"Huh?"

"That postcard," she said. "It's a clue. She may not even realize it consciously, but she wants you to track her down. She needs to know that you're willing to make an extraordinary effort, that you care as much about her as you do, say, about one of your cases, or about trout fishing. She wants to know that you're willing to climb tall mountains, brave stormy seas, confront a den of angry lions for her."

"That's what this postcard is all about?"

"Of course it is."

"Why are women so devious?" I said. "If they want something, why don't they just ask?"

"They shouldn't have to ask. They expect you to love them so much that you'll make the effort to figure it out for yourself."

"Julie," I said, "what the hell are you getting at?"

"San Francisco, dummy. Go. Find her."

I laughed. "Right. Just go and wander around a city of what, about a million people, hoping to bump into her?"

"If necessary."

I stared up at the ceiling for a minute. Then I looked at Julie. "She's not in San Francisco."

"What makes you say that?"

"Evie hates cities," I said. "She wouldn't even stay overnight in San Francisco if she could help it."

"But that postcard . . ."

"If you're right," I said, "if this postcard is some kind of clue, then she's near there. If you're right about Evie, she would not expect me to wander aimlessly around the city. She'd expect me to know she hates cities. She'd expect me to figure out where she is." I poked my finger at the picture of the Golden Gate Bridge. "You and Edward were out there last winter. When you take this bridge out of San Francisco, what's on the other side?"

"The first exit is Sausalito. Then you come to Mill Valley, and then San Rafael, and—"

"Sausalito," I said. "What's in Sausalito?"

"Houseboats," said Julie.

Julie booked me for an early Saturday flight. I landed at the San Francisco airport around eleven in the morning, picked

287

up my rental car, and I crossed the Golden Gate Bridge a little after noontime.

It seemed like a quest that would make Don Quixote roar with laughter. But here I was in California, looking for Evie.

I took the first exit after the bridge and found the houseboat colony in Sausalito. There were many long wooden docks reaching out into the quiet bay, and scores of houseboats were moored there—houseboats of every conceivable design, size, shape, and color.

I cruised the parking areas, and finally I saw what I was looking for—a black Volkswagen Jetta with Massachusetts plates.

I found an empty slot in an area marked Guest Parking, retrieved my old L.L. Bean backpack from the backseat, and started prowling the docks.

Those houseboat dwellers were no seafaring roamers. Maybe they hadn't put down stakes, but they had dropped heavy anchors. They grew flowers and vegetables in big container gardens. They dressed their windows with lace curtains and parked supermarket carriages at the ends their gangplanks. Some of the boats sprouted television antennas.

The village seemed deserted on this Saturday afternoon, and I walked up and down three or four docks before I came upon a woman who was being tugged around by a pair of Jack Russell terriers on leashes.

When I said hello to her, she looked me up and down and said, "Are you lost?"

I took out the picture of Evie I'd brought for the purpose and showed it to her. "I'm looking for her," I said.

The woman glanced at the picture, then said, "Does she want to be found?"

"Yes, I think so."

"We're quite protective of each other here," she said. "We

don't like strangers wandering around, peering in the windows."

"I don't blame you," I said. "Her name is Evelyn Banyon. I've come from Massachusetts to see her."

"But you don't know where she is."

"I know she's here somewhere."

The woman smiled. "You came all the way from Massachusetts to find her?"

I nodded.

"And I suppose you won't leave until you do."

"No," I said. "I won't."

"Because you love her?"

"Yes."

She smiled and nodded. The terriers were tugging in opposite directions on their leashes. The woman said, "Sit, both of you," and they both sat.

Then she pointed across the row of houseboats to the next dock. "It's on the left about halfway down. White with red trim and a stained-glass window. You can't miss it."

I thanked her, bent down and scratched each terrier on the muzzle, and went over to the next wharf.

I found the red-and-white houseboat with the stained glass window and called, "Evie?"

No reply came. From where I stood on the dock, I could see no sign of life in the houseboat.

I called Evie's name again.

No reply.

So she was out, but she couldn't be far. Her car was in the parking lot.

I'd wait. I'd come this far. I'd wait forever if I had to.

I leaned against a piling and lit a cigarette, and a couple of minutes later a door on the houseboat opened and Evie came out. She smiled at me and said, "Hi."

I lifted my hand. "Hi yourself."

She was wearing cut-off jeans and a man's shirt knotted across her flat belly and sneakers without socks. She'd picked up a tan the color of honey, and her silky auburn hair hung in a long, loose ponytail down the middle of her back.

My belly did a flip-flop, she looked so good.

She leaned her forearms on the boat's railing and looked up at me. "So you found me," she said.

"It looks like I did."

"Why?"

"I wanted to make sure you knew I loved you."

She dropped her gaze to the water and mumbled something I didn't understand.

"What did you say?" I said.

She looked up at me. "I said, it would be easier for all of us if you didn't."

"Didn't love you?"

She nodded.

I spread out my hands, palms up. "Can't help it," I said.

At that moment, the houseboat door opened and a man stepped out. He was tall and skinny, with a deeply tanned, sun-creased face and long, gray hair. He wore khaki shorts and an unbuttoned blue shirt and a necklace of little seashells around his neck.

He stood beside Evie at the railing and put an arm around her shoulders. "What's up, honey?" he said to her.

She pointed her chin at me. "That's Brady."

He squinted up at me and nodded.

I nodded back to him. About then, I figured I had the picture.

"Look," I said to Evie, "I have something that belongs to you. Let me return it to you and I'll be on my way." I reached into my backpack, found the carved wooden bobwhite quail I'd bought for her on the Cape, and showed it to her.

She said something to the man, who nodded, patted her shoulder, and went back into the houseboat. Then she came up the walkway onto the dock where I was standing.

I handed the quail to her. She took it and ran the tip of her forefinger over it. "Thank you," she said.

"Sure," I said. "No problem. I'll leave you alone now."

I turned and started to go.

"Brady, wait," she said.

I stopped.

"So what are your plans?"

I shrugged. "Mission accomplished. You got your bird. Guess I'll mosey on back to Boston."

"In a hurry?"

"Things are pretty hectic at the office."

"It's not what you think," she said. She came up to me and touched my arm. "That man is my father."

I looked at her. "You never said anything about your father."

"There's a lot I never said."

I shrugged.

"So," she said, "is it all over?"

"In Cortland, you mean?"

She nodded.

"Yes," I said. "It's all over."

"I want to hear about it."

"It's a pretty long story."

"This is California," she said. "We always have time for long stories."

I smiled.

"We've got a kettle of jambalaya on the stove and a six-pack of ale in the refrigerator," she said.

"Sounds good."

"Then you can call Julie, tell her you'll be home in a few weeks."

"A few weeks?"

"We've got a lot of catching up to do," she said. "I figure we need at least one week to prowl around. I haven't been to Yosemite yet, and there are the wineries in Sonoma and Mendocino, and you've got to see the redwoods in the Muir Woods, plus you still owe me at least one day at the beach. Then it'll take a couple weeks at least to load up the Jetta and drive home. There's a lot to see between here and there. It'll give us the chance to talk about all the things we've never talked about."

"You're coming home?"

"Home is where you are," she said.